CITY OF STEEL

A Damascus Love Story

Amber Wiser Thompson

Madison + Park

Copyright © 2024 Amber Wiser Thompson
Written by Amber Wiser Thompson
Published by Madison + Park

All rights reserved. No part of this book may be reproduced, stored, or transmitted by any means—whether auditory, graphic, mechanical, or electronic—without written permission of both publisher and author, except in the case of brief excerpts used in critical articles and reviews. Unauthorized reproduction of any part of this work is illegal and is punishable by law.

ISBN: 979-8-9918122-0-7 (Hardcover)
ISBN: 979-8-9918122-1-4 (Softcover)

Because of the dynamic nature of the internet, any web addresses or links contained in this book may have changed since publication and may no longer be valid. The views expressed in this work are solely those of the author and do not necessarily reflect the views of the publisher, and the publisher hereby disclaims any responsibility for them.

Published 2024
United States of America

DISCLAIMER

This is a fictional story. All characters, events, and even some places are fictitious. Any resemblance to actual persons or other real-life entities is purely coincidental. City of Steel is a painting, not a photograph. It is a departure from our reality and for entertainment purposes only. If you want to learn more about Syrian history or the events leading up to the war, please check out notable historians and journalists from inside and outside the country.

And what is it but fragments of your own self you would discard that you may become free?

—KHALIL GIBRAN, *The Prophet*

CONTENTS

1. Damasco & the Other Son   1
2. Welcome, Welcome   15
3. It's a Free Country   29
4. TUZ   37
5. Super Syr   47
6. Storytellers   63
7. O Bar   75
8. *Muy* (Water)   87
9. Big *Wasta*, Small *Haram*   99
10. *Aweeyay* (Strong Woman)   117
11. Everyone Knows Everyone   127
12. *Heleh, Baadain* (Now, Later)   143
13. Muhammed Omar Sunni   151
14. Blonde Bar   159
15. What's Obvious   165
16. Alawhat?   171
17. Same Letter as *Arse*   177
18. *Wainuk, Akhi?* (Where Are You, My Brother?)   183

19. *V is for Visa* 189

20. *Meen Inti?* (Who Are You?) 199

21. *Yelli Aajbo...* (Whoever Likes It) 209

22. *Akbar Minek* (Greater Than You) 225

23. Don't Believe Me, Believe In Me 233

24. *Min Eedi* (From My Hand) *241*

25. M 259

26. *Boukra Bil Mushmus* (Tomorrow in the Apricot Season) 269

27. Kiss Me Again 283

28. SOS 289

29. Ramadan 297

30. Stay Small 315

31. Kind of Safe 325

32. God's City 333

Glossary 341

Acknowledgements 343

CHAPTER 1

DAMASCO &
THE OTHER SON

I found God in an apricot I stole from an orchard in Sonoma. Spring is too early for ripe apricots, and their season is deceptively short, so while I was taking my daily run, the velvety fruit that looked like a blazing sunset caught my eye. My father told me once that the Portuguese call this enchanting fruit a Damasco. The travelers, wild as they were, found no finer apricots than the ones in Damascus and then compared all others against them. The fruit reminded me of my father and all the mystery that surrounded the city of my birth. According to him, the best of everything came from Damascus: the sweetest apricots, the strongest steel, the most fragrant rose.

I stepped on the split wood fence that separated me from the tree and grabbed the apricot. Halved, it tasted both sweet and tart and entirely heavenly.

As it turned out, the same day, maybe even the same moment I sunk my teeth into the apricot, my father was in a fatal car accident outside Damascus. As soon as I got the news, I left Sonoma to return home. I was in a daze at first, not quite believing what happened, but knowing everything had changed. On the day of his funeral service, I stared into my bathroom mirror, trying to lift myself out of the fog I was in. I pulled my hair, thick and black, up into a high ponytail, letting it fall down my back. I splashed cold water on my face and, between splashes, forced oxygen into my lungs. I propped my eyes, blue like my father's, open with my fingertips. Then I ran my palms down the front of my white dress, as my mother insisted we all wear white, to smooth out any wrinkles. I took one last look at myself in the mirror, noticing that the person looking back at me wasn't the same person who, months earlier, left for an internship in California wine country.

I hurried downstairs and outside to our patio where I sat next to my mother in the front row of chairs facing the Pacific. Cascading arrangements of white roses graced our patio along with oversized framed photos of the three of us playing on the beach. Nothing pointed to my father's heritage or where he'd been when he died. It all felt like a lie or a terrible misunderstanding.

"Dad is Muslim," I whispered to my mother as I watched a man with wispy, gray hair blowing in the ocean breeze, his belly protruding, read from the Bible. I vaguely remembered seeing him at one of the church services my mom used to take me to with my grandparents when I was younger.

"Laila," she sighed and absently placed her white-tipped nails against her lips and shook her soft, blonde waves. "I begged him not to go."

"It's where he wanted to be, Mom. You can't blame all of Syria."

"Oh yes, I can."

Upon hearing the news of my father's accident, my mother had tried to make arrangements to have his body shipped back to the States. She'd been told by my father's family in Syria that the authorities insisted that, due to the severity of the accident, there was no body to ship or bury. When pressed for more details, we were told there were no witnesses to the accident. It had been decided that his family would have a traditional funeral in Damascus, a proper Muslim ceremony within three days of his death, and my mother would hold a service at our home in Orange County for her side of the family and close friends. It seemed even in death that my father was torn between two worlds.

I glanced sideways at the two rows behind me which were filled with my father's former patients, all of them in fitted white dresses crying quietly behind their black sunglasses. My father was one of the best plastic surgeons in Orange County and his patients loved him. They must have felt safe revealing their deepest insecurities and trusted him with their vulnerable pieces. I kind of resented having to share him with them as I had no doubt they would find new surgeons.

As the priest continued, my mind wandered to thoughts of his funeral in Damascus, but I couldn't even really conceive of what a funeral there would be like.

Out of the corner of my eye, I saw my father's oldest and dearest friend, George, standing by the pool. George was from Beirut and fled during the war years. He bought a small vineyard in Sonoma and never went back. I had grown up calling him 'Amou', the Arabic word for Uncle, specifically a father's brother. It was the only thing I ever remember calling him and one of the few Arabic words I knew. Now he wore a starched shirt, arms folded across his chest, a chunky gold ring on his pinkie finger. His thinning hair was slicked back and he looked older than he did the last time I saw him at his vineyard in Sonoma just days before.

"Hi, Amou." I walked over to him and kissed him on each cheek. "Thanks for coming."

"Hi, *habibti*," he said, "I'm so sorry." He held my hand for a moment before he turned to admire the flower arrangements and trays of hors d'oeuvres. "Your mother—" he shook his head, smiling, "she did a beautiful job."

"Yeah, she did," I agreed. My mother had to be my father's greatest challenge, which just proved how much he loved her. Sometimes I thought about what his life might have been like had he married a Syrian. But, then, of course, I wouldn't be here.

"Don't worry. Your father would have seen the humor in it."

"When she wasn't driving him crazy, she definitely made him laugh. It's just how she's dealing with it," I said, even though we both knew I didn't have to explain my mother to him.

"I still can't believe it," he said, knitting his eyebrows together.

"You can't believe it or you don't?" I forced myself to look away when I said this, but when I looked back toward him, I caught a glimpse of worry on his face. It seemed impossible that I was the only one to doubt the story of his accident.

"Are you arguing semantics with me? You know I am an expert in more than one language."

"Yes, I know," I said, feeling a linguistics lesson coming on, though I was grateful for his ability to make light of a serious situation and distract me from my dark thoughts.

"You know Arabs don't say 'I love you' that much? Not as much as Americans, obviously." "Obviously."

"I mean, we say it sometimes, but we prefer sentiments without the separation of 'I' and 'you.' We say things like *hayati, elbi, amri*: my life, my heart, my years. At least, us old timers."

"It sounds wildly romantic," I said.

"Laila, what do you know about romance?"

"I hear things. But you were saying about Arabs . . ."

"In Arabic, your dialect, *abooyi*, my father, is one word. No space," he said. "Even in death, you can't be separated from each other."

"Yeah," I said, clearing my throat because I didn't trust my voice. Amou had handled the situation with so much care. He was the first to come and find me in the vineyard when the news came, as he knew I never carried my phone with me. Still, he was probably the only one who would even hear me out. "Actually, I have been thinking about the last thing he said to me."

"Hmmm," he said, nodding, probably expecting something sentimental and profound and comforting.

"So," I paused to consider what his reaction might be and blurted it out before I could stop myself. "He told me that all Syrian authorities are full of shit."

"Those were his last words? Out of nowhere?"

"He was in his office, on the phone after he had packed all his bags. I overheard him because he was angry, arguing with someone in Arabic—"

"That's just how we talk. For some reason, we are very loud on long distance—"

"No, Amou, I never heard him so angry like that before."

"So, what are you saying?"

"His accident was so terrible that there is nothing left of him and nobody saw a thing, but they are one hundred percent sure he was at fault? Come on."

"*Habibti*, we know for sure he was in the wrong place at the wrong time. If I told you how many people I have lost to car accidents in the Middle East, it's more than the war. It happens all the time. I wish it wasn't true, too."

"Yeah."

"Every daughter thinks her father is invincible, that nothing could ever happen to him. I agree with you, it probably wasn't his fault."

"There's no way."

"Laila, just know that he will always be with you. And I will be here for you as though you are my daughter. Anything you ever need, I am here. But we have to accept it."

"I am trying," I said, even though I was nowhere near acceptance.

"You must. If the Syrian government says 'this is what happened', end of story. We don't go digging for more details, okay?"

"Sure."

"Please, come back to Sonoma while your mother is in Damascus. You can stay with us until she comes home. I don't think you should be here by yourself."

"Damascus? My mother? No way." "Yes, definitely."

"She hates Syria. That's why she never let me go."

"As his wife, out of respect for his family, it will be expected."

"She'll do whatever she has to do not to go."

"She has, at least, to sort your inheritance issue. I don't know how she can avoid it this time."

Amou knew as much as I did how resistant my mother was to going there or having much connection with it.

"I'm sorry," he said. "I thought she would have told you by now."

"Of course, she didn't tell me because she knows I will want to go with her."

"It's not a good idea, Laila. Your mother and I always agreed on this."

"Dad didn't."

"It is what your father wanted. Otherwise, he would never have brought you to California, to begin with. What do you want with Syria, *habibti?* You belong here."

I knew it was a long shot, but I was secretly hoping Amou would be an ally in finding out the truth about what happened to my father. Maybe he really thought I was doing the natural part of grieving or maybe he wanted to protect me from a truth more devastating than the one I was being asked to believe. Either way, I knew my father would want me to go to Syria. He would want me to find out the truth about what happened to him. My mother would hate the idea as she had kept me away from there for most of my life. There was no way I was letting my mother go there without me.

After saying goodbye to Amou George, a few of our neighbors, and my dad's office staff, I found my mother standing in front of the kitchen sink. For the first time in the days since we heard the news, she wasn't doing anything at all. She wasn't on the phone or making a list or on her way out the door. She stared out the window and watched the caterers clean up the last of the teacups, stack the chairs, and take down the easel that held my father's photograph. I stood next to her for a minute without speaking. The house had been a whirlwind of food and flowers and comforting voices, but it would just be a matter of time before everyone else went back to their lives, and my mom and I were left to building a new life without my father.

"Mom, are you okay?" I asked.

"The white roses are so tasteful, don't you think?" My mom, curvy and petite, had honey-brown eyes, a silky blonde bob, and freckles that sparkled against her pale skin. "He loved roses."

"Yeah," I nodded in agreement, even though I knew red roses were his favorite. He was always more sentimental than my mother.

"Did you say goodbye to George?" "I did."

"He said he loved having you at the vineyard."

"He told me you are going to Damascus, is that true?" She hesitated. "Yes. I wish I didn't have to."

"Why wouldn't you tell me you were going?" "Because I know you would want to come with me." "I am coming with you."

"No. Absolutely not. Anyway, I really need you here." "For what?"

"To feed the cat."

"Mom, that cat hates me." "She still needs to eat." "Mom."

"Why don't you have a couple of your girlfriends come stay while I'm away?"

"They are in school, Mom. They won't be back until the end of the semester."

"Then George would love to have you back at the vineyard. He will help keep your spirits up."

"I just lost my dad. It's the only place I want to be. You're not seriously thinking about leaving me behind?"

"You can't run in Syria," she said, pulling what I hoped was her last card, her final line of defense.

"I am sure I can run somewhere in the city."

"I'm just telling you, you can't do all the things you love, there are different rules."

"It's 2011. I'm sure it's changed since the 90's." "I am sure it hasn't," she said.

When I was little, I'd overheard many heated conversations about my going to Syria. My father had always wanted to take me back, and my mother had always come up with a million reasons why it wasn't possible. My father always backed down in the end, saying, "*Tayyib*, okay."

"Dad always—"

"He wanted to take you when you were younger, but as you got older, he really didn't."

"He got tired of arguing with you about it."

My mother took a deep breath. "I know why you want to go. I understand this is your father's family and you were close to him. You want to know him and where you came from, but Syria—"

"So let me find out for myself. If I go and hate it, then you can say I told you so."

"You won't hate it. Not at first." "What do you mean?"

"It can be deceiving. I know you, Laila, you'll love it. You'll love all the attention, the food, the people. They'll spoil you rotten."

"And that's bad?"

"What I am telling you is that Syria is dangerous, regardless of what your father may have wanted you to believe." When she saw my raised eyebrows, challenging her calling my father a liar, she gently took my face between her palms. "He only wanted you to be proud of your heritage, but there is a lot you don't know." Her fear of my father choosing Syria over her was one thing; me choosing Syria over her was a whole other matter.

"He would have wanted me to go," I said, raising my voice as much as I thought I could get away with.

"Only if it's safe for you," she said, matching my tone. "Now you know they drive like maniacs." And then she turned abruptly and went back out to the patio to pay the caterers.

I walked slowly up the stairs, to the door to my father's office at the top. I pushed the door open and found the cat curled up in his desk chair.

"Guess it's just you and me now," I said, as she hissed at me and pounced down from the chair leaving me alone in the room.

I remembered a conversation we had a few years earlier, on New Year's Day, which was also my birthday, and we had just finished our annual family brunch to celebrate. It was after that phone call that he first started making more frequent trips to Syria. I was on my way out for a run and overheard him speaking on the phone in Arabic. He rarely raised his voice and had never argued with his family in Syria. I took my headphones out of my ears and listened by his closed door.

All of it was in Arabic except one sentence which came through very clearly. He said, "Not Laila, not now." The cat slinked up the stairs and brushed past me, pushing her nose in the doorway and cracking the door open all the way. When he saw me standing there, he said goodbye to whomever he was speaking to about me and set the phone down on his desk.

"Dad, what's wrong? Is it the family?" I asked as I came into his office.

"The president's son is dead."

"Of Syria? Oh my God. I—" I didn't know how I was supposed to feel. Although he never said anything directly critical, his attitude toward the government seemed more like they were just a nuisance, an obstacle to get around so he could do his work there. Now, the way his shoulders were hunched forward at his desk made it seem as if we had lost a member of our own family. "Did you . . . know him?"

"No, I didn't know him personally, but he was a young man. He was supposed to be the next president." He shook his head absently, his eyes flitting about his desk as though there may be something he missed. "It's very tragic."

"How did he die?" "Car accident."

"Oh." I wanted to ask who he was talking to and why he mentioned my name on the call, but I could see he was distracted by the news, and I didn't want to seem insensitive.

He looked up at me suddenly, as though something important just occurred to him. "Of course." He was looking at me, but he seemed to be talking to himself. "The other son."

"The other son will take over?"

"I have to make some calls, Laila. Are you on your way out?"

"Yeah, I'm going for a run, start the year off right. You sure you're okay?"

"Yes, I'm fine, thank you."

"Dad, I'm sorry about the president's son, the one that died. That must be . . . sad for Syria?"

"Indeed, it is. But I don't want this to ruin your day. I will see you later . . . I have a nice surprise for you."

"You're taking me to Damascus with you?"

"Not this time. You don't want to go now. There will be a mourning period . . . it will be so dull and depressing."

"Right." There was always a reason. I bit my tongue again not to ask about the conversation I overheard.

"No, you and Mom will both like this surprise."

The surprise was definitely a good one as it distracted both my father and me from the Syria call. Though I never asked for one, he bought me a white SUV wrapped in a big red bow, which meant my mom wouldn't have to drive me to cross-country meets or pick me up late from school.

I went around the desk to sit in his chair, still warm from the cat. I tried to quiet my mind and figure out what he would have wanted me to do. I didn't know what he had been arguing about that day or with whom and why he had mentioned my name. The news of his death had come to my family from the military. If I told anyone what my father had said to me, they might also say denial was a natural part of the grieving process, or worse, keep me from going to Syria altogether.

I wasn't going to get anywhere asking questions over the phone or through internet searches and my mother definitely had no intention of searching for answers while she was there. She had already accepted what happened regardless of the details. I wasn't sure what I thought Amou could do, but he was no help either.

Now, standing in his empty office, I understood the sentiment behind Amou's words about how I would always be connected to my father, but the truth was I had never felt farther away from him. All I knew for sure was that he would want me to go. It was slowly dawning on me that the truth about my father, and maybe even my own history, was in the city of steel—the city of apricots—and no one, not even my mother, would keep me from going back.

CHAPTER 2

WELCOME, WELCOME

"Damascus." My mother removed her black Chanel sunglasses and placed them on the ticketing counter when we checked in at the airport, "Syria?"

"Ah." The ticket agent's smile remained indifferent as she clicked away on her computer. "Very good, Mrs. Abdullah. Who are you traveling with today?" she asked, without lifting her head.

"My daughter, Laila—same last name," my mother answered as she handed my passport to the agent and turned toward me. "Are you sure you want to do this? We could be there for a while."

Her manicured nails, a barely-there shade of pink, rested on the handle of my suitcase, her wedding ring catching the morning sunlight. After my parents met at UCLA and got married, my father convinced my mother to move to Syria before she had me. She moved us all back to California when I was four years old, and my father have been traveling back by himself at least twice a year ever since.

"I have never been more sure of anything," I said, taking the suitcase from her and placing it on the scale.

I was confident my bag was not going to be overweight, but even I was surprised at how few possessions mattered enough for me to take for such an extended stay. She eyed my suitcase as the agent tossed it on the conveyor belt.

"What did you pack, Laila? I hope appropriate clothing."

"Mostly running gear."

"That is all you brought?" she asked, looking panicked.

"How better to learn my way around the city?" I asked. "I brought some other stuff, too."

"I hope you brought loose-fitting track pants, at least.

I brought your black prom dress."

"My prom dress?" I rolled my eyes; it was so like her.

"Yes, the prom you didn't attend," she reminded me. "You will need something black. And at some point, you might need something nice."

"Nice for what?" I caught the ticket agent's eye and we traded worried looks as my mother put our passports away. And who could run in long, baggy sweatpants? It was a conservative country, but that couldn't apply to athletic wear? It was a desert, and summer was a few weeks away. Syrian runners must wear shorts out of necessity. In any event, I had packed one pair of long track pants, and I didn't want to raise any doubts in my mom's mind about me going. "What else did you bring?" I asked, eager to shift the focus back to her. It usually wasn't difficult.

"I brought everything black. Syrian widows wear black," she said, putting her sunglasses back on.

"Mom, that's so not you," I said, as gently as possible but finding it hard to imagine my mom wearing all black everything for weeks on end.

"I know it's not. But we have to make an effort to fit in for as long as we need to stay there. I want no problems... we draw zero attention to ourselves, okay?"

"Sure."

"Laila?"

"Zero attention. Got it."

When the agent handed us our boarding passes, she smiled and said, "Safe travels."

To convince my mother to take me with her, I told her the family would be offended if she showed up without me, my father's only child, and what possible excuse could she give them for me not being there. Even if she told them I was going to school in the fall, that was still months away. I even called my cousin, my father's favorite nephew, Mazen, so he could reiterate to her how disappointed his mother and father, my aunt and uncle, would be if she didn't allow me to go. I felt a little bit guilty about bringing the pressure of the entire family on her, but my mother could be stubborn, and I was not going to let the opportunity pass. Eventually, we convinced her, and my father's family was now very eager to have us.

The airplane was crowded with people freshly showered, excited to see their loved ones, slightly distracted by the worry that they'd left something behind. I sat down next to my mother and buckled my seat belt.

"Was I well-behaved on the flight over from Damascus?" I asked.

"You? You were a little terror. I pretended I didn't know you."

My father wanted more children after me, but my mother always said having me was like having three. She seemed to enjoy me more the older I got.

"Just curious, why are we staying so long?"

"Because we are going to Syria. Everything moves slowly there, especially when you have to deal with the government."

"What do you mean?"

"I have to play their game by their rules if I want to accomplish anything." Before I could ask her what exactly she was trying to accomplish, she turned her attention back to me, "What are you going to do there?"

"I am going to run, learn the city, get to know the family, fact-check all of Dad's claims about Damascus. I mean, is it possible that everything from there is the best?" I asked, smiling at how familiar we both were with his 'back home everything is better' speech, at his insistence that the fruit, the flowers, the tea, the dinners were all superior.

"Hmm," she smiled and said, "What are you reading?" She nodded her head toward my tablet.

I had downloaded a few articles in case I was quizzed at customs. I knew what happened in Damascus a thousand years ago, but I was embarrassed to admit I had no idea what modern Syria would be like, and I didn't remember much from when I was there the first time. Mom always accused my father of wearing rose-colored glasses when it came to his country and said that nostalgia keeps people stuck in the past. She wasn't there when he told me that the authorities were full of shit, so I knew my father loved his country but he wasn't delusional. Between my father's romanticism and my mother's stubbornness, I needed a more neutral source.

"Let's focus on the facts." I opened the articles on my iPad. "The Syrian Arab Republic is a secular country with an elected president," I read aloud for her. "How nice."

"They hold elections only so they can say they did." She rolled her eyes and moved a piece of hair behind her ear.

"Seems like a lot of trouble to go to just for show."

"Nothing you need to know about Syria is going to be on there. Really what we need is a little *wasta*, the currency of connections. You can't get a thing done without it, so this is a concept you need to get comfortable with."

"So I would say, 'I have lots of *wasta*' or 'May I have some more *wasta*, please?'"

It was the first time I heard her laugh in what felt like forever. She imitated me placing my hands together in Christian prayer. "'May I have some *wasta*, please?' You're cute, Laila, that might actually work for you." She shook her head, still smiling. "You could also use it as a noun, like, 'She's a big *wasta*' or 'They are big *wastas*.'"

"Got it."

"You really just have to know the right people. And you have to have a strong enough relationship to ask for favors—and be able to give something in return. *Wasta* isn't free. Remember that."

Her smile had all but disappeared as she pulled her black cashmere sweater tighter around her shoulders. She suddenly appeared smaller to me, more vulnerable, her resistance to Syria being more about not being able to control everything around her and less about hating it.

She continued, "I am hoping Mazen will be able to help me. You know I have always thought small *wasta* can be more beneficial than big *wasta* because you don't need to kill a mosquito with a cannonball, right?"

I nodded, but I was pretty sure Confucius wasn't referring to the *wasta* system when he said that. Something told me, even though my mother's heart was pure, that she was also flesh and blood, and had she and my father been "big *wastas*" in Syria, they might never have left in the first place.

My memories of Damascus came to me in fragments: boys playing soccer in the street, watermelons resting in a shallow river, being chased through an orchard, a relentless sun. Then they slipped away, diving back down into a deeper part of my subconscious that I could never completely reach. Everything fit together, somehow. I started to get restless somewhere over the Atlantic.

"Mom," I whispered. She lifted her pink, silk eye mask over one eye. "Why do they keep watermelons in the river?"

"Watermelons?" She lifted the mask off completely and faced me. "Oh, the watermelons! I can't believe you remember that. On Friday afternoons, everyone goes to these gorgeous outdoor restaurants in the mountains, and your table sits right next to the river. The water is so cold they put whole watermelons in to chill."

"Like literally chill?" I asked.

"Yes, Laila, as in to keep them cool. I am sure watermelons have reached a perfectly Zen state on their own."

"If we decide to visit one of these restaurants by the river, as you call them, then I'll have to remember to take a black marker to make them some sunglasses," I said.

"Or nipples, they're easier to draw." She giggled.

It brought me comfort that my mother kept her naughty sense of humor. She reached for my hand and said, "I am really glad you came with me. I don't blame you for wanting to get out of the house. Everything at home reminds me of him."

I just nodded my head, happy to hear some emotion in her voice, but thinking it mildly ironic that she was going to Syria to get away from his memory. In her mind, his heart belonged only to her. She pulled her eye mask back over her eyes and slept peacefully until we arrived.

When we touched down safely on the runway of the Damascus airport, I was surprised when the other passengers started clapping.

"Was there any doubt?" I turned to my mother and asked.

"You know they believe nothing is in our hands. They live by *inshallah* rules. If God wills it, then it will be."

I giggled but joined the clapping, just in case.

"We could just thank a well-trained pilot who knows what he is doing." She took a deep 'cleansing' breath, the way she did in her yoga classes or before she entered a specialty boutique. I had a moment of doubt that maybe this whole trip was a terrible idea. But it was way too late for that, and I had to push it away from my mind.

The airport was chaotic, with people pushing and shoving to get to the front of the line to go through customs, the agents all dressed in green military uniforms. Syrian flags and pictures of the president hung everywhere, and an overpowering scent of cologne lingered, underlined by stale cigarette smoke.

"It's so retro, like '70s style," I said, as we stood in line. "So cool."

"It's not retro, Laila; it has always been like this. Although they did get computers—that's an improvement."

"They didn't have computers in the '90s?"

"And they could still keep track of everyone," she said under her breath. The last in line, we finally stepped forward to give our passports to the agent. He looked up at us briefly, stamped our passports, and waved us through.

My mother's heels clicked on the white tile floor as we went to claim our luggage. The sun had already set, and the night sky could be seen through Islamic designs cut into stone walls and interspersed with floor-to-ceiling windows. Despite the military presence, I got the distinct impression Syria was a friendly place. When you smiled, people smiled back. The baggage checkers said, "Welcome, welcome," even as they looked through all our luggage, admiring my mother's clothes. When they saw how many pairs of running shoes in every color of the rainbow I'd brought, they paused.

My mother gave me a stern look and said so only I could hear, "They will think you are trying to sell them."

"I am a runner," I said turning toward them and making a running motion.

They shook their heads and laughed, then closed our suitcases and said, "Okay, you are welcome, you are welcome."

We were the last ones to walk out from baggage claim, and I assumed Mazen would come alone to pick us up, so when I walked through the exit, I was surprised when I heard a female voice call my name.

In the next moment, Mazen's sister, Noura, her hair tucked carefully into her headscarf, emerged through the crowd to greet me. Cousins of all ages, dressed in jeans and bright t-shirts trailed behind her like a bunch of balloons. Soon I was drowning in hugs and kisses and questions and prayers. They all wanted to touch my hair and take selfies with me, almost as if to make sure I was real.

"Why you don't put on makeup?" one of the girls asked, giggling and pulling my ponytail around to the side of my face.

"I am not really into that stuff."

"You don't need it, *habibti*," Noura said, grabbing my face and pushing my lips into a fish face. "*Inti amar.*"

"You are a moon," my young cousin translated. "See, Mom? In Syria, I am a moon," I bragged. "Yes, darling, you are definitely out there."

It was only for a brief moment that I felt as if no time had passed, and I had never left, and then the guilt of barely remembering this place set in. They all knew who I was, and I was ashamed at how little I knew about any of them. My uncle, my father's brother, stood waiting next to my cousin, Mazen, and before my brain could register otherwise, I thought he was my father. He brought such strong memories of my father that I had to search his face to find where the differences lay. He had equally wild eyebrows, though they had turned white, and his eyes were a deep brown while my father had the same blue eyes I saw in the mirror. When I was sure I wasn't in danger of crying, I walked over to them and kissed my uncle on each of his cheeks as he thanked God for my safe arrival. Finally, I turned to my cousin.

"Mazen!" I said, throwing my arms around him. "Laila, when did you get tall? You used to reacmy knee." His wild, curly brown hair was the same but his face was chiseled, his features more defined than I remembered.

"And your English has got so good. Have you been taking classes?"

"YouTube," he answered as one of the little girls pulled at my shirt sleeve.

"*Shoo jibteelee min America?*" she asked.

I looked to Mazen to translate, but he hesitated. "Come on, Mazen, tell me what she said."

"She wants to know what you brought her." Mazen gave her a reproachful look.

I knelt to look her in the eye and pointed toward my mother, who had hung back a little, her sunglasses on even though by then it was pitch-black outside.

"Talk to that lady, she has the good stuff." I knew my mother had brought gifts, her way of saying she was sorry, and I hoped the awkwardness of our extended absence would be lessened by the loss we all felt. She lowered her sunglasses and smiled as the little girl hid behind me, her knuckles in her mouth.

"You are welcome, Amy. Come," my uncle said to her, reaching for her carry-on, probably thinking it was her only bag. He led us out the doors and into the night air while Mazen pushed the trolley piled high with suitcases behind us. I expected still desert heat but instead was greeted by a dusty, arid wind and a cool temperature. We were glad for the three cars they'd brought because my mother needed the extra trunk space. After he loaded the luggage, Mazen got in the driver's seat with his father on the passenger side, while my mom and I rode in the back. Before he could take off, I wrapped my arms around

Mazen's neck and kissed him on the cheek. I hadn't realized how much I'd missed him. It felt surreal to touch him, soak up his scent, and hear the sound of his voice after years of scrolling through his life and watching him out of the corner of my eye on social media.

"I am sorry for your father's passing. *Allah yerhamo*, God have mercy on his soul," Mazen said, patting my forearms and releasing me before starting the car.

"I am sorry we couldn't be here for the funeral," I said. "Did you have it at your house?"

"Yes, my mother arranged everything. So many people came to pay their respects. People I have not seen before from all over the country."

"Really? From where?"

"Yes, from Homs and Deraa and Aleppo. Your father was very well known," he said.

My father's visits to Syria included work with a medical nonprofit, mostly doing surgeries for children with a cleft palate or other birth defects. I hadn't realized how many lives he had touched here too, and it was strange to hear how he'd had this whole other life that didn't include me.

My mother rolled down the window, letting in a cool breeze. Tall, metal street lamps lined both sides of the highway, a vast emptiness extended beyond the bustle of the airport, and the air smelled of truck exhaust and gasoline. Even the gasoline smelled different, stronger, rougher, with more jagged edges. I looked over to her to see if she had been listening, but she continued to stare out the window, her sunglasses pulled over her eyes again. Her chest rose and fell as she took deep breaths, and I wondered if the air felt the same as it had fifteen years ago when she was last here.

When we arrived at my uncle's house, Mazen carried our luggage to our rooms, and we all turned in, deciding it was best to take the tour the following day. I collapsed from exhaustion for a few hours, but then jet lag or adrenaline kept me from sleeping, so I rolled out of bed and unpacked my toiletries, and folded my clothes into the dresser. My room used to be Noura's before she got married and moved into an apartment in a newer section of the city. It was nothing like home, but it had all the necessities. Except for the window, all three walls were bare. I had a bed that was firmer than I was used to, a closet, a trash can, a dresser, and a nightstand where I placed my worn copy of Khalil Gibran's *The Prophet*. The bottom of the closet was filled with extra bedding, so I lined up my running shoes, one pair for each day of the week, against the wall by the window. I made a mental note to ask Mazen where they kept their shoes.

My mother was in the bedroom next to me, the one she used to share with my dad. I put my ear against the wall to see if I could hear any signs of life. I was both relieved and disappointed to hear silence.

The next morning, Mazen appeared at my door as I sat on my bed, reading. "*Sabah al khair*, Laila—good morning."

"Morning," I replied, not trusting my tongue to get around all those words in Arabic.

"I remember you used to speak Arabic very well," Mazen said. "In fact, your mother was worried about your English. I am sure it is in there." He pointed to his temple.

"Yes, I am sure it is," I said although I really wasn't sure. I didn't know if my Arabic was stored as a memory or a fantasy about a place and a life that I longed for but never really felt I had. "Mazen, where do you guys keep your shoes?" I gestured toward the row of mine.

"We keep them downstairs, by the door," he said, eyeing all my running shoes. "We don't wear street shoes in the house. We put on house shoes, *shahatta*, when we come inside."

"Oh. Okay, I will check that out. Thanks."

"Laila, when you are running, you wear—shorts?" He hit his thigh with the side of his palm. I got the sense he had been speaking to my mother.

"Is it not allowed here?" I asked.

"It is not 'not allowed' but it is not advisable." "Khalil Gibran says modesty is only a shield against the unclean eye," I said.

"Gibran knew the *shabbab* well—the young men on the street," he replied, gesturing toward my book. "Their eyes are definitely not clean, and they will give you a hard time."

"When you say a 'hard time,' what do you mean?"

"They will throw rude words to catch your attention. They will follow you—they won't leave you alone."

"For wearing athletic gear? That's really stupid."

"Laila, I would prefer you don't run at all. For such a small thing, it is a headache we don't need."

"Running is kind of who I am, you know what I mean?"

"Maybe it is only the American side of you," he said, handing my book back and leaving me to finish getting dressed.

Running was not a "side" of me. It was not a "small thing" as Mazen put it. Running was my sanctuary. I couldn't imagine not doing it. I was willing to assimilate and do my part to fit in, but there was no way in hell young men catcalling in the street was enough to keep me from running.

CHAPTER

3

IT'S A FREE COUNTRY

I woke up every morning at sunrise to the call to prayer. My mother refused to suffer from jet lag and used a sleep aid on day one, but I secretly enjoyed being awake at odd hours. Jet lag kept me in a constant dream-like state, never fully awake or totally asleep, making my re-entry into Syria that much more surreal and oddly clear at the same time. Since no one in the house was ever awake this early, and it was safe to assume all the *shabbab*— the young men Mazen had warned me about—were still sleeping, I decided it was the best time to run.

Many Damascenes were naturally nocturnal, so only the faithful who rose to pray knew the Damascus sunrise was spectacular, especially in the springtime. The air was crisp and slightly cool, perfect weather for running. I dressed in a cotton t-shirt, pulled my sweatpants over my shorts, and tiptoed across the courtyard and out the door. I jogged first through the narrow streets of old Damascus, the canaries tweeting at the rising sun and the scent of jasmine filling my lungs. My muscles were stiff and lazy at first, punishing me for not having run in more than a week and the narrow cobblestone streets were harder on my soles than the soft California sand.

The old city was filled with Damascenes of all kinds. Whether they tied headscarves or crosses around their necks, their homes, fates, and stories were pushed so tightly together that you couldn't tell where one neighbor ended and the next began. I passed a donkey loaded with burlap sacks filled with vegetables, and I could smell the fresh soil that hadn't been shaken from the tops of the carrots. An older gentleman in a white, fitted lace cap, a robe, and house slippers, cleaned the sidewalk with a hose. He pointed the water away from me, putting his hand to his head as I passed.

My muscles began to loosen and my breathing deepened as I continued running until I reached the area with shops and cafes. I stopped to quickly pull off my sweatpants and tie them around my waist. They felt bulky and weird, and I had to wrap them around me twice, but I couldn't take running in them for one more minute. The merchants were hours from opening; wavy steel gates were pulled down over the storefronts and padlocked at the bottom. As the sun climbed higher, I passed the Roman columns of Jupiter and entered the *Souk Al Hamidiyay*, a long street of merchant shops covered by a metal dome, beams of sunlight streaming through bullet holes left by the French. Though they always pushed occupiers out, Syrians didn't ever seem bothered by foreigners and embraced what they left behind.

I took the same route back instead of risking getting lost. I finished my run at the parking lot outside my uncle's neighborhood, untied my sweatpants from around my waist, and put them back on before entering my uncle's street. I did this for several days without drawing attention to myself until Friday, when a guy about Mazen's age, with a beard and a long white robe, spotted me from across the parking lot. When I stopped to make my change, he stared at me. I leaned against a parked car and slipped back into my track pants. His surprise turned to disapproval as he saw what I was doing. I ignored him and continued toward my uncle's house.

I walked down the street feeling rejuvenated but judging from where the sun was, I knew I was a little later than usual. I didn't know if I was slowing my run or slowly but surely adjusting to local time. I made a mental note to pick up the pace the next day.

I pushed open the heavy wooden door and stepped lightly down into the courtyard of my aunt and uncle's old Damascene home. I knew everyone was awake because the water was bubbling in the courtyard fountain; someone must have turned it on. The intoxicating scent of jasmine floated in from outside the courtyard's walls and was enhanced by the two men playing backgammon. My uncle and Mazen sat facing each other across a small wooden table, their eyes downcast in concentration. The mother-of-pearl in their backgammon board caught glimmers of sunlight, throwing them like dice across the white tile floors. My uncle wore a long, white robe and held prayer beads made of amber between his fingers, absentmindedly counting each stone worn smooth by worry and prayer. As they studied the board, I noticed how much they had aged into each other, wrinkles like memories etched into their bronzed skin. They seemed immersed enough in their game that I could sneak past them, but Mazen looked up and caught my eye. They both stood as I came toward them, and when Mazen smiled I breathed a sigh of relief. He wasn't angry that I had been running. After all, he had said he *preferred* that I not run, not that I was not allowed. He gave me his chair while his father excused himself to feed his birds, so Mazen took his chair and sat facing me.

"I didn't see a single one of those mouthy *shabbabs*, only a donkey and some old men," I said, as soon as my uncle was out of earshot.

"Laila, tell me something—did you leave someone special in California?" Mazen asked, disrupting my train of thought.

"What?" I shook my head and smiled at how suddenly he had changed the subject. "No, not really. Why do you ask?"

"I am happy to hear you say this. You're young to think about marriage."

"In America, young people don't think about marriage at all. Relationships are for having fun or hanging out with someone, that's all."

"Hanging out? What is the purpose if it does not lead to marriage?" Mazen asked.

"Maybe to feel free, even in a relationship. It doesn't have to have a label. Sometimes it is what it is—you know what I mean?"

"Free? No label? It is what it is?" He turned his head from one side to the other with each question. "I have no idea what you are talking about. You either belong to a man or you don't."

"Mazen, your attitude is how Arab men get their reputations, you know."

"And your attitude is how American girls get their reputations."

"Mazen, are you starting with me?"

"I don't understand. Why does this idea bother Western women?"

"Because we don't like being told what to do, and we don't like to think of ourselves as property with a fluctuating market value. Who would?"

Mazen sat thoughtfully for a moment before replying. "This is a wrong interpretation of our culture. Women are very precious to us. We are responsible for you; we are supposed to protect you and provide for you. Of course, you are not property. *Bil akis*, it's the opposite, as men we are supposed to give you everything. It is our only job in life."

"What if we want to give ourselves everything?"

"Then you don't need us. This is a sad thing. We belong to each other, *sah walla la?* Is it right thinking or not?"

I understood where he was coming from, but my mother's voice still echoed in my mind about being independent and having a future that I chose, even though it was usually her that was trying to choose for me. I wanted to see if Mazen's arguments could stand up to scrutiny on their own. I wanted to hear it from his mouth and not my defense of Arab men, so I allowed him to continue.

"When I say 'You belong to him,' it means you are very special to him and only him. That he loves you in a way nobody else can."

I laughed. "Then I definitely didn't leave anyone special behind."

"And you were not 'hanging out' with anyone?"

I shook my head. "First of all, you know my Dad. That was never an option for me. Secondly, I'm an athlete. All of us had to give up socializing so we could train. And in order to compete, we had to keep our grades up."

"I understand," Mazen said.

"So, maybe it's easy to believe my life in California was all beach parties and cute guys, it wasn't at all like that." As difficult as it was for me to admit, given where I had grown up, and that I enjoyed challenging Mazen's old-fashioned ideas, I secretly admired, or at the very least, was intrigued by the defense of his thinking. I didn't want to encourage him too much given that he was already trying to get me to stop running.

"That is the reason I am asking. Your father, may God rest his soul, passed, and there is no other man in your life, that means now it is our responsibility to look after you."

"Listen, Mazen, about the running—it's not my 'American side.' When I'm running, it's the only time I really feel in the world like I am a part of it. Do you understand?" I could see I hadn't convinced him.

"Laila, I know this is what you are used to, but you cannot do this here. It is not safe for you."

I felt a little bit guilty resorting to the one thing I knew Mazen would have difficulty arguing against: "It's how I . . . pray."

His left eyebrow shot up. "This is not how we pray."

"I know it's not how 'we' pray. But it is how I pray."

"I see," Mazen said. "I may have a solution for you. I will let you know."

"Thanks." I kissed his cheek and turned to leave the courtyard, restoring Mazen's peaceful sanctuary.

I was relieved to hear him say he was going to help me because, while I had no intention of giving up running, I was also risking getting sent home if my mom got wind of what I'd been doing. Not to mention how much she loved finding fault with Syria and proving her point that it was a dangerous place for me, and I would never understand it and never fit in. I could hear her saying, *"This is the problem with a sexually repressed culture—women dressed in bikinis aren't harassed in California."*

Before I reached the stairs to leave the courtyard, I turned back to Mazen and said, "Please don't tell my mother about any of this." Mazen didn't like keeping secrets, especially from family, unless it served some higher purpose. "Unless you want me to go home— back to California."

"This is the last thing I want. *Khalas*—it's between us."

"*Khalas*," I said, liking both the sound it made at the back of my throat and the confidence that came with such finality.

CHAPTER 4

TUZ

I found my father in everything. While I had to pause my morning running routine, I focused more on what was happening in the house. I found him in the distinct aroma of rich Arabic coffee in the morning and in the sound of the spoon clinking against the small metal pot as it was stirred, forming a deep black in the center and froth the color of roasted chestnuts around the edges. I felt him in the sound of Fairuz's voice, one of the most beloved old-school Arabic singers my aunt listened to on a small kitchen radio while she did her housework. My mom used to roll her eyes when my father played her music at our home in California. I recalled one morning, I was sitting in his office while he drank his coffee and listened to her music when my mother poked her head in the door.

"She sounds so," she wrinkled her nose, "sad?" In her mind, no sadness couldn't be fixed or erased.

"Yes, Amy, she is." He swiveled in his chair to face the door, nodding his head and smiling as though this was the point of it, and some pains could not be erased. My mother shook her head, smiling back at him. "I'm getting the tweezers later." She patted the spot between her eyes and then pinched her thumb and forefinger together. "I love you."

Fairuz was sacred to him, transcendent even, as she wrapped him in her sultry voice, taking him home. I always imagined her with a cigarette in her hand and a beautifully decorated coffee cup in front of her while she sang to him.

"Why do you only listen to her in the morning?" I asked, always amused by his routine.

He looked at me as if he didn't realize he could listen to her any time of the day. "Fairuz? I don't know, to be honest. Does her music make you sad?"

"Yeah, but it doesn't bother me." I rested my head on the arm of the chair in his office. By then, I was getting too tall to curl up in them as I had as a child. "But then again, I am not overmedicated either."

When I saw his reproachful look, I figured I might as well make my point. "Dad, Mom has no feelings. We were watching that movie *The Patriot* for my history class, and she didn't even flinch. Even the part when the little girl goes 'Papa, I'll say anything—please don't go' as he goes off to fight the war. You are made of stone if that movie doesn't make you cry."

"I love that movie; Mel Gibson is so good in it. Just because she doesn't cry doesn't mean she doesn't care. She loves you very much, you know. And me."

"When you are who she wants you to be." I patted the spot between my eyebrows the same way she had.

He laughed and said, "And when *I* am not. You may disagree with her sometimes but your mother has done everything for you. I was raised to believe mothers walk on water and yours is no exception."

"Okay," I sighed.

"Anyway, you let me take care of your mother." He had finished his coffee and turned toward the window, drumming his fingers on the desk. "You take care of—who do you have to take care of?"

"Nobody. You didn't give me any siblings." "I wanted to."

"Or a dog."

"No, Laila," he said, clicking his tongue. "Dogs are dirty, and they can't be trusted." He never felt comfortable around dogs no matter how long he was in the US, even though I had begged for a puppy when I was a kid. I had fantasies of running on the beach with a golden retriever at sunrise. "Let me get you a canary."

"A canary? How am I going to run with a canary?" I laughed and stood up, kissed his forehead, and left him and Fairuz in peace.

As promised, a couple of days later, and because I had been driving Mazen crazy, he drove me to a newer area of the city where the sidewalks were broader and less crowded with people. We walked through the park Mazen said was called Jahez, though it still wasn't clear what he had in mind for me. We walked past a playground, painted wooden benches, and manicured patches of grass. I was trying to work out how much distance I could get if I used the paved walkways, but Mazen kept moving toward the exit, so I followed him. When we left the park, crossed the street, and came down the sidewalk, I noticed on the other side of the street a walled-in section that took up an entire city block. All I could see were the tops of buildings and trees. When Mazen told me it was the American school, I became more interested.

"My father always told my mom if she moved back I could go to this school. Do you know anyone who went there?"

"No, Laila, this school is for *wasta* people and foreigners. But I think they have places to run and maybe you can talk your way inside."

"Will you come with me?"

"It's better if you go alone," he replied. "There are guards at the gate."

"Oh, yeah. And it looks like they have guns," I said, squinting at the guards in military uniforms.

"Yes, but they do not have bullets," he assured me.

"How do you know that?" I asked. Then I realized I wasn't asking the right question. "What's the point of having a gun?"

"You will have a difficult time in Syria if you ask questions like these. Go try. I will wait for you here."

"Should I tell them I am American?" "No."

"Why not?"

"Because they will think, 'You are American? *Tuz*.' They need a better reason to allow you in." He sat on the ledge of the building across the street from the school.

"So what is my reason? What is *tuz*?"

When Mazen finally stopped laughing, he said, "It means fart. It is our way of saying, 'So what?'"

"My passport is a fart?" I asked over my shoulder as he shooed me towards the school's entrance.

I jogged across the street and slowed to a walk when I reached the school, dragging my fingertips along the sand-colored wall, the kind of wall designed to keep people in. Even with the armed guards, who seemed pretty harmless, I liked the energy of it, and I had always fantasized about what my life would have been like had I gone to this school and if I would have found my own tribe behind these walls. It seemed like a place where I could have wandered more but been less lost. I planned to walk through the gate like I had walked through those gates a million times—confident that I belonged, and who was anyone to stop me?

I smiled at the guard and tried to continue through the front gate, but he put his hand up and pointed to a sign-in sheet. I wrote "Laila Abdullah" as clearly as possible, and then in the space marked "Reason for Visit" I put "Running" thinking Mazen would be proud of me. But when I saw next to it a space for nationality, I panicked after what he had told me. It was a few minutes after three o'clock, so students and teachers were coming and going through the gates. People were standing behind me waiting to come through the door. I scanned the list above my slot filled with 'SYR, CAN, AUS' so I scribbled in the space the first thing that came to mind and kept moving.

What waited beyond the slightly intimidating metal gate made me wish I could turn back the clock and relive my childhood here. The leaves from the palm trees created a shady canopy at the entrance, and tiled walkways, a faded red, led to a courtyard of grass and manicured hedges. Walkways bent in every direction through the courtyard toward white, chalky buildings with red roofing. Beyond that, I could see what looked like a playground and maybe a soccer field, so I knew the track couldn't be far.

Just when I thought I was inside safely, and soon free to run in shorts, I heard a deep, male voice behind me say, "Hey."

I wasn't surprised but disappointed that I was probably going to get kicked out of the one place where I might get away with wearing running shorts. I wished I could have at least seen the track. I slowly turned around to face him.

"Do you go here?" he asked. He looked too young to be a teacher, but a little too old to be a student. A pair of earbuds hung loosely across his shoulders, and he held a basketball against one hip.

"Yeah, I go here. Uh-huh." I bit my lip, feeling silly for using an exaggerated American accent.

"That's funny, I haven't seen you here before." He studied me like he was trying to place me, as Mazen's voice rang in my head. *Tell the truth.*

"I *could* have gone here."

"Ah, and you're from a place with the acronym T-U-Z?"

"You've heard of it?"

"I know it well." He smiled.

"So, is it okay for me to use the track?"

"I am not really sure." He pushed his curly, sandy hair off his forehead. "But you are here now, so—"

"I'm—"

"Laila Abdullah?" he said, switching the basketball to his other hand so he could shake mine. "I'm Omar. I actually did go here. Would you like me to show you the track?"

"Please." We walked back to the soccer field and outdoor basketball court, the track circling them both. He pointed out the gym, tennis courts, and cafeteria, and I noticed that all the kids were wearing shorts.

"The guards aren't sure what to make of you, so—" he pointed at me as he prepared to leave.

"—the guards know you?"

"Since I was a little kid, so if it turns out you're a troublemaker, I'm going to look like a real asshole."

"Best behavior, promise." I gave him a little salute. "Okay, see you around, Laila."

For the next few weeks, Mazen took me to the school and dropped me off for a couple of hours so I could run. I even veered off the track sometimes and explored the campus. It seemed that these kids could have gone to school anywhere in the world but chose this place. Sometimes I watched them on the soccer field, the black and white of the ball blurred until one of them stopped it with their cleats. When they yelled at each other in Arabic to pass or shoot, brothers and sisters bonded through blood and sweat, I wondered how many of them were fighters, and how many peacemakers. They barely noticed me so I watched them from the bleachers, curious to know what their futures would be like, how many of them would marry each other, and if they believed in themselves.

Omar played basketball with a couple of his friends almost every time I was there. Even though I became unofficially known as "Omar's friend," and he always said hello, he also seemed to keep his distance. Life at my uncle's house was entertaining, but I was hoping to make friends outside of my family, and for whatever reason, I felt immediate ease with Omar, like he understood all sides of me. One day, as I was running on the track and coming up on the side of the basketball court behind the hoop, I heard him shout, "Agh! Kiss me again!" missing the shot completely. I had been watching him the whole time and it seemed as though his friends weren't coming. Then, the ball landed lightly in my hands.

I raised my eyebrows at him and asked, "What did you say?"

"Nothing. Sorry," he said, walking over to me and taking the ball.

"Can I play?" I asked.

"Sure." He wiped the sweat from his brow with his sleeve. "But just so you know, I don't care if you're a girl, I will foul the shit out of you."

"Whatever, just pass the ball."

Omar and I played until the sunset, and he stayed true to his word, fouling me at least a hundred times. I loved his playfulness, that he didn't take himself or me too seriously, and he didn't try to be cool. By the time we called it a tie, we were sweating and red-faced, unaware of how much time had passed. We crossed the track to the white stone water fountain lined with multiple drinking spouts. After we drank, I wiped my mouth with the bottom of my t-shirt as he lowered his head to let the spray cross his forehead and sandy hair and run down the bridge of his nose.

"Can I give you a ride somewhere?" he asked, pulling his hair back and wiping the water from his face the same way I had.

"Thanks, but my cousin will be waiting outside for me by now."

"Okay, I'll walk you out."

We found Mazen sitting in his car across the street, and I thought it might be a good idea to introduce him.

"Omar was the one who told the guards to let me use the track." He shook Omar's hand, and they went back and forth in Arabic for a while. To my surprise, Mazen seemed to enjoy the conversation. After they traded phone numbers, and Omar went his own way,

I got in the car with Mazen and asked what they were talking about.

"He is looking to hire someone for his office. Someone with either a marketing or business degree who speaks English and Arabic. I told him I would love to come and speak with him about it."

"He might give you a job?"

"*Inshallah.* We will see." A huge smile crossed Mazen's face, and for a second, he looked like the teenage boy I remembered, instead of the serious grown man who picked me at the airport.

And Omar was the kind of guy friend I would have loved to have had in the States. By the time I walked back through the gates to find Mazen that evening, I had already forgotten I was only pretending to belong.

CHAPTER 5

SUPER SYR

The aroma of Arabic bread baking in a stone oven filled the early morning streets of Muhajireen. In front of the bakery, bread graced the hoods of cars and the backs of bicycles in tall, lazy stacks as the steam poured out of the pockets. A sunrise the color of ripe apricots promised another day of sunshine in Damascus.

"This is the best bakery in the city, I promised my mother I would stop on my way." Mazen parked on a side street and we all got out of the car. He planned to take my mother to Kora Al-Assad, a suburb of Damascus to see the house my parents owned and my mother was trying to sell. It was too early in the morning for them to drop me at the school, so he let me ride with them to the bakery. I wore the baggy sweatpants and the only top I thought would be suitable, a black tank that wouldn't draw any attention. I had to keep pulling it down to cover a tiny bit of midriff. I shrunk myself to appear smaller in the hopes the tank wouldn't ride up in front of my mom. We let Mazen walk ahead of us so my mother could fuss over me on the sidewalk.

"The pants are fine but your stomach is showing. Pull the shirt down," my mother said, as she tugged on the fabric. "Honestly, Laila, you young girls, crop tops are so '90s."

"Were you ever happy here?" I asked.

"In the '90s?" She smiled, turning to follow Mazen down the steep hill. "Yes, I was young and in love. I was so happy here."

"What happened?" I asked, falling in step next to her.

"I didn't want your father to have to worry about messing up someone's nose or having his practice taken out from under him because he didn't pay the right bribes."

"Dad is the best surgeon in the world. He would never mess up a nose job."

"Even so, the reality of life here is that everything you work for and even the people you love can be taken from you, in the blink of an eye."

"Did you ever think about looking into what really happened? I mean, there has to be some official record or investigation. A death certificate, at least."

"I asked Mazen; they said it was raining and he was driving too fast and he lost control of the car." She rummaged around in her purse for her sunglasses case and put them on.

"Dad was a good driver." "I know he was."

"You think it's possible . . . ?

"That someone else was out there with him? Absolutely. Someone with more *wasta* who could pin the accident on him because no one important would come asking questions."

"Like his family?"

"Let's just do what we came to do and try not to draw any attention to ourselves while we are here. We sell the house and we go home."

"I still think we have a right to know the truth."

"The truth doesn't matter here, Laila. And it *really* won't matter if..." "If what?"

She looked up and down the street to make sure Mazen or anyone else was out of earshot.

"We don't know what's going to happen here. It could blow up into revolution tomorrow."

"No way. Mazen said everything is okay here. People are happy."

"How would we know if they weren't? And there are protests outside the city, Laila..."

We continued down the crowded street and as Mazen came into view, I watched him waiting patiently in line for bread. He smiled and waved, watching us come down the street. We walked side by side in silence until we reached the main street bustling with people and traffic.

"Are you sure you don't want me to go to the house with you?" I asked.

"I don't want you and Mazen ganging up on me and trying to talk me out of anything."

"I want to see the house, too."

"The Bible says it's never a good idea to get emotionally attached to real estate."

"The Bible doesn't say that."

"How would you know?" she asked, putting her arm around my shoulder as we reached Mazen in front of the bakery.

"Fresh from the oven, you must try." Mazen handed my mother the tea first and then gave me a piece of flatbread with thyme spread over the top. "*Zaatar*, it's delicious."

I took a bite and was momentarily stunned by the flavor and aroma of bread, *zaatar*, and olive oil. "Wow," was all I could manage with my mouth full.

"You don't eat these things in California?" Mazen asked.

"No, I eat as much protein as I can. Food is fuel."

"Fuel? Like I put benzene in my car?" Mazen asked, looking at my mother and back to me. "This is the saddest thing I ever heard. We are not machines."

"Bread is all carbs. It has zero nutritional value," I said, taking another bite of heavenly *zaatar*.

"Never say this. Bread is . . . sacred," he said.

I smiled, showing all of my teeth full of seeds. "It is pretty amazing."

"*Yalla*, we will drop you at the school now," Mazen said after he carefully stacked the bread in one hand.

"I can find my way." When Mazen hesitated, I added, "I will take a cab."

"Laila—" My mother was always ready with a reason why my ideas weren't good.

"Actually, Auntie, we are going in the opposite direction, and the school is not too far from here," Mazen assured her. "But Laila, please go straight to the school, okay?"

"Okay," I said as Mazen stopped a cab for me and told the driver where to take me. I stood between the curb and the street with the door open and watched Mazen and my mother get a safe distance from me.

"*Khalas, yalla,* bye," I told the driver and slammed the cab's door. He turned around and twisted his fingers to the sky. I was proud of myself for using my one full Arabic sentence on a real person but I still couldn't explain to the driver how I wanted to explore the city on my own. He shrugged and pushed back into traffic.

As I backed away from the curb, across the mess of cars and buses, horns honking and people shouting orders at the baker behind me, his store filling up more now the sun was high, a young man in a military uniform on the other side of the street caught my attention. As soon as I looked up, our eyes met, a sea of chaos between us. His green eyes widened as his expression turned from stoic to a gentle half-smile like there was some familiarity between us. Although it looked like he wanted to cross to my side of the street, he didn't seem like he was in a hurry. Standing much taller than the other men on the street, he held his space with confidence, everything around him keeping a respectable distance.

I half smiled back at him not wanting to break his gaze, but Mazen's warnings about the *shabbab* surfaced, forcing me to lower my head and turn, weaving my body through the thick pedestrian traffic. As soon as the sidewalk cleared, I started to run. While my father's words about authority figures were never far from my mind, it was Amou's voice now that rang clearly through my head. What did he always say? God Bless *Jaysh a Soori*? A smile pulled at my lips at the memory of Amou's stories about playing cards in the Beirut mountains with the Syrian army back in the day.

I took a deep breath through my nose, exhaling through my mouth. I pushed the image of the handsome soldier out of my mind and focused on getting myself oriented. As long as Qasioun mountain was behind me and I turned left at some point, I was going in generally the right direction to get to the school. I had seen pictures of a sword the size of a tall building in the center of the newer part of the city, and I hoped it might appear somewhere on my horizon. During his many history lessons my father explained that Damascene steel was so superior (of course) to all other materials in sword making that if you threw a piece of silk in the air, the sword could cut it in half. Why it would ever be necessary to cut such a delicate fabric as silk with a steel sword remained a mystery. Still, Damascene steel was one of the many treasures the Crusaders were after.

I crisscrossed the residential streets, making the descent from the mountain more gentle, and unlike my uncle's neighborhood, the sidewalks were broad and not as crowded with people. Occasionally, a woman would poke her head over a balcony, curious only for a moment before she turned back to her own business. Nobody was at all concerned with me, and I was excited to have discovered a new running route. The sword never did appear, but it was a matter of time. How long could a sword the size of a building hide from me?

When I reached the gate of the American school, I stopped to catch my breath as a shiny black Mercedes with tinted windows pulled up beside me. A picture of the president, the ailing father, hung prominently inside the back window, Syrian flags on either side of the poster making the car look like it was wearing a cape. The window on the passenger side opened and Omar said, "I came to rescue you."

"Rescue me? From who?"

"The *shabbab*. I talked to Mazen. He said he had a feeling you were running alone in the streets somewhere between Muhajireen and DCS."

"Mazen called you?" I had been so careful to make sure Mazen and my mother were well on their way when I let the cab go.

"Actually, I called him. I wanted to speak with him about the job, and he asked if I was in the neighborhood. He told me they're going to be late coming back and if I wouldn't mind driving you home."

"Somehow I survived the mean streets of Malki by myself, but if he insists." I opened the passenger door and slid in next to him.

Instead of his usual basketball shorts, he wore jeans and a polo shirt. He even had his curly hair under control with what looked like gel.

"Even with your stomach showing like this from Muhajireen to here, not one man said anything or even looked at you?"

"My stomach is not showing. Maybe one guy noticed me but he didn't say anything." I had a feeling the soldier didn't care at all what I was wearing.

"I don't believe you."

"I totally blend in here." "You don't blend in here." "What do you mean?"

"Girls don't run in the street." "Why not?"

"Because it's weird. And they don't want to be harassed."

"Other than running, I totally fit in?" "You're also tall for a girl."

"I'm average height."

"I'm average height for a man and you and I are the same."

"I think I am a little taller than you," I said. "No, the same."

"Okay."

"Do you mind if we stop by my office? I have some materials I would like you to give to Mazen."

"Sure," I turned to look at his back window again, "So, what exactly does your company do?" I asked.

"We are a private marketing firm, but we mostly do government contracts," Omar said.

"What kind of contracts?" I asked.

"It's a lot of event planning, we also work with television producers, radio personalities, we develop content for newspapers and magazines..."

"Propaganda?"

"Branding," he said, smiling in my direction. "My job is to create a narrative that includes Ba'ath Party ideology, a touch of theology, and a heavy dose of national pride so the lines between them become so blurred they can no longer be separated in people's hearts and minds."

"Which theology?" I asked.

"Non-specific." He paused, squinting at me before he said, "You did an internet search before you arrived?"

"I know Syrian politics, a little." "What do you know?"

"I know the president is not in super great shape." "Not true! He has a very small flu."

"He's pretty old. What happens when he is you know, 'out of office'?"

"If, God forbid..." "God forbid."

"Something terrible would happen, his son will be considered and is able and willing to run in the next election."

"God willing."

"God willing, *akeed*. And then his son will take over the way I took over my father's business."

"The business of running the country?" "Yes."

"When is this totally unnecessary election happening?"

"We are a country of laws, Laila, he has to run like anyone else. Between you and me, it's looking more and more like it will happen soon," he said, as parked on the sidewalk in front of his office building.

"You don't think there will be any problems?" "How do you mean?"

"I mean, not everyone is a huge fan, right?"

"Laila, I can tell you with absolute certainty that we will get nothing less than a landslide."

"So, you did your job well?" We got out of the car and I followed Omar up a short flight of stairs until we reached a set of double glass doors.

"I won't take all the credit, but yes," he said, as he opened one of the doors for me.

His office was in an older residential building turned into a modern workspace; a photo of the Damascus skyline hung carefully against the white wall spanning the entryway. He led me back to his own private office where his glass desk was piled high with documents, thick folders, and magazines. I sat on his plush leather couch and scanned the bookshelves of mostly framed photos of him and friends on yachts and snowy mountain tops and at elegant black-tie parties.

He excused himself to take a phone call behind his desk where two floor-to-ceiling windows were separated by a small wall space. A picture of the president hung directly above Omar's head when he sat in his chair. I hid my smile as his assistant came in and asked if I would like Nescafe. Instant coffee with milk is something I never would have had at home but here it tasted delicious. I nodded my head yes and moved to one of the chairs in front of Omar's desk. He put his earpiece in and stared directly at me, occasionally nodding but saying nothing back to his caller. I hadn't noticed before that he had a small scar above his right eyebrow. While he was undeniably cute with his sandy, curly hair and warm brown eyes, I was not attracted to him, which would explain my ease and comfort with him. Something reminded me of the soldier with the green eyes and the half-smile that revealed beautiful white teeth against his bronzed skin, which, while delicious, didn't make me feel exactly at ease.

When Omar finished his call, he pulled his earpiece out and called for his assistant. "Nadia!"

"She makes a yummy Nescafe," I said, sipping from my mug.

"Oh, yeah with coffee and tea, she's perfect. With organization, not so much," he said, gesturing with both hands to the mess on his desk.

Nadia came in carrying a stack of folders and magazines. She cleared a space and stacked the materials on his desk in front of me.

"These will give him an idea of what we do so he can prepare for the interview," Omar said.

"He has to study all this stuff, huh?"

"*Khalas*, between you and me, he has the job." "You already decided?"

"Yes, but I want him to know this company inside and out because he will have to speak with my father."

"Your father?"

"Yes, I run the company but he owns it. And he hates the whole *wasta* thing when people get or expect jobs because of who they know."

"You had to interview for your job?"

"Interview? I had to get my MBA before he would even consider me, and he is still on my back all the time about everything."

Omar seemed confident in his decision, but a small part of me couldn't shake what my mother had told me that *wasta* was never free and Omar barely knew Mazen. Regardless of whether he called it a favor or not, Mazen would not have the job without me.

"Why Mazen?"

"He will be working on messaging with me. I could use his insight into what would resonate with people his age with the same background. Slogans, visuals, uh, points of contention."

"But you and Mazen are the same age."

"Yes, but Mazen grew up differently than me," Omar said. In a less formal setting, like on the basketball court, I would have said, *"You mean he is not a pampered little wasta boy who went to the American school?"* But it seemed like it was not the place or time. Luckily, Omar continued, "Mazen is a product of the public school system, from a conservative middle-class family, and a former soldier. I am interested in knowing him better, what his ideas are about the country's future."

"You seem to know a lot about Mazen." "I know a lot about everyone."

"How?" I couldn't help asking.

"Damascus seems big, but it's a small town. Everyone knows everyone. And just so you know, Laila, this is not a favor."

"Of course. I mean, why would you do me a favor?" "Mazen will get the job on his own merit."

"He will work really hard for you. He taught himself English on YouTube. He is a serious guy. He would never take an opportunity like this for granted." Omar could not possibly understand that this was not just an opportunity for Mazen; it was potentially life-changing, and no one deserved it more.

"And this is for you," Omar said, as soon as we got back in the car, handing me a rolled-up poster.

"What is it?" I asked, taking it from him.

"It's a gift," he said, smiling enough to show me all of his teeth.

I unrolled the poster to find a picture of the president at the top, whose face was now familiar to me, but in this version, he was not alone. A young man with light hair wearing aviator sunglasses and a military uniform was to the left of the president, the Syrian flag behind him. To his right, there was another man only slightly older and darker complexioned, with a beard cut close to his skin. "So, which one will be the next guy?"

"This one." He pointed to the fairer of the two, the one to the left of his father, and I was immediately reminded of the conversation I had with my own father. In his office when he got the news the president's son had died, and he remembered there was another son. It all seemed so distant then, an alternate reality. But here I was, all three of them staring back at me.

"He looks intimidating," I said, and I meant it.

"He should. That's who you want on your side," he said, as I rolled the poster back up. "You should hang it in your bedroom." He laughed and put his hands up to protect himself as I swatted him with it.

"I have the perfect place for it." "You won't throw it away." "How do you know that?" "You won't."

On the way home I noticed how, the closer we got to my neighborhood and the farther away from

Omar's, the president's picture hung everywhere. Paintings of him on canvases were draped from buildings, posters were hung in stores, and car windows. It wasn't that I had not seen the pictures before, but now this was Omar's business, so it had become more interesting to me.

"You seem to know your way around my neighborhood," I said, as Omar weaved in and out of traffic and sped down side streets and alleys I hadn't discovered yet.

"I own a bar in the old city. I'm usually there on Thursday and Friday nights. You should let me know if you ever want to stop by."

I considered what Mazen and the family would say if I told them I was going to a bar to hang out with a guy. I didn't want him to think I didn't appreciate the invitation, but I didn't want to agree until I knew I could go without causing a problem at the house. "Thanks, I will."

"I will pick you up and drop you back home, it's no problem," he said, as though reading my mind.

"Thanks, Omar."

After he dropped me home, I threw the poster in the trashcan next to my closet, took off my sweaty running clothes, and went to take a shower. It was a relief to finally wash the day away and have a moment of solitude with so much on my mind. Though Omar was such a find, a guy that I really got along with and there was no attraction from either one of us, I didn't have him quite figured out. Still, my father would have wanted me to help Mazen in any way I could, and I hoped he would not be resistant to what Omar's company did. There was also the memory of a handsome soldier smiling at me from across the street that gave me the warmest, tingling sensation until I came to my senses and decided he was, most likely, a mirage. A mirage in an oasis? "Yes," I told my foggy reflection in the bathroom mirror. "Absolutely."

When I got back to my room, the poster rolled up in the trash can seemed to be calling me. I lifted it from the pile of tissues and airline luggage tags, not understanding exactly why I felt bad. Although, it was a gift from Omar so it was kind of rude to throw it away. I decided I would hang it, but ironically. That made me feel less guilty. I found a roll of tape in the nightstand drawer and a pair of scissors. I cut four pieces of tape and managed to hold the poster and tape four corners to the wall next to my dresser and mirror. I stood back to admire my decorating project and decided I liked it. I wasn't buying the narrative; I was just playing along. As I started to take off my towel to put my clean clothes on, I realized I couldn't see the blonde one's eyes behind the aviator glasses. I quickly pulled my towel back up over my breasts.

"Don't you have any sense of privacy?" I asked him. His answer was obvious so I moved to the other side of the room while I dressed to where he was facing the opposite direction. That might take some getting used to.

"Oh my God, Laila, are you serious?" Mazen asked, immediately seeing the poster when he came into my room later that evening.

"I'm totally Syrian."

"That is . . . very wrong," he said, a look of disgust on his face.

"That is hilarious, first of all," I said, giggling at the president and his military-clad sons. "They could cut you with these strong jawlines."

"What is the second of all?" Mazen was not amused.

"What? Oh, well, secondly, it was a gift from Omar. This is what his company does."

"This," he asked, pointing to the poster, "is his company?"

"Yes," I said, pulling the stack of materials Omar gave me from my nightstand and handing them to Mazen. "And you need to know all this stuff before the interview."

"Wow," he said, taking the heavy pile from my hands. "I don't know, Laila. Maybe this is not the right thing."

"Listen, Mazen, Omar says that it is just business. Branding, you know?"

"Branding," Mazen said, shaking his head and examining the pile.

"Just go to the interview and see what happens." I didn't want Mazen to feel any more pressure so I didn't mention that Omar already decided to offer him the position. "Who knows? You may not even get it."

"Well, at least now that I live with a Ba'athist, no one will ask about my loyalty," Mazen said, smiling and heading out the door with his new reading materials.

"You better watch out . . ." I said, as he rolled his eyes and shut my door behind him.

CHAPTER

6

STORYTELLERS

I dodged wooden carts loaded with candies and nuts as I ran through the cobbled streets of the old city. The carts, pushed by boys who were not yet *shabbab*, were piled high with brightly colored treats and sugar-dusted, rainbow-colored gelatin cubes. A thin sheet of plastic shielded them from light rain. The boys always lowered their eyes shyly when they saw me, struggling with the weight of the cart and not wanting anything to fall. The scents of the spice souk, cinnamon, cardamom, and dried flowers to make chamomile tea, followed me out of the market.

The streets of my uncle's neighborhood were narrow and crowded and I felt mostly safe inside their historic walls; other times I felt suffocated by them. Running gave me the freedom to experience the city in the only way I knew how to enter the world.

When I popped out into the busier main streets, I ran in and out of the traffic flow, which made the taxi drivers yell out their windows at me, '*lik ma fi mukh!* crazy!' putting their index finger to their temple and then twisting up to the sky. Even when they were yelling at me, they were smiling good-naturedly, so I just waved over my shoulder and kept going.

Mazen was interviewing with Omar, so he couldn't drive me to the school's track even though he begged me to take a taxi there or wait until he got back. Mazen had no reason to be concerned. Other than cabbies, and if I kept my track pants on and still woke up relatively early, no one paid much attention to me. The *shabbab* didn't like early mornings or rain and losing the shorts was a compromise I was willing to make.

After the official mourning period ended, the family opened their home back up to receive visitors for the first time since my father's funeral. Aside from my uncle, my father had two older sisters. When my aunts came over, they grabbed me and kissed me hard several times on each of my cheeks. After reciting Koranic blessings over me, they sat close enough that I could smell their breath. Their idea of personal space was much smaller than what I was used to, but while my mother was visibly uncomfortable, it made me think of my father. I loved how they wanted to bring me close even though we couldn't understand each other. Initially, they all spoke to me in rapid-fire Arabic, and they only laughed when they realized I didn't understand a word they were saying. When they grew tired of speaking to me, they turned to each other to talk about me.

Then, my younger cousins moved in on me and, with devious looks in their brown eyes, asked about my life in California. None of them spoke much English, but somehow all knew the word "boyfriend." I imagined they thought I had a life of partying on the beach and that a blonde surfer with a six-pack was waiting for me to come back. They seemed equal parts relieved and disappointed by discovering I was more like them than they expected me to be, even if it meant I didn't have any good gossip.

Mazen's mother was the only one who didn't see the humor in the fact that I only knew three words in her language even though it was once my native tongue. When I first arrived at her home, she held my chin in her hand and inspected my face closely then looked me up and down until she was satisfied she knew me. "The Laila she knows speaks Arabic very well," Mazen explained. She continued to study me and then crossed her arms and said, "*Tayib, maalishee, min aalima.*"

"She said it's okay, we will teach you," Mazen translated. She returned to her cooking like someone who had a lot of work ahead of her.

Being with all the relatives kept my mind occupied, but I was not used to being around people all the time or being the center of attention. Though I loved the feeling of coming home I needed running to remain the sole thread of who I was, who I am, and who I would always be, even as the world around me shifted.

To learn or relearn Arabic was on my to-do list, but I was more curious about the city and the Damascene way of being in the world. I was amused by their near-obsession with tissues as there was a box in every room in the house, in every taxi cab, and one in the fist of every woman over 50. It was funny how they loved Nescafe and how men held hands in the street as a sign of friendship. Because they shared water bottles they turned their heads to the sky and tipped the bottles high above their mouths. With the ever-present sun at their backs, it seemed as though they drank from a waterfall cascading from the heavens.

When I came back to the house, I was surprised to find my mother sitting in the courtyard alone, drinking tea. I didn't have a chance to speak to her earlier.

"How is the house?" I asked, plopping down into the chair across from her.

"They call them villas." "Ooh, sounds fancy."

"Not ours. For starters, nothing works properly. We need electricians, plumbers, landscapers, it's a mess."

"Didn't Dad ever spend time out there? Doesn't sound like him to let it go like that."

"No, he always stayed here and he worked all the time. He wanted to do as much in the hospitals as he could."

"That does sound like him."

"Oh, we also have squatters. Apparently, it's very rude to ask people to leave so we have to find them a place to live, and then we can start renovations."

"So when do you think that will be?"

"Their timelines begin and end with *inshallah*. I can't book tickets home with *inshallah* dates."

"I guess it's not in our hands," I said with a smile, my palms to the sky.

Mazen came through the front door carrying plastic bags of fruits and vegetables. When I went to help him, he asked, "Did you go running? At the school? You will get sick if you run in the rain."

"That is such an old wives' tale and it was barely raining, Mazen. It was like not even enough to get wet."

"I wish it rained more. Everything is getting so expensive," he said, walking into the kitchen. We dropped the bags on the kitchen table, and I followed him back out to the courtyard.

"Hey Mazen, do you know where the big, steel sword is?"

"Yes, it's in *Umawiyeen* Square. It's not made of steel, it's a building, how do you say, a monument? I will take you there," he said, taking the stairs two at a time to find his mother.

"Laila, he is not your driver," my mother said, as I sat back down with her.

"What? He didn't have to offer."

"They always offer and they will never tell you 'no.' Be careful what you ask of them. This could be an extended stay and I don't want them to feel we're taking advantage."

"Mom, we're family." "*You* are family."

"You are Dad's wife," I said, as she lowered her head and looked into her tea glass. "Mom? Are you okay?"

"Laila," she said, looking up to meet my eyes. "I choose not to indulge my feelings all the time and in every situation, but that doesn't mean I don't have them."

"So, you are feeling sad?" I asked. My uncle's canaries tweeted from cages in the fruit trees but other than that we were alone for what seemed like the first time since the flight from California.

"I feel like they hate me. I don't ask anything of them and they still hate me."

"That's not true." "It is."

"Did you ever consider that they think you don't like them very much?"

"What on earth would give them that idea?"

"I don't know, maybe that you have nothing positive to say about their country? And you didn't come back here once in fifteen years even to visit?"

"My reasons had nothing to do with them. They know that."

"That doesn't mean it doesn't hurt," I said. "I know you think not asking for anything and keeping to yourself is polite and respectful but they don't see it that way. They want you to need them."

"I don't know how to do that."

"I'm sure with all the renovations on the house you'll need Mazen's help. And why are you drinking tea by yourself? Drink tea when they drink tea, with them."

"Laila, I have to say I'm a little worried about you."

"Worried? About me?"

"I know how much you want to be here. But I don't want to see you get lost in Damascus. I would like to see you getting serious about going to school. Your internship at the vineyard was fine but now it's time to figure out your next step. There's no future for you here."

"Sure, yeah." I had not given one thought to what I would do when I went back. I hoped I wouldn't have to. "I will get right on it."

"The best thing for both of us is to keep moving forward." My mother finished her tea and took her glass to the kitchen.

At sunset, Mazen drove me to see the sword. "What is this place called again?" "Ummayad Square."

"Oh, it's a circle."

"It is a square," he said, as we circled the roundabout, a fountain at its center. "There's the sword." We found a parking space in the hotel across the circle and walked toward the monument.

"So how did the interview go?"

"Very well." Mazen described in more detail what Omar's company did and how they needed someone to help them develop a narrative surrounding the new president that would resonate with young people. "I would work with media to create the image of a reformer, Western-educated, but with strong nationalism. Also, his military background is very important. My generation likes this."

"Yeah, he's cute."

"Some people say he is already running the country, but we have to wait for his father to die so we can have an official election." Mazen lowered his voice as he said this and looked back at me. "Cute?"

"Some people say change is coming to Syria, so maybe—"

"Be careful, Laila, there is a difference between talking about reform and talking about real change. This could get you into trouble."

"But Omar says—"

"Omar says? Omar is with the regime. He is one of them and they know how to find troublemakers. They make them feel as though they can speak openly."

"But they really can't?"

"*Walla*, the regime will put this sword in your ass if you challenge them, kabob style."

"Wow." I had to laugh hearing Mazen loosen up around me, he always seemed so mature and polite. I decided I liked that he was getting more comfortable around me.

"Yes, wow. Please do not forget."

"What do you think Omar wants with you?"

"I am sure he does want someone like me. I have the language skills and the background. But I am nobody and he is giving me an opportunity that has nothing to do with *wasta*. This shows people they are fair and they are doing things differently. But the job itself is repeating the same message I have heard all of my life. Nothing is changing."

"Oh."

"Even with a new president, this is the same family, the same people around him, telling us the same stories we've all heard before."

We walked around to the other side of the sword, amazed at how much taller it seemed compared to the aerial photos I had seen on the internet. The stained glass swirled with red, blue, and yellow, transparent enough that you could see only the change in light without being able to see directly through to the other side.

"By stories do you mean bullshit?" I asked, careful to use the right word.

"Not bullshit, no. As Damascenes, we are storytellers and lovers of stories. We use them to understand our situation. These stories are a reflection of who we are as a people. The good and bad. The right and wrong. But that does not mean we don't know this is a story."

"So maybe now you will get to help write the story?"

"To be honest with you, it is a very good opportunity. My family cannot look for a wife for me if I have nothing to offer her. This job could make me . . ."

"A big *wasta*?"

"More *wasta* is more problems, so only a small amount of *wasta* is enough for me."

When we arrived back home, the murmuring from the television in the sitting room mingled with my mother's voice. It sounded like my cousin Noura and my aunt were trying to explain what was on. Mazen and I stood on either side of the door to the sitting room and I put my finger to my lips to indicate I wanted to eavesdrop.

"*Akbar*," my mother was saying over and over and they would respond with "*Akhbarrrr*," trying to get her to roll her r's.

"It's the same," she insisted.

"No," Noura said, giggling. She must have been wagging her finger, making her gold bracelets jangle.

"*Akbar* is like the call to prayer *Allahu Akbar*, God is greater. *Akhbarr* is just the news. It changes the meaning completely."

Mazen and I left them to their Arabic lesson and tiptoed across the courtyard before I started to crack up at my mom's pronunciation. I didn't have much room to talk as my time was also coming. First, I wanted to tell Mazen I appreciated him, and I didn't see him as my personal driver.

"Thank you for taking me to see the sword."
"Welcome," he raised his hand to his head.

As I started up the stairs, I remembered our earlier conversation. "Hey, Mazen," I said and turned to look back down at him. "You are not a nobody. You are everything to me," he smiled and nodded. "You should do what makes you happy."

"*Inshallah habibti, inshallah.*"

※

There was no wireless access at my uncle's house so, when he needed to, Mazen went to an internet cafe where the download speeds were slow and the cafe was often crowded. I called Omar and asked if I could use his computer to print information packets for UCLA and a couple of other schools in San Francisco in case I decided to move closer to Amou. I was also hoping to check my email and social media. It felt like ages since I checked in with the world outside Damascus.

When I walked into Omar's office I saw him chewing on something while holding a brown paper bag folded around the edges. "What are you eating?" I asked when I came into Omar's office.

"*Bizr*, watermelon seeds," he said. "Why?"

"I used to be fat," he said, as though it was obvious. "You were fat?"

"Yeah, and then I started eating *bizr* and I got thin. It turns out I am a nervous eater. I am sexy now, right?" he said, black shells sticking to his lower lip. "*Bizr*."

"Omg, eating *bizr* is not sexy, I am just saying."

"Why do you say omg? It's the same number of syllables to say it properly."

"Why do you say 'kiss me again' when you miss a shot on the basketball court?"

"It's vulgar, you shouldn't say it." "Tell me what it means."

"Why do I have to be the one to tell you these things?" "Okay, then I will ask Mazen."

"No, no, no. A kiss in Arabic is the slang word for a girl's uh, girl parts. It's also a verb in this context."

"I don't get it."

"When you feel like the universe keeps fucking with you, you say 'kiss me again.'"

"Oh. So weird. And sexist a little bit?" "It's a rough translation. So?"

"I don't say 'oh my God' because it seems disrespectful." "To whom?"

"To Him," I said, lifting my eyes upwards.

"Ah." He leaned back in his chair, nodding his head slowly.

"But now that sounds pretty lame after the whole 'kiss me' thing."

"Yeah. You seem older than you are." "Really?"

"Not when you say, 'omg', but sometimes. And you practice our religion in a strange way."

Remembering the apricot I pulled from the tree in Sonoma, I wondered if Omar would ever be a close enough friend for me to tell him why I came to Damascus but it definitely wasn't the time yet. I was also curious how he knew so much about my family even though we hadn't known each other very long.

"How do you know I'm Sunni?" I asked. "The same way you know I'm Sunni."

"I know because you just told me."

"You didn't know before? I may as well be named Muhammed Omar Sunni. Everything we need to know about each other is in our names. Laila, you have so much to learn."

"So, what are you nervous about?" "What do you mean?"

"You said you're a nervous eater. What's up?"

"Believe it or not, one day I might actually tell you," he said as he stood, offering me his chair. "For now, my office is your office. Just hit the print button on whatever you need and Nadia will bring it to you."

"Thanks," I said, sinking into his comfortable leather chair.

As soon as he left and I turned to face his computer, a framed photo on the edge of his desk caught my eye. I picked up the photograph of him and a couple of his friends on jet skis and studied it closely. Though it seemed an impossible coincidence, I couldn't forget the green eyes and thick black hair of the soldier I saw in the streets of Muhajireen. Only he wasn't in uniform, he was shirtless with blue swim trunks and a deep tan. Of course, they weren't wearing life jackets. What were the odds Omar knew him? He did say he knew everyone but it's impossible to know absolutely everyone. I put the photograph face down on the desk and forced myself to focus on college and, for the next hour, I poured my energy into UCLA's admissions requirements as well as San Francisco State and Berkeley, to make my mother happy. The admission deadline for the coming fall already passed and the upcoming application which hadn't even been posted yet would be for the following year. I happily ran through an ideal timeline in my mind that included a lengthy stay in Damascus.

"Nadia's busy, and apparently, I work for her." Omar came back into the office and handed me the printouts. He sat on the edge of the desk facing me.

"She's a boss lady," I said, hoping he wouldn't notice I hadn't put his frame back up.

"Yeah." He followed my eyes to the frame. "It was distracting," I explained.

"You like the water?" He lifted the frame back up. "Definitely. I miss it a little bit."

"I will bring you to Latakia with me sometime. But more importantly, when are you coming to my bar?"

CHAPTER 7

O BAR

"A Muslim walks into a bar . . ." It was the same day my father left for Syria that he stood in the center of my parents' bedroom, two suitcases open on the floor.

I stood in the doorway patiently waiting for the punchline but none came. "That's the joke?"

"Yeah," he said, as he laughed and snorted. "We are not supposed to drink, you know?"

"I know. But because we do, it makes the joke not funny."

Undeterred, he continued, "Okay, what does a Muslim say when he walks into a bar?"

"*Allah ou akbar?*" I asked, willing to play along but, as usual, embarrassed by my inability to speak Arabic properly.

"*Akkhhhh,*" he said, holding his forehead and stumbling backward as though he were in pain. "He walked into a bar. He says what anyone would say when he bumps into something and gets injured."

"Dad, seriously. Who tells you these jokes?"

"My patient. Americans are funny people. He tells me the same jokes every time I see him and would you believe he makes me laugh every time? Maybe because it makes him laugh so much," he said, as he walked back and forth from his closet, pulling green, blue, and orange polo shirts and jeans and tossing them in stacks in his suitcase. The other suitcase held deflated soccer balls, tubes of face cream, and lollipops.

"You're doing a lot of surgeries this time?"

"There's a waiting list, even. *Inshallah*, I get to everyone who needs me."

Though he never said it, I always had the sense he felt he was just another plastic surgeon in Orange County, but in Syria, he could actually make a difference. I was happy he was in better spirits than the other day when I ran into him coming out of his office. I wanted to ask him about the Syrian authority figures he was angry with, but for some reason I was afraid. Afraid of what he might say. Then again, maybe it had to do with the surgeries he wasn't able to do. Nothing bothered him more than not being able to get to people who needed him. People he knew had no one else.

"Wish I could come with you," I said, sitting on their king-size bed while remembering jumping into their bed when I was younger and swimming in a sea of pillows. I sat up a little straighter now. "Did you talk to Mom about it?"

"You know, Laila, sometimes I wonder if she was right to keep you here. Even though I still wish she let me get you an Arabic teacher, I may have been wrong to want to take you there all these years."

My mouth dropped open. "Uh, this is new. Why are you all of a sudden changing your mind about this?" Though he always backed down in the end, he never suggested my mother was right for keeping me away. "I am nineteen now, I can go if I want to."

"Do you really want to? Or would you want to do it to make me happy? Or even to defy your mother a little bit?"

"Of course, I want to go. How many years have we been fighting Mom? I thought we were together on this."

"We are. You know I always support you in whatever you want. But she's right that you have to choose it because you want it." I got the sneaking suspicion he was choosing his words way too carefully.

"How can I choose? I never had the chance to even know it."

"*Inshallah, habibti*, one day everything will work out the way it is supposed to."

"I mean, I guess so," I said. "I know so," he said. "Okay, Dad."

"We have a nice life here."

"Yeah, definitely. Tell Mazen I said hi?" "Yes, of course."

"Bring me something?" "Anything."

"Choco Prince?"

"Of course, *hayati*. I always bring you Choco Prince."

"You okay, Dad?" I was disappointed that his mood turned more serious than when I first found him and I felt guilty that it was me who reminded him of whatever was upsetting him.

"Yes, sweetheart, I'm fine."

I got up to leave and when I reached the doorway, I remembered what I wanted to ask. "Hey, Dad, your patient, the guy that you think is funny?"

"Yes, what about him?"

"What work did he have done? Just curious."

"This guy was in Iraq. He was in a roadside bombing. I fixed some of the burns on his face. He is a young man, *alhamdid Allah*, he is healing well."

"Oh. That's good."

If my father were a different man, he may have taken offense at his joke. If this young man were different, he might take a hostile posture toward my father. He was always teaching me not to take offense too quickly, and to be a little less sensitive and a little more caring. I remember wondering at the time if we could ever get to a higher place or would we always inevitably retreat to what we know.

❦

Omar's bar was tucked into a cozy side street of the old city, a remodeled Damascene home, much like my family's, but twice the size, and everything freshly restored. A sign with the bar's name hung modestly from a lamp post outside the front door.

"You named the bar after yourself?" I asked.

"The success or failure of any bar or nightclub depends on one thing only and that is if the hot girls hang out there."

"I get that. What does that have to do with you?"

"Every girl in the city knows me. They love O Bar," he said as we walked in.

"It stands for oasis!" A guy about Omar's age with fair skin and freckles, dressed in a light orange linen button-down shirt, shouted from behind the bar. I assumed he was Omar's business partner and he had had this conversation many times before.

"It was the only way I could get him to agree to name the place after me," Omar said.

"It is not after you," he insisted, inspecting a martini glass against the pink uplighting behind the bar.

Omar winked at me and nodded.

"It stands for the oasis, like Damascus is an oasis and we are an oasis inside an oasis," he continued, revealing a slight lisp and a gap between his two front teeth.

"This is why I handle the branding. This is Gabriel, he handles, what do you do?" Omar asked him.

"All the work? And I serve our Christian friends so we don't have to close for a month during Ramadan," Gabriel snapped a white cloth out and cleaned the edge of the glass with it.

"Laila. Nice to meet you, Gabriel."

"Everyone calls me Gabby." He set the martini glass down and shook my hand. "Nice to have you, Laila."

I took a seat at the bar and looked around. The actual bar stretched from one end of the courtyard to the other, string lights twinkled in the lemon trees, and plush white couches lined the outer edges. We were the only ones there besides a few people in uniforms carrying trays of glasses and setting out ashtrays.

"Do you drink?" Omar asked me, as he slipped behind the bar.

I hesitated before I said, "Yes. I was actually doing an internship at a winery before I came."

"You are not even allowed to drink there yet."

"After hours." Late evenings at Amou's vineyard were mostly older people, who couldn't tell whether I was nineteen or twenty-nine, but there were always interesting guests coming and going and part of my internship was hosting them.

"Well, here it is not a problem." "The drinking age here is eighteen?"

"The drinking age is whatever we want it to be."

"I also would not drink in front of Mazen." I felt the need to clarify in case it ever came up.

"Ah, he is your keeper."

"It's more out of respect for him. My family's conservative, so I try to—"

He laughed and held his hand up to stop me. "Laila, listen to me. You don't have to explain any of that stuff. I drink with my father's side of the family; I go to the mosque with my mother's side. I get it."

"Does that make you feel weird though? Or like you're betraying one side of the family?"

"No. We can hold two contradictory truths in our heads at the same time."

"But which one is right?"

"I'm Muslim, but I don't think I am going to hell because I drink."

"Maybe for another reason but not drinking, right?"

"Exactly. Would you like an apricot margarita?" "Are you kidding?"

"We only make them for a short time, their season comes and goes quickly."

"I love apricots."

"In Arabic, they're called *mush mush.*" "*Mush mush,*" I repeated, giggling.

"But, in some parts of South America, they call them Damasco, because apricots from Damascus are the best in the world."

"Of course they are." I smiled thinking about all the times my dad said the best of something was always from Damascus.

As Omar grabbed bottles and scooped ice into a shaker, he explained what he was using: fresh apricot juice, lime, tequila, and a little orange-flavored liquor. I could tell from the way his hands moved expertly from one step to the next, not even looking at what he was grabbing, he had done this many times before.

"How is Mazen? Is he considering my offer?" He poured the drink into a margarita glass in front of me. I put my lips to the glass and sipped through the froth, a delicious blend of sweet and tart. I smiled my approval and wiped the excess from the corner of my mouth with my fingertip. "Good."

"Mazen or the margarita?"

"Both. He is definitely interested. I think he wants to make sure it's the right thing."

"Why wouldn't it be? I mean, if you don't mind me asking."

"It's just, Mazen wants to make sure his family is okay first. That he can work for his father and you."

"Of course. Fair enough." "Aren't you having one?"

"I don't drink while I'm working."

I shrugged and continued to sip my drink.

"Tell me, where did you hang it?" he asked, trying to mask his amusement.

"Hang what?"

"The gift I gave you." "The poster? Oh, I didn't."

"Laila," he said, putting his hand to his chest, feigning heartbreak. "How could you not hang this great work of art? It's an original print, you know."

"I didn't have time." I hoped he would forget about the poster because I wasn't even sure why I lied about hanging it up. Maybe I was worried he would think it was normal to hang a picture of the president in his bedroom.

"Don't worry, we are not asking you to pledge your allegiance to anything." He rested his forearms on the bar and met my eyes, "Yet."

"Haha."

Omar and I talked about our hobbies and families and it came up again about his boat at the coast. Even though my comfort with Omar was growing I had to stop myself from asking him about his friend that I had seen in the street and the photo on his office desk, if it was even the same guy.

"So, is this a permanent move or do you plan to go back to California?"

"I'm not sure." While my mother had no intention of staying any longer than we had to, I didn't want Omar to think I was leaving any time soon.

"Maybe you will meet someone here, fall in love, have a couple of Syr babies?"

"That is never going to happen." I started giggling but stopped when Omar's smile disappeared from his face.

"Why not?" he asked, crossing his arms across his chest. "You wouldn't go out with a Syrian guy?" Just then we heard a loud crashing sound through the kitchen door, like a tray of glasses hit the tile floor. Omar shook his head and went to take care of it. I sipped my margarita and watched as people started to trickle in, tingly from the drink.

"Easy, Laila, there is a lot of tequila in there." Omar came back to the bar, texting on his phone.

"Really? I can't taste any alcohol."

"Because the apricot is sweet. I should have held back a little on yours." He looked up from his phone.

"My father doesn't allow me to have boyfriends from anywhere. He didn't even let me hang around my friends' boyfriends."

"So he wanted to keep you in the house forever?" He raised one eyebrow.

"He was weird about boys, that's all. As far as future stuff, we ... didn't have that conversation."

"Wow."

"Anyway, I would never make a life-altering decision for a ... guy."

"No?"

"I have seen so many girls change their lives for a relationship."

"If he can provide a nice life for you, what's the problem?"

"Omar," I said, "you sound like Mazen. Would you want a girl to give up everything for you?"

"Yes," he said, a smile playing on his lips. "Tell me, Laila, and we're being serious now. Who's waiting for you in California?"

"Nobody." I didn't think about the future much at all and I could only have guessed my father would have wanted me to get married one day. He was a hopeless romantic who changed the direction of his life, gave up ambitions, and being close with his family, all for my mom. Maybe he didn't want me to have those complications or maybe he hoped I would stay at home forever. For reasons that had nothing to do with religion or culture, my father didn't ever want me to have my heart broken.

Someone must have turned the music up because it was getting loud and we had to shout at each other to be heard.

"Look up," Omar said. I tilted my head back and noticed for the first time the moon was full and, with the lights turned down, the stars filled the sky. The courtyards were becoming my favorite place in Damascus. Even inside, all you had to do was look up to see the sky and everything greater than you. "This is God's city, Laila. You belong here."

After Omar dropped me off at home, I found Mazen in the courtyard. I wanted to bring up the subject of Omar's job offer without seeming like I was pushing my own agenda. After catching up on each other's day, I decided it was best just to put his mind at rest.

"Mazen, they are not all hard-core Ba'athists."

"With these people, you are either in or you are out. And I am not sure I want to be in with these kinds of people."

"I see how Omar can be a little intimidating. But deep down he is just like us, Mazen. I trust him, he is one of the good ones." I continued because it was too late to backpedal, and I was ready to back off if this one final play didn't convince him. "If my father were here, he would tell you this is an amazing opportunity. One that may not come again. Didn't you say you want to save money so you can buy a house and get married?"

"Yes." Mazen sat back in his chair, swinging his car keys around his index finger.

My mother walked out of the kitchen with a glass of tea in her hand. "I hate to say it Mazen but she's right. If your uncle were here, he would say take it."

"Do you think so, Auntie, really?" He stopped swinging his keys and looked at my mother, surprised by her enthusiasm.

"Yes. This is exactly the kind of thing he would have wanted for you. This is your chance, Mazen."

"Omar wants you for a reason. He grew up in a different Damascus than you, he knows that. He wants you to help with messaging, reaching other people like you to find out what your ideas are for the future. This is your chance to write a new story. How could this be a bad thing?"

When I turned in that night, still buzzing from the apricot margarita Omar made me, I slept with the deep comfort of feeling complete. Damascus was starting to feel like the paradise my father had always promised.

CHAPTER 8

MUY

I woke up to the sound of my aunt yelling at my uncle to bring her more water.

"*Muy*," I repeated and wiped the sleep from my eyes, pleased with myself for immediately knowing the word for water in Arabic. I pulled a pair of jeans on, then shuffled out of my room in *shahatta*, slippers, and poked my head over the balcony to see my aunt ironing in the courtyard. She was suspicious of most modern technology, her iron an ancient relic which seemed to heat to a thousand degrees, steam blasting from its edges and a cord so long it disappeared into the sitting room or what they called a *'salon.'* My aunt insisted everything done the old way was the right way and even from the balcony, I could see Mazen's white button-down shirts were pristine.

The whole house was buzzing about his new job. As soon as she found out he accepted Omar's offer, my aunt started ironing his entire wardrobe, even sending his shoes out to be professionally cleaned. It didn't seem necessary to tell either of them Omar usually wore polo shirts and jeans to work. It wouldn't have changed

Mazen's mind anyway. His look was always immaculate and slightly overdressed.

The only person who seemed uncertain was my uncle. He and Mazen had gone back and forth several times since his interview and I could gather he was trying to tell him he could work for Omar during the day and then go to his father's shop in the souk in the evenings, which was their busiest time. I couldn't tell if it was the nature of Omar's work and his proximity to the government that was troubling my uncle or maybe the disappointment that he could not provide an opportunity the way a twenty-nine-year-old kid like Omar could. While I was sure he was happy for Mazen, he was not happy to let him go, and he certainly didn't like that his business could not support all three of his sons.

As I made my way down the stairs, my aunt disappeared into the kitchen and came back out with a rolled-up sandwich and a peeled cucumber in a plastic bag. "*Ay mab tarif shoo besir. Berkey ma bit hib aklato,*" she said when Mazen raised his eyebrows at her.

"She said you don't know what will happen. Maybe you don't like their food," he smiled, taking it from her and putting the sandwich bag against his heart. "And thank you, Laila. Really." My aunt looked me up and down and then hurried back to the kitchen.

"Please. You didn't need me. All I did was sneak into the American school, which you helped me do anyway."

"Cream always rises to the top, Mazen," my mother's voice rang out over the balcony.

"Okay, Auntie," Mazen answered politely, having no idea what cream rising had to do with him.

"Don't leave yet. I have something for you." She came down the stairs, a green silk tie in her hand. "I found this in our bedroom. I know how happy he would be to see you wear it."

"Thank you, Auntie." He draped the tie across his shoulders but fumbled because of the sandwich bag when he tried to tie it.

"Let Laila, she knows how."

I adjusted the ends of the tie around his neck, a vision of my father's face when he had to attend medical conferences moved through me as my fingers remembered how to cross the fabric over, under, and through the loop.

"It's okay?" Mazen asked. I had to admit that the green tie stood out against his pressed white shirt.

"Perfect. Very patriotic." I pinched the center knot to give it a dimple, my father's favorite last touch.

"I'm having coffee with the landscaping lady, and then she's driving us up to the villa. Do you mind dropping me in Muhajireen to meet her?" my mother asked Mazen.

"Of course," Mazen replied as my mother hurried up the stairs to finish getting dressed.

"I have something for you." He reached into his pocket and pulled out a cell phone. "You can use it for now and then maybe we can bring you another one."

"Oh thanks, Mazen. Cool."

It looked slightly used, and when I saw the screen saver, a picture of me in mock terror, with a cat on top of my head, her claws in my hair, I knew who it belonged to. The photo was one I sent to shame him when he got me a cat instead of a dog, a compromise from the canary. My voice caught in my throat, and I was silent, concentrating on the phone so I wouldn't cry. My aunt came back and handed me a rolled-up sandwich.

"I didn't know, maybe it makes you sad?" Mazen said. "I believe it is still working."

"It's just . . . it doesn't look like a phone that has been in a fatal car accident, does it?" I asked, taking the sandwich from my aunt with my free hand.

"No, he forgot sometimes." He shrugged his shoulders. "He has all his music here."

"Omg, God only knows what's on here," I said, turning toward the stairs. "Thanks. I will go check on her for you."

"Please." Mazen would never try to rush my mother, he would wait forever.

I slipped my father's phone in the back pocket of my jeans and found my mother in front of the mirror that hung above the dresser in their room. "I have been meaning to tell you, not that it matters, but as long as we're here I hope you know not to take Syrian men seriously. They are outrageous flirts."

"Okay. If you're talking about Omar, he doesn't flirt with me." I sat on the bed and leaned back against the headboard, eating my *lebneh* sandwich. Her tactics were always amusing but none of her discouragement was going to work now that I was here. "There is really no interest from either of us. We're just friends."

"They flirt with the foreigners, they marry the Syrian girls," she continued as though I hadn't said anything. She opened her eyes wide, pulling her lashes with a mascara wand.

"I was born in Damascus, remember? I'm pretty sure you were there."

"God, how could I forget? I remember thinking how weird it would be for a California girl to die giving birth in Chami Hospital."

"And yet here you are."

She looked at me in the mirror. "And here you are, my love."

"Anyway, Dad didn't." "Didn't what?"

"Marry a Syr, obviously."

"He almost did." She dabbed a little lip gloss on her lips. "Laila, why are you eating so much bread?"

"Because it's sacred," I said, my mouth full of food. "What do you mean he almost married a Syrian girl?"

"Oh, I have to go; I don't want to make Mazen late. I love you." She kissed my forehead with her fresh gloss and headed out the door.

"I love you, Mommy."

I popped the rest of the sandwich in my mouth and took the phone out of my back pocket, studying the picture of myself. It was so like him to use this picture as his screen saver. I wondered what his young dreams were like when he slept in this bed and if he sensed my American mother and me waiting for him in his future. He hadn't mentioned he was engaged to a Syrian girl, although I had never thought to ask. I was learning more about my father since I arrived and if I didn't dwell too much, curiosity seemed to keep the grief at bay.

I wandered back to my room and realized that, with my mom and Mazen gone, the house was quiet. On the plus side, it meant there was nobody to micromanage me. I pulled my jeans off and picked out a pair of black leggings and a long-sleeved black workout top I would have only worn on chillier mornings in California. It was a fair compromise in my mind. As I pulled my black sneakers on, I heard a knock at the front door. I waited to see if anyone else would answer, but the knocking continued so I assumed my aunt and uncle were out grocery shopping.

When I opened the door, a young man wearing a long white robe, fitted white cap, and thick beard stood staring back at me. He looked vaguely familiar, and it took me a minute to realize he was the one who was watching me in the parking lot when I finished my run and put my sweatpants back on over my shorts. It had only been a few weeks but it seemed like a lifetime ago that I was running in my shorts in the streets of old Damascus. Only in retrospect did I understand how crazy that was. Was he here to tell on me? I pushed the thought away, realizing how ridiculous that would be. He doesn't even know me.

"Hi," I had to assume he was a relative or friend, otherwise he wouldn't be here, and I didn't want to embarrass my family by being unfriendly. "Can I help you?"

"Is Mazen here? I was hoping he would come to the mosque with me." It took me a moment to realize he was speaking English, perfect English with a British accent.

"No, he left already," I answered. "He has a new job so..."

"A new job?"

I nodded but didn't offer any more information. "I'm Laila, by the way." I offered him my hand to shake, hoping he didn't remember seeing me.

He eyed my outstretched hand and then placed his hand on his chest, this time careful not to look me in the eye. "Mahmoud." I pulled my hand back, embarrassed he left me hanging. "Please let him know I stopped by."

"Sure." As soon as I started to close the door, he added, "Oh, Laila, I am sorry for your father's passing. May God have mercy on his soul." While his words were technically polite, his tone was cool, his eyes full of judgment in place of sympathy.

"Thanks." I shuddered as I shut the door behind him. Why would Mazen be friends with someone so creepy? I would have to tell my mother she was wrong and that not all Syrian men were flirts.

I asked the taxi driver to drop me at Chami Hospital, the place where I was born and my mother 'almost died'. I planned to run down the hill from the hospital, cut across the Sheraton hotel, around Umayyad Circle-Square, past the sword, and come back up the hill on the other side of the street. I plugged my earbuds into his phone, turning it up loud enough to drown out any comments.

All my muscles were stiff and lazy, so I pushed them gently as I worked my way down the hill. I deepened my breath as I picked up speed and I could feel myself getting in step with the city, my pulse lining up with the lifeblood of Damascus like when I first entered the world.

My sneakers tapped against the pavement, my ponytail swinging behind me. As soon as I started running, I felt how long it had been since my last run. I was used to the heat, but I hadn't realized how much drier it was in Syria, and I regretted not bringing my water bottle. As hot as it was, I realized I wasn't sweating and I licked my lips to wet them. I pushed the sleeves of my shirt up and tried to lift my leggings up a little to cool down, renewing my annoyance at not being able to wear what I wanted.

My father's playlist was predictably hilarious. A mix of eighties and random American pop music, a song about raining in Africa and another that I suspected was off one of the Rocky movies. Was it possible to miss someone more and feel closer to them at the same time?

Nobody paid any attention to me as I ran through the guest entrance of the Sheraton. As I exited on the other side of the hotel, I was met by the intoxicating aroma of garlic, tomato, and brick oven pizza. The sun was high now, but the outdoor pizzeria was still pretty empty, as lunch in Syria was considerably later in the afternoon than what I was used to.

A smallish man, who looked no more than a boy, in a red vest and black dress pants, walked a few steps ahead of me, a case of bottled water on his shoulder. I wiped the sweat from my brow and thought how hot he must be in those clothes in addition to carrying such a heavy weight. I didn't want to slow my pace, so when I stepped off the curb to pass him, I must have startled him. He turned toward me and dropped the case of water. The plastic case broke open in front of me, bottles rolling in every direction. I jumped to avoid tripping over them and smashed straight into a tall, sturdy structure. When I looked up, the green eyes I thought I had imagined in the streets of Muhajireen until I saw them again in the photo on Omar's desk gazing back at me.

Oh. It was like looking at the sea though we were nowhere near the coast. His palm rested lightly on my arm to steady me as I tried to catch my breath, Rihanna still singing *SOS* in my ears. I swallowed to keep my mouth closed, and I was reminded of my thirst. He smiled the same half-smile I was finding so familiar in my mind's eye, revealing white teeth against bronzed skin.

"*Muy,*" Was the only thing I could make come out of my mouth. He nodded in agreement as if I had just stated the obvious until he realized I was referring to the cold water bottle he was holding and slowly handed it to me. I took it from him and put my mouth directly on the bottle as I had not yet mastered the Syrian trick of drinking without touching.

He stood staring at me in his military uniform, the steel sword in the distance behind him. It was like we were lost in time and space for a brief moment until my thirst was quenched, and I handed his water bottle back to him. I waved apologetically to the boys in vests who were gathering the bottles and looked to have been watching our exchange with some amusement.

I knew simple phrases like 'thank you' and 'I'm sorry', but I couldn't make any of those come out of my mouth. I gave him a little salute instead and turned around and kept running.

The phone started ringing, cutting into my thoughts and music. "Hello?" I sounded like a four-year-old answering her Dad's phone.

"*Allo*, Laila, what problems are you causing today? What rules have you broken and it's not even lunchtime?"

"What's up, Omar? Omg, you are my first phone call."

"Mazen gave me your number. Listen, I'm having a party Thursday night at the bar, will you come?"

"Let me check if I have anything else going on."

"I already asked Mazen. He said you're always free."
"Oh. How's it going by the way? Is everyone being nice to the new kid?"

"They love him. He brought a sandwich to work, this guy is hilarious."

"I know. Are you doing curls right now?" "Triceps."

"I think the two of you need to get back to work. I'm not seeing nearly enough propaganda on my running route."

"We don't need it in this neighborhood. But I like the way you think."

"So, let me ask you something. If a total stranger took a drink from your water bottle, would you be disgusted?"

"Is she hot?" I was on the brink of overheating and dehydration.

"Very," I said, confident in my answer.

"Did you put your mouth on it?" he asked, trying to mask his laughter.

"Maybe." A little more hesitantly. "Laila, we don't do it like that."

"Hey, how did you know I was running in your neighborhood?"

"I'll pick you up at eight; be ready," he said and hung up.

When I got back to my Uncle's house, I saw the bathroom door open and found Mazen shaving. I stepped in and sat on the edge of the bathtub.

"Why do Arab guys shave twice a day?" I asked, even though I knew the answer.

"Because we have no choice." He used a shaving brush working it into a big, white lather. I loved the old way of shaving; especially when my dad did it, it always looked like whipped cream. Then I remembered the beard from earlier that day.

"Your friend was here earlier today, Mahmoud? He was asking if you wanted to go to the mosque," I said, with raised eyebrows. "I told him about your new job."

"You told him?"

"Also, he wouldn't shake my hand, how rude is that?"

He stopped shaving for a minute. He laughed and tapped his razor blade against the sink. "No, he doesn't shake hands with girls. If people at the mosque knew him before..."

"What do you mean? What was he like?"

"He was drinking, smoking, chasing girls. He always wanted me to go out with him."

"You didn't like hanging out with him?"

"I didn't mind it but he used to get so drunk. Then all he would talk about was his dream to move to America where he could see girls in bikinis everywhere."

"He never got to go?"

"His visa was denied many times so he went to England to study because they gave him an easier time. He came back very religious. I don't know what happened over there."

"But you said he wanted to go to the States?"

I felt a pang of sadness for Mahmoud, maybe even compassion, then remembered his coldness toward me in the doorway earlier that day. I brushed it all aside. "So, tell me again why are you friends with him?"

"He's our neighbor, we have always been family friends. He knows you too, from when you were young."

"Really?" I was hoping Mahmoud had not mentioned to Mazen about the shorts. Mazen knew I'd been running but the shorts were still my little secret. They were a silly mistake I made early on that I wanted to forget. I wanted to change the subject of Mahmoud completely. Part of me felt sorry for him and a part of me strongly disliked, maybe even feared, him.

"So, did you know my dad was engaged before he married my mom? She said it was to a Syrian girl?"

"Mmm yes, it's true. I remember." "What happened?"

"With her, I don't know. Maybe he knew to that marry your mother was the right thing from the beginning."

"Yeah, could be. You're coming to Omar's party?"

"No, I have to go to the souk. Work, *ya* Laila."

"After?" When he shook his head vehemently, I asked, "Why not? It's fun." I was hardly a wild partier, but even by my standards, Mazen could definitely loosen up a little bit. He was twenty-nine going on fifty years old.

"I don't drink, Laila. Why would I spend time in a bar with all these big *wasta* people?"

"Just to hang out."

"You Americans love to 'hang out.'" He threw his towel at me. "A man needs to sleep."

CHAPTER 9

BIG *WASTA*, SMALL *HARAM*

"You said eight." I stood in the parking lot in the beam of Omar's headlights when he finally picked me up from my uncle's house.

"Yeah." He stood on the driver's side of his Mercedes with his elbow on the open door, pointing to the watch on his wrist.

"You called and said you were 'on the way', that was hours ago, what the hell?"

"Laila, what kind of Arab are you? Everyone knows 'on the way' means I am nowhere near ready."

"If I had known you were going to take so long, I would have taken a nap," I said, holding my space in front of the car.

"I'm sorry, Madam Laila, I promise I will make it up to you." He placed his palms together against his chest. "*Yalla* please, let's go."

"Oh, now you're in a hurry."

"Laila, no one goes out this early. It's my party and I wouldn't show up before ten."

I could tell he was genuinely surprised that I was upset with him. It made me worry I was acting more like a girlfriend and less like a cool friend and I didn't want to give him that impression, but I didn't want him to think I was some pushover either.

"Look, I had to take a shower then deal with my girlfriend . . ." He sighed deeply, letting his head drop forward. He looked back up to meet my eyes. "Sorry."

"Girlfriend?" I repeated, feeling relief and suspicion at the same time.

"Yeah," he lowered his voice and eyed a few passersby who were pretending not to watch us in the parking lot. Of course, Mahmoud had to be one of them. Why did he always seem to be lurking at the most inopportune times? I turned my attention back to Omar. "I will explain, please just get in the car."

"Fine," I said, walking over to the passenger door and sliding in. "So? Why didn't you mention her before?"

"You didn't ask, first of all. Secondly, I didn't think it mattered to us. We're friends, right?"

"Yeah, but does she care that we hang out? Is that why you were fighting with her?"

"Believe me, you are not the problem."

"Why then?" I asked, "Omar, I don't like secrets—" "She is Christian, Laila. Her family doesn't know about me."

"Oh," I replied after a while. I wasn't sure what question to begin with. For some reason my mind wandered back to Mahmoud walking through the parking lot a moment ago and a word I had heard in the house, *haram*, or sins in Islam. "Is being in love with a Christian *haram*?"

"No, love is never *haram*. I only wish she didn't have to lie to her parents, this part kills me."

"You don't know, maybe they would be okay with it."

"No, they wouldn't. Christians, they don't like their daughters with Muslim guys. None of the minorities like intermarriage."

"Marriage? I mean if you guys are serious maybe you can convert?"

"No, *habibti*, she will convert."

"Why does she have to change?" I fired back a little too quickly.

"Oh my God, Laila, it's not for me. My family is very open-minded, but for some legal issues, it's much easier if she's Muslim. I love Christmas and Easter bunnies and all these funny things she likes, and we will celebrate however she wants. But for the future, it benefits her to convert."

"What will you teach your kids?"

"*Inshallah*, we teach them to be good people who respect all faiths. The details are minor."

"I wouldn't say 'minor.'"

"This is a major issue for you, I can tell."

"Yeah, it's not easy being half and half. When you're a kid, you just want to be like everyone else, you know? Not a weirdo."

I wasn't sure about his idea that she should automatically become like him, but it was a nice break from my own story, and I did like that I was becoming part of his inner circle. As he weaved in and out of traffic and through the narrow streets of old Damascus, I thought of my father and wondered if he and my mom had these same conversations about her becoming Muslim. I couldn't imagine how my mother would have responded to such a request. Not because she was such a devout Christian but because of her resistance to change and adherence to a particular worldview. I never doubted her love for him despite their differences, maybe even somewhere deep down she loved him because of their differences. The more I learned about Omar the more curious I got about all his motivations.

"So, why are you spending so much time with me?" I asked.

"I like you. I know how it is to be somewhere new where you don't know anyone."

"It's weird, though, because I am not new, you know? I was born here."

"So you are saying you don't need me?"

"No, I do. I mean, I hang out with you because I like you, too, but I don't need you to babysit me. I could totally meet people on my own."

"Really? How? By drinking from strangers' water bottles in the street? I think you could use my help."

I sighed, conceding the point. "So your girlfriend, what's her name?" When he hesitated, I said, "I won't tell anyone about her, I promise."

"Sabrina." He smiled broadly, showing all of his teeth. He couldn't even say her name without smiling. "Her name is Sabrina."

"Does Sabrina come to O Bar?" I asked, hoping I could meet her and see what she looks like.

"Not really, no."

"Why not? You could pretend not to know each other," I said, thinking it seemed a perfect way for them to see each other without being found out.

"First of all, she doesn't really like, you know, *dowjay*, loud places. Lucky for me, she only likes fancy dinners and things like this, which is better for me because if any guy tried to talk to her, I would have to kill him. That's not good for my business and then everyone would find out about us," he said, pulling into a side street close to O Bar. I had never witnessed even a hint of a violent streak in him but the way he said he would kill a guy for talking to his girlfriend left little doubt that he was exaggerating.

Before we got out of the car he turned and said, "People hide their girlfriends all the time here. Only my close friends know about her. If anyone else found out, it would be over tomorrow. Please."

"Your secret is safe with me." "You said you don't like secrets."

"Secrets to protect people I love, I don't mind." "Thank you."

When we walked into O Bar, I saw his business partner, Gabby, was already there, making drinks for a few early guests sitting at the bar. There was a DJ setting up his booth in the far corner, and low tables with flickering tea light candles lined the side of the courtyard that sat opposite of the bar, and lemon yellow throw pillows popped against the white couches. It smelled of men's cologne and freshly lit cigarettes.

"Where are the 'hot girls'?" I asked, just to poke fun at him for bragging that all the hot girls in the city hung out at his place, and yet his bar full of young men smoking and drinking scotch. These were probably the 'big *wastas*' Mazen was talking about.

He smiled, slipping behind the bar. "They'll be here, don't worry. They're, uh . . . getting ready."

"It took me fifteen minutes to wash my hair and be totally ready."

"Yeah," Omar said, nodding while trying, unsuccessfully, to hide his amusement.

"You're wearing house slippers at a bar," I said, crossing my arms.

"I'm a guy. These girls are basically ... full-on. They will come with hair, makeup, the whole thing."

"Oh." I looked down at my flip-flops and torn jeans and wondered if maybe I should have put on a little mascara.

"It's confident," Omar assured me.

Before I left my uncle's house, my mother brought a little black dress to my room, one she had been trying to get me to wear for ages. She had bought it for me in California for my senior prom. The prom I 'didn't go to' she liked to point out.

When she handed it to me, I held the dress in my hands, remembering how it looked hanging on the back of my bedroom door in California and how my father really didn't want me to go, how much I didn't want to disappoint him. I felt a pang of resentment at the time at what I had missed out on in high school because of the many times I couldn't go to parties or hang out with friends because boys would be there. Having the dress in my room in Damascus made it seem silly to keep hanging on to my old life. What difference did it make? What if I had gone to the prom with a real date? If I had fallen for him, would I have come to Syria? Of course, I would. I would come for my father under any circumstances, so it worked out for the best anyway.

"Dad didn't want me to go," I had reminded her, handing the dress back to her. I couldn't believe she brought it all the way from California.

"He said it was fine."

"He said 'tayyib, okay', which means he was getting tired of arguing with you. He didn't want me to go, Mom."

As much as my mom and I disagreed, she must have sensed I was having some guilt about hanging out with Omar—all the more reason to be relieved to find out about Sabrina.

"He knew he was going to have to let you go at some point," she said. "I mean, obviously, I don't want you to meet anyone here . . . I am just thinking you might not be used to the way people dress here when they go out. It's pretty over the top and I want you to feel comfortable."

"Mom, you know Omar and I are just friends, right?" I asked, but something else had already caught her eye. "What is that?" She pointed at the poster on the wall of the president and his sons that Omar had given me. I had gotten so used to having it there. I had even taken to having daily conversations with the future president, the young one with the fair hair and aviator glasses. I chose him over the darker complexioned one, the son who had passed, because I couldn't get anywhere talking to the dead. The young one seemed more open and playful, despite the aviators and fierce expression. Speaking to him made me feel less crazy, and when I said it out loud what I really felt they didn't sound as scary on the outside of my head. He was a very good listener, and I never felt judged. I made a daily habit of telling him '*khalas yalla bye*' before I left the room, if only so I could practice my main three words of Arabic.

"It's the first print. You'll be seeing the young one's face all over the city soon. You know after the father dies."

She gave me a reproachful look but said nothing. I wasn't sure whether she was responding to my hanging the poster, to begin with, or that I said 'when the father dies' because officially no one was allowed to acknowledge the illness of the current president even though we all knew his son was already running the country. Knowing my mother, it was probably the former. Her experience of Syria was still that of a critical, although largely disinterested, observer.

Now I watched Omar make my drink in his *shahatta* and tried to get his attention. In an effort to be discreet, I made a circle with my index finger and thumb and put my other index finger through it, gesturing to the guy sitting a few stools down from me at the bar. Omar's eyes went wide as he said, "Dude . . ."

I leaned over the bar to whisper in his ear. "Inner circle? Is that guy in your inner circle?"

"Oh! Which guy? The chubby one?" Omar said, loud enough for him to hear.

"Omar!"

"What? He knows he's fat. Look at him, he doesn't give a fuck." 'The Chubby One' started beating his belly like a drum as soon as the DJ began playing Arabic pop music. Omar shook his head at me and lowered his voice. "I'm already regretting telling you."

"I just want to know who's who. You have to help me out."

"He's a friend but not part of the inner circle. The less he knows the better it is for him. And," he nodded in the direction of the kitchen, suddenly sounding serious, "Gabby, for sure, no."

Omar placed a full-to-the-rim apricot margarita just out of my reach on the bar and met my eyes. Understanding his meaning, I said, "Okay, Omar, I got it." I pulled an invisible zipper across my lips and reached for my drink.

"Laila, seriously," he said, still holding the drink back.

"You either trust me or you don't. I'm sure I will have a secret one day that I will ask you to keep," I said.

"Oh, fuck. That's for sure." He slid the glass my way, obviously reassured, and then half jogged, half skipped into the kitchen, dodging Gabby on his way. I found mild amusement in how confident he was that I would get into some scandalous situation that would require his secrecy.

I watched as the newer partygoers arrived, everyone kissing on both cheeks, the girls taking extra care not to smear lipstick on each other by lightly tapping each other's impossibly high cheekbones and kissing the air. As soon as I was emboldened enough by the tequila, I turned to my neighbor, the so-called 'Chubby One' at the bar, and I was grateful he spoke first.

"How are you?" he asked loudly speaking with a thick Syrian accent. I got the feeling he was one of those people who it didn't matter what he said, everything came out funny.

"Good!" I yelled back so he could hear me over the music. I moved a few stools closer to him. I didn't know how long Omar would be, and I thought I might as well meet new people. "Is this why Damascenes stay out so late? With all the kissing it takes an hour to get into a party."

"Go to Beirut, there it's three kisses." He flashed his middle, ring, and pinkie fingers. "They stay till the morning."

"Kissing?"

"Kissing, drinking, dancing . . . that is what war does to people."

"I think I like Beirut," I said, remembering suddenly all of Amou's stories at the vineyard and how close they seem to me now instead of a mythical, magical place.

"You will love Beirut."

"More than here?" I was sincere in my efforts to fill out applications to schools in California, but the American University in Beirut did pop up in my research, though I doubted Mom would ever agree to let me go.

"No, Damascus is home, but Beirut is . . . something else."

"Yeah?" I prodded.

"Damascus is like a good wife, special, home, there's no one like her. Her love is pure. Beirut is like a wild mistress, good for a weekend here and there, but you can't stay. It's too easy to get lost in her. You forget who you are."

"Wow. Now, I have to go," I said, as soon as Omar reappeared from the kitchen.

"You should go with Omar. First, let him take you to Latakia, the coast. He has a boat there."

"And jet skis, right?" I asked, my mind wandering back to the photo on Omar's desk of him and his friends, one of them the impossibly hot soldier in the street with the water bottle.

"Yes. My name is Amer, by the way." He offered me his hand.

"Laila." I was glad not to have to call him 'The Chubby One.' Amer was distracted by one of his friends shouting at him in Arabic, so Omar lowered his voice to speak privately with me.

"By the way, Laila, this—" he made the same symbol I had before, making a circle with his thumb and forefinger, and sticking his other forefinger through the circle, "is the international symbol for fucking. It does not mean 'inner circle.'"

I had to smile at his ancient reference. "Omar, seriously, you are so vintage."

"I am twenty-nine."

"I know, right?" I started laughing when someone coming through the swinging kitchen door caught my eye. Maybe it was his bronzed skin against the bright white of his polo shirt or the electric currents that coursed through me the same way they had when I first saw him in the street in Muhajireen and then again in the photo on Omar's desk. It was even intensified when I stood close to him, and he handed me his water bottle by the hotel. I blushed at how unintentionally intimate a moment it was, in retrospect, to share with a stranger. While he didn't speak a word to me, I felt I knew him.

When he saw Omar behind the bar, he tilted his head back as a way of saying hello but kept moving. From where I was sitting, I couldn't tell if he saw me or not. The kitchen was behind the far end of the bar and the place had filled up significantly since we had arrived. From the corner of my eye, I watched him make his way to the tables and couches where all the girls in tight dresses and blown-out hair sat giggling and waiting.

Part of me wished he would come down to where Omar and I were, part of me wished he would stay on the other side of the world forever.

The couches that lined the outer courtyard were elevated a few steps above the bar and fountain which sat in the center of the dance floor. Everyone stood up when they saw him. His back was to me as he took the three marble steps up to greet his friends. The guys shook his hand and then pulled him in to slap him on the back. Girls in short skirts stood on their tippy-toes to kiss him on both cheeks and he listened politely to their chatter, having to bend down to hear most of them because of his height and the loud music. I turned my attention back to the bar when I realized Amer and Omar had both been staring at me. I was embarrassed that they had caught me watching him so I slid my empty glass in front of Omar to shame him for leaving me dry. He looked past me so I followed his eyes to find the beautiful soldier, having greeted almost everyone else in the entire place, was now looking back at me. His flirtatious green eyes reminded me again of the sea and, for some reason, above the loud music and shouting in Arabic and laughing and glasses clinking together, I could hear the water flowing into the fountain in the middle of the now-wild dance floor. I thought how serene and fresh it sounded, how like home it felt.

He stepped down into the courtyard which was now wall-to-wall people. He was tall enough to look over everyone's heads, only breaking his gaze with me when one of the guys clasped his hand as if they were going to arm wrestle but instead pulled him in, close to their chests. People kept grabbing him to shout something in his ear and it was taking time to close the distance between us. That's when I panicked as the thought occurred to me that he might not speak English. And he doesn't know I don't speak Arabic.

Still, he was looking at me—me, with my ripped jeans and flip-flops, the girl who probably spit in his water bottle. He wasn't paying attention to the voluptuous girls with bandage dresses, sky-high heels, and expertly applied cat eyeliner. I licked my teeth to make sure there were no bits of apricot in them and ran my hand over my ponytail to smooth out any flyaways.

When he finally reached me, I smiled, exhaling, "*Marhaba.*"

He laughed and said, "*Marhaba.*" He tilted his head to the side, patiently waiting for me to say something else. "So *muy* and *marhaba*, that's it?"

"You speak English."

"I do. The question is why don't you speak Arabic?" He smiled and gave me his hand. "I'm Ali."

"Laila." When I took his hand it felt like electric currents ran up my arm, and I forgot what I was saying. His hand was warm like he had been in the sunshine, and his grip was firm without being harsh. "I also use *khalas yalla bye* quite a bit."

"No, I hate that one."

"Hate? That is a strong word."

"I mean it strongly. You can throw that one in the garbage."

"I'm not sure I can afford to." "I'll teach you better words." "That's so charitable of you."

"I am a charitable guy," he said, resting his hand on his chest. "So, don't take this the wrong way," he lowered his voice and got close to me as though he were sharing a secret, "but only foreigners say '*marhaba*.' And old men."

"Awesome. I am so happy I have the vocabulary of an older gentleman."

I found myself wishing I could touch his hand again; his touch was soft for such a big, muscular soldier. I felt tingly and calm at the same time, still unsure if he was real and speaking to me with an almost (but not quite) American accent.

He searched my face, his eyes subtly flitted over the length of my body. "Is this your first time in the city?" It was almost as if he remembered we had only just met.

"No. I was born here. We left when I was young," I answered.

"You don't remember anything?"

"Bits and pieces. I remember playing foosball and I could barely reach the poles, and watching the Smurfs in Arabic. I thought they were Syrian for a long time."

"Yeah, me too," he said. "You know, I didn't realize they spoke English until I moved to the States. They're actually—"

"Belgian," we said, at the same time. "Yeah. You lived in the US?" I asked. "Six years. Undergraduate and master's."

"Tell me the truth, was the master's necessary?"

"Between you and me, Laila, no. But don't tell my father that."

"You didn't want to come back here?" I asked, loving my name on his lips.

"It wasn't that. I knew I would have responsibilities when I came back. Syria would wait a few more years for me."

"Yeah, I see that," I said, glancing at the table of girls who had been vying for his attention since he left them.

"Omar is taking good care of you?"

"Yeah." I nodded at my empty martini glass. "So, is the kitchen the 'big *wasta*' entrance?"

He laughed and said, "What *wasta*? I can't even get a drink in this place. No, I was starving. You should be careful who you hang out with."

"I've been told."

"This guy is a big-time *arse*. Stay away from him." Omar came back down to my end of the bar and winked at me so I knew instantly that he and Ali were actually good friends.

"Why are you talking to this guy? Look at his shoes. I don't want to see the toes of the guy making my drink," Ali said, as he wiggled his fingers in front of him. I always thought it was hilarious how offended Arabs were by feet and toes in particular.

"I think I should get going," I said, as Omar looked at me with surprise.

"*Bakir*, it's early." Omar gestured to his watch again.

"I know, but I don't want to push my luck, you know?" I answered, hoping Omar would remember how I didn't have to explain family dynamics to him. He nodded his head and went to grab his car keys so I turned to Ali. "I never got to thank you for the water," I said, for the first time acknowledging we had seen each other by the hotel.

"My pleasure."

"I wanted to say it then, but I didn't think you spoke English and I didn't want you to know I didn't speak Arabic."

"Why didn't you want me to know that?" he asked as Omar returned with his keys, ready to leave.

I gave Ali a wave, grateful I didn't have to answer that question right away. "It's a long story."

"For next time?" "*Inshallah.*"

In the car, I must have been smiling, because Omar kept looking at me sideways.

"What?" I asked. "You what?"

"Nothing. I had fun. I am not allowed to smile for no reason?"

"All the chicks love O Bar," he said, shaking his head.

"Whatever, dude." But I think Omar knew it was Ali that had me lit up like a Christmas tree. It was the first time since my father's accident that my heart felt light.

❧

"What is the difference between *memnou* and *haram*?" I found Mazen lying on the couch in the living room when I got home and figured I might not have that many chances to ask him. He opened one eye and answered.

"*Memnou* means something that is prohibited by some form of man-made law. *Haram* is a religious, spiritual offense. Although, a *harami* is a thief. Any kind of thief."

"So, *haram* is like a bigger deal?" I asked.

"There are big and small *harams*." He kept talking but put his elbow back over his closed eyes. "A big *haram* would be drinking during Ramadan. A small *haram* is if you let a piece of bread touch the floor or if you run in the souk with shorts on." He smiled and pulled his arm away from his eyes to look at me. "Mahmoud mentioned this to me."

"I see that it's stupid, but it's not *memnou*. Why is it *haram*?"

"Where you were running is very near to the mosque. You didn't know and you weren't inside the mosque, so it is only a small *haram*."

"According to who? Mahmoud? He can kiss my a—"

"According to me, Laila. And everyone. Anyway, now you understand."

"I really don't like that guy. He's always spying and skulking around, making everyone feel dirty."

"*Khalas mat ridee alay*," he said, his arm draped back over his eyes. "Don't answer him, don't give him any face."

"Face?"

"Don't give attention to him."

"Don't worry, I want nothing to do with him."

"But you really need to remember that you speak Arabic," he said.

"Yeah, I'm working on it," I said, smiling as thoughts of Ali Jaysh returned.

"You are?" Mazen looked at me in surprise.

"I'm making new friends who could probably teach me a lot."

"Another friend? Isn't Omar enough? Who's your new friend?"

"Ali," I said, trying not to smile. Until that moment I had forgotten what Omar said, that here, everything we needed to know about each other was already in our names. When Mazen suddenly sat upright and wide awake I was taken aback. "What?"

"He is a friend of Omar?" Mazen asked, looking down at the carpet with his head slightly tilted to avoid my gaze. When I nodded, he asked, "His name is Ali? What is his last name?"

Judging by the look on his face, I instantly regretted telling him. What was I thinking? "Jaysh?" When I saw Mazen's increasing look of worry and disapproval, I said, "He's serving his country, just like you."

"He's serving his country," he repeated, still looking at the carpet, it seemed like he forgot I was there.

"What's wrong with that?" I asked more timidly than before, although I knew it wasn't the military that was the problem.

"If he is a friend of Omar, I am sure my place in the army was very different than his place in the army." He looked back up and toward me.

"What difference does it make? Mazen, he is a friend of a friend, that's all."

"Laila, you should be careful who your friends are. A girl's reputation here is everything. You should think about your future, like going to university."

I smiled, relieved he didn't want to get into any more details tonight. "Okay, Mazen, I will start working on my future right away." I kissed his cheek and headed for the door.

"At least find some people who are girls!" "You too, Mazen!"

CHAPTER 10

AWEEYAY

While the merchants slept and the partiers recovered, the faithful prayed and the bakers made miracles, the intoxicating perfume of roses and jasmine pulled me awake. The sun rose, bending time around the city whose ancient walls pulsated with the energy of believers and skeptics, coffee makers and storytellers, perfumers and sword makers.

Though I tried to ignore them and focus only on my breathing, thoughts of Ali followed me through the narrow streets, down alleyways, and past the closed shops in the souk. The way he tilted his head, his half-smile revealing his white teeth, the deep bronze of his skin, and the green of his eyes warmed me inside. Pieces of our conversation moved through me as I felt a new surge like I was being pulled toward a life in front of me, the one that I was truly meant for, and a life that was freer than the one I left behind.

After meeting Ali Jaysh (officially) for the first time, even the air seemed lighter, as though there was more of everything for everyone. My early morning run in the old city was the best I had had since my arrival and I had to keep checking that the soles of my feet were actually touching the cobblestone streets as I ran. Luckily, Mazen had all but given up trying to get me to run only at the American school. It was a nice track but nothing compared with the experience of running through the old city.

When I came back, sweaty and invigorated, I found my mother in her bed with an ice pack across her eyes. Spending time with my father's family had given me the sense that the weight of the grief at the loss of my father was more evenly distributed but, as usual, my mother didn't feel the same way. I hadn't seen her for a while and I was curious to hear what she had been up to.

"What's with the ice pack, Mom, are you okay?" I asked, plopping down on the bed beside her.

"The endless parade of coffee, tea, and visitors. I haven't slept in days. I think I popped a blood vessel in my eye."

"Oh, sorry. Have you seen Mazen this morning yet, Mom?"

"I haven't *seen* anything today." She sighed and removed her ice pack. "It's Friday, maybe he went to the mosque with his father. Can we give him one day off from us, darling?"

"I was going to ask him to take me to the internet place. You know I have to check my email and work on my college search." I made sure to emphasize the last part.

"You mean your social media? Oh, Amou called here yesterday. He said he hadn't heard from you. You should check in with him, he was worried about you."

"Funny, I was just thinking about him." The only day everyone had off was Friday, so Omar's office was probably closed and I didn't want to bother him. I wondered if he went back to the bar after he dropped me at home. "Amou went to the American University of Beirut, right?"

"Yes," she sighed audibly so I quickly changed the subject. "So, what's going on? What's with all the coffee and tea?"

"Well, you haven't heard?" she asked, pleased with herself for knowing something before I did. "Mazen wants to get married now, so we put the word out and we have to go visit with all these potential brides' families."

"I knew he was planning to look for a wife after he started working for Omar, but I didn't think he was going to get started this soon," I said, still feeling uneasy about our last conversation.

She shrugged her shoulders. "Normally, because we are the groom's family we would go find a bride, but now he's a big *wasta*, and the phone hasn't stopped ringing. You should hear the thinly veiled reasons they give for calling and inviting us. The whole thing is so funny."

"Why is he in such a hurry?" I sat up on the bed, tucking my legs underneath me.

"He is twenty-nine, Laila, that's a long time to wait. He wanted to wait until at least one year had passed since your father, but I told him it would be nice to have something to celebrate. Your father wouldn't have wanted him to put anything off for him."

"Have you seen any of the girls?"

"Yes, there's one I think he'll really like." "You mean he hasn't met her yet?"

"No, when they've narrowed it down to three then he can meet them."

"So, they looked for a wife for Dad?"

"Yes, before he left Syria, obviously," she smiled, shaking her head.

"What did they think of you when they met you?"

"Believe it or not, they liked me a lot back then. They only wished I spoke Arabic. That's why it's hard to be close to me."

"That's what makes it hard to be close to you? Mom, they still like you. And I heard you trying to learn," I teased, reminding her of how much she botched the rolling of the letter r.

"Well, now it's more about taking you away from here and never visiting and all that. Now, it wouldn't matter if I spoke perfectly."

"Okay, Mom. Hey, where are your sleep aids?"

"I'm already out. Anyway, I am trying to put only good things in my body. I would kill for vodka and soda. I should have asked you to bring me one from the bar last night."

"I have a better idea."

I went downstairs with a bag full of bathing suits—I couldn't decide between a bikini and a one-piece, I would figure it out when I got there—and bottles of sunscreen, leaving my mother in her room to finish getting ready. I found my aunt and Noura sitting at the kitchen table. They were surrounded by piles of photographs and a small notebook. I put my bag down and sat at the table with them.

Noura explained that my aunt kept a running list of families who had daughters of age. She wanted someone educated but who would also enjoy and appreciate domestic life. My aunt seemed to find problems with each girl.

"What's wrong with this one?" I asked, picking one up from the slippery stack.

"*Barday iktir.*" Noura translated that '*barday*' literally meant cold, but in Arabic, it didn't mean unfeeling, it implied she was slow in her movements and speech and generally lacked enthusiasm.

"She'll never finish cooking a meal, or a sentence. We will spend our lives waiting for her." Noura shook her head, setting the photograph into a separate pile.

"Okay, that one is no. How about her?" This time I picked a photograph of a girl in a pink blouse with loose, auburn hair that fell in waves around her face. I started to enjoy the game and forgot for a moment its purpose.

"*Useerah.*" Short.

"*Iktir taweelay.*" "Too tall, like a tree," my cousin added.

"*Ghaleeza.*" Silly. "*Melounay.*" Tricky.

"*Kaslanay.*" Lazy. I wondered how far I would have gotten in this process. Not past the first round for sure.

"What about this one?"

"*Aweeyay.*" Strong. "*Mitlik.*" My aunt added, snorting and laughing.

I raised my eyebrow at my aunt and cousin as they were the toughest chicks I knew. I never saw anyone boss everyone in the family around as they did. Maybe that was why they were rejecting her; they didn't need another.

"Not strong in a nice way. Like she is too much," Noura said when she saw my expression. "Don't take us wrong. We like them all, but for a wife, we have to be careful."

I held up the next photograph, "*Yainee. Shayfay hala shway.*" She "sees herself" meaning she is a little full of herself. I studied her picture closely, to see any signs of overconfidence and found none. A brown scarf covered all of her hair and was pulled tightly down over her forehead almost reaching her eyebrows. She wore no makeup or expression.

"She is too religious," Noura said, taking her photo from me and placing it on the pile of those girls who were 'too much' of something.

"I thought you said she was full of herself."

"She is. She fasts one minute longer than everyone else, she prays at every prayer. She never touched even a man's hand before. It is always like a competition with this girl. She thinks she is here," she put her hand to the sky, "and the rest of us are down here." She put her hand close to the ground. "We don't have time for her."

"Yikes. She sounds like Mahmoud," I said, as Noura nodded her head in agreement. I picked up another photo.

"*Msayfay hay,*" my aunt shook her head. Noura laughed and said the word literally translated to 'summer' as a verb.

"She summered?" I asked.

"Like she is on vacation. But all the time." Mazen came into the kitchen and whistled while he made a circle in the air with his index finger.

"Omg, what are you wearing?" I asked, trying not to laugh. I had never seen Mazen wear anything but dress pants and starched button-down shirts since we arrived.

"For exercise. This is what we usually wear on Friday." He wore a matching Adidas jacket and track pants made of noisy parachute material and finished the look with spotless white sneakers.

"Maybe she is fun but not for a wife, not a mother for his children," Noura said, bringing my attention back to the photograph of the 'summered' girl. Mazen filled a coffee cup from the pot on the gas stove, amused but surprisingly disinterested in the whole conversation about the girls.

Seeing him made me realize one of them was going to be his wife. It forced me to see him as a man and not my young cousin anymore. He was always tending to everyone else in the family; it also made me see him as someone with needs and dreams and, unlike me, clarity about the future. Without even looking at any of the photographs, he started back out the narrow kitchen door. I jumped out of my chair to follow him.

"Mazen, hey, uh . . . how are you?" I asked as he turned toward me at the fountain. He put an apple slice in his mouth, balancing the saucer that held his coffee cup with his other hand.

"I am fine, Laila," he said through his apple, amused by my awkwardness and formality. "How are you?"

"Are you going for a run?" I asked, pointing to his workout gear.

"No," he said as though the answer was obvious and ignoring that he had just told me his outfit was made for exercise.

"Are you playing soccer today?"

"No. When I play soccer, I don't wear this."

"What do you wear?" I asked, as innocently as possible, but he knew I was trying to trap him.

"Laila, my shorts and your shorts are two different sizes."

"Whatever. Listen, it's just that... doesn't this whole thing make you nervous?" I said, gesturing toward the kitchen which held the photograph of his future wife.

"Why would I be nervous? I will love the woman my family chooses for me; I will love her completely."

"What if they choose the wrong one? Don't you worry there's someone else out there that's better for you, that will maybe make you happier? I mean, it's kind of old-fashioned, right?"

He pulled a beige plastic chair and motioned for me to sit while he balanced his coffee and grabbed a chair for himself.

"If you have too many choices, too many possibilities, you are always worried, so you end up missing what was written for you."

"But you can't choose who you fall in love with."

"You can choose who you spend your time with, and you can't fall in love with someone you don't know."

"But you don't know any of these girls," I said, pointing back at the kitchen and feeling like I couldn't back out of the conversation now so I might as well make my point.

"It doesn't matter. My family, they know me, and I know what I believe."

"What do you mean?" I asked, genuinely curious what his beliefs had to do with marriage.

"I believe in one God and Muhammad is his messenger, I believe my future wife is the sun, and I believe in my country. That's all that I need," he said. "This is how we choose to live our lives. But thank you for asking about me."

If I were being honest with myself, I was bothered because I just got my favorite cousin back in my life, and now I was going to have to share him with some girl I didn't know and probably had nothing in common with. When I told him the other night that he should hang out with more girls, I didn't think he would immediately look for a bride. Part of me felt immediately guilty that if I felt that strongly why didn't I insist my father bring me here? Before I had a second to remind myself why I didn't get to spend time with my Syrian cousins over the years, my mother came down the stairs in her flip-flops, her hair covered with an enormous black straw hat, and pink gloss on her lips. She already looked to be slightly cheered up, so that ebullient feeling, the one I had on my morning run with thoughts of Ali, returned.

"What's up?" she asked, as Mazen rose to give her his chair.

"Mazen believes in God, his wife—even though he doesn't know her yet—and his country." I checked them off one by one on my fingers and asked, "Did I get them in the right order?" Mazen blinked once, which I learned was enough to mean yes.

"Just like his uncle." My mother shook her head and beamed at him. In her eyes, he could do no wrong. How she didn't see that everything good in him and, for that matter, in my father came from here, I didn't understand.

Maybe it was my father's situation with my mother that made me afraid for Mazen, the worry that he may miss out on true love the way my father almost had. But who was I to question generations of tradition? Who says he couldn't find true love through an arranged marriage?

CHAPTER 11

EVERYONE KNOWS EVERYONE

My mother and I took a taxi to the same hotel where I ran into Ali Jaysh a few weeks before. I was reminded of him when the steel sword the size of a building appeared and we drove around the Ummayyad Square, which is actually a circle.

"It's kind of romantic if you think about it," I said to my mother in the taxi as we pulled into the hotel entrance that led to the pool.

"I don't know if it's romantic, but for Mazen, it's the best thing. He's not going to meet girls at the bar."

"I know, I tried to get him to come with me." "Laila! You know he doesn't drink."

"I know that, but he could just hang out and meet people."

"Mazen doesn't just 'hang out.' I am surprised he didn't insist on picking you up."

"I think he trusts Omar. He seems good with him."

"Even so, Mazen has always been very protective of you."

"I guess I get where he's coming from with the whole shorts thing. Sort of," I said, remembering all the girls in miniskirts at O Bar that made my shorts look conservative.

"Not just that. When you were little, you and Mazen ran around the neighborhood together. The park, the corner store, the soccer field; he took you everywhere. Well, I don't know if you remember, but the neighbor kid, Mahmoud? He followed you all the time, wherever you went, he was there. He never said a word but he was always just there. It was like he was obsessed with you."

"Omg, creepy." I closed my eyes and shook my head to clear the image of Mahmoud following me around when I was a kid.

"Very. So anyway, one day at the playground he pulled you by your ponytail, and you fell off the swing onto the concrete. Mazen walked right up to him and clocked him, knocked the kid off his feet."

"Concrete on a playground?"

"Don't get me started on the lack of safety standards here, but, yes, you really could have been hurt."

"I didn't know Mazen was a fighter." I just couldn't picture Mazen hurting anyone, let alone punching someone in the face. I was happy it was Mahmoud on the other end of his fist.

"Mazen definitely isn't a fighter, normally. Everyone has something or someone that pushes them to that point."

"Why can't I remember any of this? And why is Mazen still friends with him?"

"Well, Mazen is a good guy and loyal to his friends ... and," she trailed off.

"And what?"

"One of the girls on the list is Mahmoud's sister."
"No! Ugh, God, that sucks. Is she the really religious one?"

"No, that's the funny thing. She's not like him at all! She's fun and *spor* . . . " "*Spor?*"

"*Spor*," she continued to struggle with the end of the word.

"Mom, it's *sporrrr*," I said, trying to show her how to roll her r as the taxi driver snickered behind the back of his hand.

Finally giving up, she said, "It means sporty like she's cool slash modern, maybe even Westernized."

"Sporty means cool? That's hilarious. But I still hope he doesn't pick her. I can't stand him." The thought of Mahmoud even as a distant relative sent a chill down my spine.

As soon as we arrived and paid the entrance fee, we put our bathing suits on in the change rooms. I went back and forth but finally opted for the one-piece, even though I brought several cuter two-pieces with me. Mazen's warnings about not attracting unwanted attention to myself were still running through my head.

The hotel was made of all white stone with greenery falling from the high balconies surrounding the pool. The sun was a constant presence. I didn't know how anyone could resist the cool, blue water. The pool was shaped like a cross that curved at the bottom, the stairs at the top end. I jumped in to swim laps while my mother slathered on her sunblock. She always said she was envious of my Arab skin, and that I could pass by a window in the winter and get a tan.

I was on my last lap, swimming underwater toward the end of the pool where the stairs led to the patio, when a blurry image on my right came into focus as I surfaced. Ali stood at the edge of the water wearing navy trunks, a deep tan, and a thin green bracelet that hung from his wrist.

"Ali, hi." I stood where the water was waist-high, curious how he seemed to get better looking every time I saw him. Having noticed that some Arab men leaned to the European side when it came to fashion, I was relieved to see he wasn't wearing a Speedo.

"Laila, how are you?" he asked. His navy trunks hung low on his hips, exposing nothing rude, only showing off his toned abs.

"Good," I replied, biting my lip to keep from smiling too much.

"And how are you liking Damascus?" he asked, as a petite blonde in a gold string bikini and matching wedge sandals came and stood beside him at the edge of the pool. She stared down at me but said nothing, and I was surprised at how scantily clad she was. Even by California standards, she would be a total scandal. Not to mention the amount of gold jewelry, the most noticeable piece a diamond-studded letter 'm' that lay right between her breasts, seemed excessive for a day at the pool.

"I like it," I answered carefully, watching her pull her loose blonde waves back in a bun clearly bored by our conversation. I couldn't really tell if she was looking at me behind her mirrored sunglasses or not, but she was not smiling and I got the sense she wasn't happy he was speaking to me.

When he opened his mouth to say something back to me, she pushed him into the pool and jumped in after him. The moment seemed longer than it was, but

I forced myself not to make up a story. Just because she was with him didn't mean she was *with* him.

As he resurfaced, the blonde came back up too, her sunglasses still in place, her jewelry nearly blinding me. Then she climbed on Ali's back and put her arms around his neck, pushing him back down under the water, not giving him another chance to talk to me. This time she was smiling and laughing. When he resurfaced, she said something to him in Arabic that, of course, I couldn't quite understand.

I decided to leave them to their play and walked up the stairs, out of the pool, and back to my mom sunbathing in a chaise lounge. That was definitely more than friendship, the way she had her body draped all over him in the pool. If she was just a friend, he had a weird idea of what friendship looked like.

There were tons of girls trying to get his attention at O Bar, but the way he was flirting with me—what I thought was flirting—didn't seem like what a guy with a girlfriend would do. I thought for a moment that I would have been better off never meeting him in person if just keeping him as a fantasy would allow me to feel as elated as I was on my run that morning.

"Who is that?" my mom asked, an unusual edge to her voice, bordering on panic.

"A girl who likes to swim with her shoes on?"

"The guy," she said, bringing herself to a sitting position and removing her sunglasses to get a better look. "Who's the guy?"

"He's a friend of Omar's," I answered, drying myself off with a towel. "I met him the other night. And I don't know who she is."

"I don't think she could have made her jealousy more obvious. She was literally drowning him."

"Jealous of what? If they are together, which I am not sure they are, then why does she care if he talks to me? I mean, he's not allowed to talk?"

"Well, stay the hell away from him for sure."

"Okay, Mom, calm down, jeez," I said, but I continued to watch them, as they got out of the water, for any signs of a serious relationship. Even I had to admit that, if they were a couple, they were a beautiful pair. Her with her bombshell curves, string bikini that could barely get its arms around her breasts, and silky blonde hair, and him with his bronzed skin and piercing green eyes. It was disgusting, and they didn't seem bothered that everyone else was staring. I let my gaze rest on them as they lowered themselves into chaise lounges on the other side of the pool. He texted on his phone while she rubbed suntan oil all over her legs. I knew for sure she wasn't at the O party or I would have noticed her. But if his body language was any indication, he couldn't be less interested in her.

I narrowed it down to three possibilities: either he was single and just had lots of girls around him, or he was taken and flirtatious with other girls, which made him an asshole, or he wasn't flirting with me at all and saw me as another foreigner, a tourist even, just passing through. I decided to set aside my questions about Ali and focus on my own path in front of me.

"So, I met a bunch of people at Omar's place and they were like, 'You should go to Beirut, they have the best schools.'" I slightly exaggerated how many people suggested I go to Beirut, and I definitely tacked on the part about the schools because I knew it was going to take some serious convincing to get her to open up to the idea of me staying in the region.

"The best schools for what? Finding a rich husband? No. Beirut is not for us."

"Well, I looked into it when I was researching..."

"For this fall? Are you serious?" she asked, even though I knew she already had the answer, and she wanted me to feel bad about waiting to fill out applications when I was doing my internship in Sonoma last year.

"No, the deadline has already passed for this fall, this would be for next year. Anyway, there's an American University in Beirut."

"I know all about it. What about UCLA? Or Berkeley? You have the grades to get in, Laila, I don't know why you are setting your standards so low."

"AUB has an excellent reputation, Mom."

"But it's here. Far from home. And Beirut, by the way, is hardly a city conducive to being studious."

"And LA is?"

"You would never have to worry about LAX getting bombed."

"Mom, the war is over." I looked back up toward Ali to see what he was up to. Before I could catch myself, I found myself wishing there was an American university in Damascus. "It's peacetime," I muttered, more to myself than to her.

"Don't you want to be close to me? Does that ever come into your research?"

I flipped over on my stomach and folded my forearms in front of me, my attention back to Ali. The girl was pushing her way back into the water, her curves creating more waves than such a small person should, but I didn't see Ali anymore. Just when I thought he must have gone he appeared to be walking toward us. I tried to think of something to say that wouldn't come across cold but didn't imply I was as interested as I may have let on before. As he approached us, I opened my mouth to say something when he spoke to my mother.

"Hello Mrs. Abdullah, how are you? It is nice to see you back in Damascus after all these years." He reached across me, shaking my mother's hand.

"I thought that was you, Ali." Lifting the brim of her hat and allowing him to shake her other hand. "You've grown even taller. And you got your braces off."

"Yes, many years ago." He smiled, revealing all his perfect white teeth this time.

I had been sitting upright on my chaise lounge, still open-mouthed, before I was able to say, "Uh, you guys know each other?"

"Your father and Ali's father used to be friends."

He turned suddenly serious and said, "We were deeply saddened by the news of Dr. Abdullah's passing. I am sorry for your loss; my family sends their sympathies."

"Did you not attend the funeral?"

"No, unfortunately, we weren't able to," he said, lowering his head and putting his hand to his chest.

"So, how have you been spending your time, Ali?"
"I'm in the army."

"Are you married?"

"No," he shook his head, looking over at me. Then he gestured over to the girl who had pushed him. "Sorry about that. She is a family friend." He took a seat on the empty chaise next to me.

"Your family has many friends." My mother looked back toward the blonde in the pool.

"You know, people keep saying Syria is 'so conservative'...." I knew it was bold of me to take a shot at his 'friend', especially after he apologized for her, but I wanted someone else's opinion besides Mazen. Between O Bar and the swimming pool, with girls in short, tight dresses, cleavage was everywhere and it seemed like everything was on display. I didn't mind following rules, I just didn't like the idea that the rules were different for me. What I really wanted to know was why she could get away with wearing a skimpy bikini, but I couldn't run in shorts.

"Yes?" he asked but without even a hint of impatience in his voice. He looked down at his bare feet so I followed his gaze to the white half-moons on his nail beds, the skin on his soles a few shades lighter than the rest of him. "Don't be fooled by the exterior, Laila. Here, it's strictly 'look, don't touch.'"

"Oh. I like that."

"You like that?" he asked, raising his eyebrows. "Yes." I could feel my mother trying to hide her smile next to me.

"Have you seen much of the city yet?" he asked, meeting my eyes.

"A little bit. I'm sure I will get around to doing the whole tour."

"If it's okay with your mother, I would love to show you around sometime. It's a matter of family honor," he smiled the half-smile that made me squishy inside, "and national pride."

I smiled back but said nothing. Then I pulled my phone out of my bag and realized I hadn't entered any of my own numbers. I opened the phone app knowing the keyboard was still in Arabic. I could hear my father's voice in my head saying, *See Laila? I wanted you to study Arabic, but, no, you wanted to run to the beach.*

Ali took the phone gently from me. "Actually, you already have my number. This is your father's phone, yes? This is me." He showed me the contact information next to his name. Before he got up to leave us, he said to my mother, "If there's anything you need, Mrs. Abdullah, please let me know." She nodded and even said thank you, though I doubted she would ever take him up on it. Even with all her *wasta* talk, she hated owing people favors.

Of course, as soon as Ali was out of earshot, she started in on him. "Family honor? National pride?"

"He's joking. All he wants to do is show me around. It's not like a date."

"God forbid." My mother continued to flip through her magazine. "You would give me a heart attack."

"Mom, what is your problem? He's so nice. Anyway, the guys here are different; they're not all after one thing. So, okay, they're flirts but you heard what he said about 'look, don't touch.' I mean, how perfect is that?"

"Perfect." Her sarcastic tone made it sound like I was giving extra credit for something that should be expected. I changed tactics to one that would resonate more with her.

"Did Dad like him? I mean, he had his number."

She sighed, taking off her sunglasses and looking over at me. "He did. Very much, in fact."

Seeing her tear up made me feel bad that I had brought up my father. But here we had a connection to him we would never have in California. These people were his tribe. Not only did my father know Ali, he pretty much introduced us. Even my mother had to admit, that Ali Jaysh couldn't have come into my life at a better time.

"Lails, I want you to enjoy the brief time we have here. I really do. But I want you to be smart about who you hang around with. And, for the love of God, watch that one," she said, gesturing as inconspicuously as possible toward the blonde in the bikini who was now staring unapologetically in our direction. Given what Ali had said about their relationship being 'family friends', I had to wonder what expression she held behind those mirrored sunglasses.

"Yeah, for sure," I muttered. A waiter approached us carrying a tray with two iced juices, slices of orange, a cherry, and pink umbrellas garnishing the glasses. I eyed the tray, wondering if there was alcohol in one of them. "What is this?" I asked the waiter as politely as possible.

"Jamaica? Orange, grenadine . . ." I loved how they said English words with an accent, making it sound like Arabic.

"Jamaica?" To my surprise, my mother threw her head back and laughed. "That is so funny. I can't believe he remembers."

"Who remembers what?" I asked.

The waiter pointed to Ali who was now standing by the pool bar talking to a few other guys his age. He smiled when he saw me and the waiter looking at him, and I couldn't help but laugh too. I took the drink the waiter handed to me and tipped it in Ali's direction. I had no idea what Jamaica tasted like, but this drink tasted like everything else I tried in Syria, absolute heaven.

"He sent me a juice. A non-alcoholic, totally innocent, sweet drink. How cute and Syr is that?" I asked my mother.

"So Syr." She happily took the other glass. "They have the best fruit in the world here, I will give them that," she said, taking a long drink.

"Mom."

"Okay, he's a little cute. I still don't think you should go out with him."

"I'm not 'going out' with him. We'll probably go sightseeing or something lame." Although I sensed no time spent with him would be lame, I didn't want my mom to think I was too excited about it, either. "Hey, does your drink have alcohol in it?"

"Mine has a little." She smiled, her lips never leaving her straw.

I could tell just by how she was smiling that hers had more than a little alcohol in it. It was risky on his part, she may have rolled her eyes at such an obvious play for her favor, but Ali continued to impress me as he knew the true way to my mother's heart. Just like my father, he wasn't intimidated by her, and his confidence cut through her nonsense. He had no way of knowing but that worked surprisingly well with my mother. She sat back in her lounge chair, suddenly looking more relaxed than I had seen her in months. She had done a 180-degree change from where I found her this morning with an ice pack across her eyes.

Before I had time to overthink it, I threw my legs over the side of the chaise lounge, holding my drink upright, and pulled myself from my chair. I followed the waiter back to the bar where Ali stood with his friends who all looked like they had just come off the tennis court.

"So, I don't know how you managed it, but my mom is actually laughing and enjoying herself and not complaining about anything."

"Good. Our moms always drank them by our pool on the weekends. I remember she liked them. I never understood why they didn't let me try theirs."

"They could have given you one of these." I held my empty glass for him to see, knowing he was the one who ordered mine a virgin.

When he saw me pouting, he said, "I will get you a proper drink at Omar's."

"Why didn't you say anything at the bar? Seriously, my mind is blown."

"Stop getting blown, this is Damascus. I told you everyone knows everyone."

"You could have been more specific. Why didn't you mention the other night that you know my family? That you knew me?"

"The Laila Abdullah I knew was very short—" "I was four."

"—and a complete brat." "I was not."

"This Laila Abdullah— . . ." he gestured toward me, not finishing his sentence. " . . . honestly I was hoping you would remember me."

"If you have your own pool, why do you come here?" "To see my friends," he said. "What's funny?"

"Just tell me the truth, is she really just a family friend or is she your girlfriend? Because if looks could kill, I'd be dead."

"That's Maya. Just to prove it to you, I would never allow my girlfriend to wear a bikini that small."

"Allow her? Are you . . . serious?" "I am Syrian, yes."

"I think you're playing with me." "I am. A little."

"Honestly, she should be able to wear whatever the fuck she wants." The daggers shooting toward me didn't change how I felt about the whole issue.

"Yes, Maya does wear whatever the fuck she wants. And you see how everyone is staring at her. You want every guy to be staring at your ass like you are a piece of meat?"

"I wouldn't wear that because it's not my style." "So, why do you care?"

"Because . . . feminism." "This is feminism?"

"They should have some respect."

"As long as girls use sex to get what they want, they will be treated as objects."

My mouth dropped open, and he gently lifted my chin back up with his fingertips. "I know you wouldn't." His tone turned more intimate and serious, and he suddenly behaved as though he had known me my whole life. "Anyway, this girl, you don't need to worry about. She could run naked through the streets of Damascus. They know who her father is, they will leave her alone."

One of his friends in a white t-shirt and shorts had been standing close enough to overhear our conversation and cut in, "Maya? If Maya dies a virgin, it means we all kept our hands." He lifted his palms to the sky.

"Welcome to Syria," his other friend said, laughing.

I nodded and smiled but let my attention drift to Maya's father as we all pretended not to watch her. She lay now half in, half out of the pool, perched on her forearms passively kicking her legs behind her. A new thought occurred to me, and I turned back to Ali. "Is that why you ignore her?" After she tried to drown him, he didn't pay much attention to her, but I still needed to hear a final *khalas* statement about the girl before I could 'sight see' with Ali.

As though he read my mind, he said, "Maya has a . . . bigger agenda." He shook his head as he watched her walk toward us. He turned back to look directly at me, revealing nothing more.

I looked back to where I was sitting with my mom, and she still seemed content. I wondered if maybe she dozed off. When I could feel his gaze on me, I decided it was time to bring our conversation back full circle. "When our moms were drinking Jamaicas by the pool, where was I?"

"Running. You never stopped."

CHAPTER 12

HELEH, BAADAIN

(Now, Later)

"Ali, Ali, Ali, catch me, catch me!" I ran past the swimming pool, yanked open the back gate, and burst out into the orchard.

"Laila, don't!"

I ignored him, knowing he was too slow to catch me before I could get out. I only wished my mother hadn't made me wear this stupid puffy dress, I couldn't climb as fast. I clamored up into a tree and continued to shout his name, barely able to wait until he got to me. I leaped out of the tree into his waiting arms.

"Kameshtek!" He twirled me around in circles, making me squeal with delight. When he put me down, he said, "Yalla, go to your mom now."

"No!" I was dizzy and giggling uncontrollably, but I kept running, fueled by fresh air and Choco Prince. "Ali, Ali, Ali, catch me, catch me!" I eyed a taller apricot tree.

"Laila, go back to your mother. We will play later!" he called after me.

"Laila, come here now!" My mother's no-nonsense voice rang out across the swimming pool. I stopped in my tracks and turned to look at him, wondering why she always had to ruin my fun.

"Go." His eyes were gentle, but his tone was firm.

I hung my head and pouted, sad that our time together was over.

"I promise, Laila. I will be waiting for you."

I slept through the call to prayer for the first time since I came. It was the first step in assimilating, though it meant I missed my sunrise run. As my eyes fluttered open, I smiled softly, not really sure if I had been dreaming of Ali or if an old memory had surfaced.

As I stretched my body, I replayed pieces of our conversations in my mind, his voice deep and steady, a slight accent hidden in an otherwise flawless English. I only wish my Arabic was half as good.

It had only been a few days since I saw him in person, but I was finding myself missing him. How can you miss someone you barely know? But I did know him. Apparently, I had known him since I was a child.

Sunlight poured through the crack in my door, and I knew my mom had already been in to check on me. I promised myself I would run as soon as I could, maybe use the school's track again. I hated to admit Mazen was right about the constant harassment. I could feel myself changing just a little bit to make my life work here.

Thoughts of my dad always stayed with me, but today I wasn't sad and missing him for some reason. I threw my legs over the side of the bed, and my feet found my slippers. I shuffled down the hall to the bathroom, splashed cold water on my face, and brushed my teeth before going back to my room to finish dressing.

At first, I was surprised at myself for speaking to the three in military uniforms in the poster Omar had given me. Now it seemed normal. I brushed my hair out and pulled it back into a ponytail and I caught them up on everything that was going on. I needed someone neutral to talk to, away from the family's concerns about me and my mom's near panic around me even speaking to Ali. But I had so much to talk about. My room was far enough down the hall from the others that no one could hear so they became like a daily diary. The father seemed a bit stern, and I wasn't as comfortable talking to a ghost, so I found myself mostly directing my attention to the fair-haired one, the one who would be the next president, 'the other son' my father had spoken of in his office that day in January when he got the news the eldest son had been killed in a car accident.

I spoke to him now as I always did while I got dressed in the morning and told him about all of my plans. I told him about Ali and how we met and that he knew my mom. I paused before dabbing balm on my lips. I imagined his eyes were softer behind the aviators, and I swore sometimes he was almost smiling. It was funny how we knew each other's plans.

"Weird, huh?" I asked as I finished putting myself together.

The future president knew a lot more about me than I did about him, he was an excellent listener, but it wouldn't be long before his story was everywhere. The rumors were his father wasn't even in good enough health to make public appearances, and his son was already making speeches and cutting ribbons.

"*Khalas, yalla, bye,*" I told him as I always did before I turned to leave my room.

My mother poked her head in the doorway. "Lails, who on earth are you talking to?"

"Nobody. How long have you been awake?"

"Ages. I've been waiting for you to wake up. Seems you're already on Arab Standard Time."

"I know! I missed my run."

"So did Ali text you finally?" she asked, pretending to be casual, which was never her strong suit.

"No."

"Well, there you go. Total player. Told you."

"He called me." I sailed out the bedroom door and down the stairs, letting her trail after me.

"Why?"

"Because he's a man." I loved that he called instead of texting. I blushed just thinking about what the sound of his voice did to me. "He even asked you for permission, Mom. Who does that?"

"Which I don't believe I gave. Did you make plans with him?"

"Not yet."

"I don't think Ali is a good idea at all." "Dad liked him."

She crossed her arms. "Dad liked everyone. He was a charitable man. He cared about people, especially immigrants."

"Mom, please. Ali was not an immigrant, he was a student, and do you really think he needs charity?" We had reached the bottom of the stairs where Mazen was drinking his coffee by the fountain. He must have choked a little, and we both stopped to look at him as he put his hand up to let us know he was okay.

"You know what I mean," she said. "And what about the girl he was with? The blonde with all the gold?"

"Maya? He's seriously not into her. He says they're friends and, to be honest, I believe him. If he wanted her, she made it obvious she's very available."

"I don't want you to form attachments here. We could be gone tomorrow."

"Mom, jeez . . . " I said, nodding my head toward Mazen, trying not to make it obvious.

"It's okay, Laila," he said, standing and coming closer to where we stood. "I agree with your mother."

"Why?"

"This group, they are different than us. You don't want to be too close with them."

"He and Omar are really good friends," I said, hinting at the new job he got because of 'this group.'

"Omar, he's okay," Mazen said.

"Laila, you can't just go running around town with some random guy you met at the pool." My mom was not going to back down, but I had one more card to play.

"Ali's random? He's known me my whole life, apparently. Did you know Dad had lunch with him every Friday in LA? Every single week for six years. Dad was obviously good with him, why can't you be?"

"He was 'so good' with him that in all that time he never once brought Ali to the house?"

"Yeah, because of you!"

"I don't make the rules here, Laila. I told you before we came there would be things you couldn't do."

By that point, I had lost this battle. I knew when my mother wouldn't budge and having Mazen on her side solidified it. My approach would have to change and, just like with the shorts, I may just have to find another way.

I had to get away from my mother and out of the house. I asked Mazen to take me to the school to run, and he agreed. As I was making my last lap, Omar appeared on the basketball court. None of his usual friends was with him.

"Hey, long time, no see. How are you?" "You've been hearing from Ali?"

"Yeah, we've been talking." "Talking, huh? And?"

"And... ask him. You guys are friends." "He told me. I want to know from you." "What did he say?"

"Laila, you are blushing. I told you, you would come here, fall in love, and have Syr babies, didn't I?"

"He wants to take me on a tour of the city, no one is making babies."

"Ah, first the tour."

"If my mother ever agrees to even let me see him." "She gives you a hard time?"

"The funny thing is she knows Ali from back in the day and my dad too. But they never mentioned him before."

"Your dad never said anything?"

"No, but he saw him all the time when he was in LA. She just doesn't want me to get attached to anything here. And actually, the whole family agrees with her, so it's Laila and Ali vs. Everyone."

"*Heleh*, worry about the family later." "How's the Sabrina saga?"

"It might be a while before it gets sorted. I want you to meet her though."

"Really? Am I still inner circle?"

"You are inner circle," he said, putting his arm around my neck and making the same gesture I made the other night at the bar.

"Shut up," I laughed and pushed him away although I realized I had missed him and how easy he was to be with.

"Seriously, come to O Bar tomorrow night."

"I thought you said Sabrina doesn't go to O Bar," I said.

"She doesn't come when we have a lot of people. I will pick you up and she will meet us there," Omar said.

"So, it'll just be us?"

"A small group. Maybe you'll see someone you know?" he added, giving me a wink.

"Oh. Okay," I smiled, shaking my head at the way Omar always seemed to have a plan up his sleeve.

CHAPTER 13

MUHAMMED OMAR SUNNI

Omar picked me up from my Uncle's at exactly 8 pm. When we walked into O Bar, there was no sign of Gabby. There was no DJ this time, only soft music playing in the background. I looked around to see if anyone else had come in but the bar was empty. The string lights in the trees were lit and all the tables had flickering candles but nobody else was there. When Omar said there would only be a small group, he didn't say how small.

"So where is everyone else, even the 'hot girls' aren't coming?"

"There's a wedding tonight. Everyone is there." "You weren't invited?"

"We declined." "Who is we?"

"Can I join you?" Ali asked, appearing next to me at the bar.

"We were hoping someone better would come, *bas yalla*," Omar answered for me.

"I'm sorry to disappoint," Ali said, directed toward me.

"This was the only invitation I got," I said. I was secretly hoping he would show up but I didn't want to be disappointed if he didn't. "So, you know the guy getting married?"

"Yes, poor bastard." "What?"

"Kidding. She's lovely, but way out of his league. He wants to lock it down before she realizes it."

"Isn't he going to be pissed you're not there?" "Mmm, probably."

"Oh," I said, hoping he would come out and say it was because he wanted to hang out with me more than he wanted to go to a friend's wedding.

Omar cut in. "Just so we're clear, I didn't want to hang out with you. I just didn't want to go to another wedding."

"Thanks, Omar."

"So, are you guys hungry?" Omar asked.

"What do you have? I don't want you to cook just for us." Omar had already gone way out of his way but dinner with Ali sounded appetizing.

"I have the most amazing fish I brought with me from Latakia. Only I can cook it properly. You guys will love it." He poured us each a glass of white wine and left for the kitchen.

"Your mom was okay with you coming here?" Ali said.

"I mean, everyone is okay with Omar, so that's good," I said. I didn't want Ali to know any of what was said at the house, but I didn't want him to think seeing him was going to be easy either. "But, I'm happy you're here."

"You look pretty," he said, kissing my cheek.

I wanted to tell him he looked nice too, and he smelled like a dream, but we were both distracted by someone else coming in the front door.

"Hi," she said, shyly, as she approached us at the bar. As soon as she came into the light, I was not surprised at how crazy Omar was for her. She was shockingly beautiful in the most understated way. Her long, auburn hair fell in loose waves around her face, her skin was light and luminous, and her lips a pale pink. The only way I could describe her eye color was like honeyed tea. It was hard not to stare at her.

"Sabrina." Ali kissed her on both cheeks and introduced us. He didn't seem surprised to see her so he must have been in on the plan too. I just wasn't sure yet if it was his idea or Omar's. I guess it didn't matter. Omar could have Sabrina for a night and Ali and I could talk face-to-face instead of just texting and calling like we had been for the past week since we ran into each other at the swimming pool.

"Sorry guys, I just came straight from school." Sabrina opened her navy blue blazer, showing us her white t-shirt underneath splattered with paint. She wore it with jeans and wedge heels, which looked fabulous to me. "Are you an art student?" I asked.

"I am a teacher. Kindergarten." "This late?"

"It never ends. I had so many things to finish before the kids come back tomorrow morning, but I really wanted to meet you."

By now, strong aromas of garlic, and lemon, and seafood were wafting from the kitchen. Omar brought out a platter of fish and white rice topped with caramelized onions. One of the young waiters, the only one working tonight, put out salads and fresh bread and the four of us sat down at a table under the stars and lemon trees.

"What are your plans, Laila? Are you going to university?" Sabrina said as she placed a napkin in her lap.

"I am not sure college is for me."

"She had scholarship offers from schools she didn't even apply to," Ali said. "She turned them all down."

"How did you know about that? My mom doesn't even know." I turned toward him without even thinking about how I might be making Omar and Sabrina uncomfortable. Still, I was taken aback that he knew such a private detail about me, and I wondered what else he knew. My father was literally the only person on earth who knew that. If my mom ever found out she would have been furious with me.

"Your dad was proud of you; he would have told everyone if he could," Ali showed no signs of regret for sharing.

"Sweet." Sabrina nodded thoughtfully as she chewed a piece of bread. Watching her and Omar throughout the dinner and how comfortable they were finishing each other's sentences and eating from each other's plates, I wondered if Ali and I would ever have that level of intimacy. Or if we would ever get the chance to have a real relationship. I was surprised at how comfortable I was sitting so near him; even when I was challenging him, he didn't seem bothered. He acted as if we had known each other all of our lives.

A couple of times during the dinner, Omar whispered something in Sabrina's ear to make her giggle. She would look back at us and shake her head like it wasn't worth sharing, but it didn't bother us at all they were having their own little dinner date. I could imagine being in a relationship with Omar wasn't easy since he could be high maintenance as hell and was always going a million miles an hour in every direction, but I was sure there were a lot of laughs between them too.

When we finished eating, Sabrina lowered her voice to speak only to Omar in Arabic so when she did, Ali and I had a chance to speak face-to-face in a way we hadn't really done before. When I first saw him in the street in Muhajireen it was more like a mirage. I imagined conversations, but he wasn't a mirage or a figment of my imagination anymore. He was very real and sitting close enough that I could smell his cologne. Even though I was slightly annoyed, like knowing so much about me he was at an unfair advantage, I couldn't deny the effect he had on me. It was like nothing could bother me ever again.

"Man, this was so much better," Ali said as they clinked their glasses together. "I wish I never had to go to another wedding again."

"Keep dreaming. You know we will pay for this."

"*Akeed.*"

"Don't say that guys, it's bad luck! You will be at each other's weddings, at least," Sabrina said, as Omar lifted his hands to the sky and mouthed *please?*

When Ali and Sabrina started chatting about the couple who was getting married, I got up to help Omar clear the dishes and ask him why he didn't tell me at the school that tonight was a dinner invitation for the four of us.

"If you told your mom you are invited to dinner with Ali she would have a problem, right? This way we all happen to be here at the same time and no one else showed up," Omar explained. "Plausible deniability, *ya Laila. Learn.*"

I was grateful to Omar for helping me spend more time with Ali without upsetting the family, but deep down I was worried we would land in the same place he and Sabrina were in, and I wasn't sure I wanted that. Not to mention the issue of my mom wanting to get me out of here as soon as she could. I pushed all of those thoughts out of my mind as Omar and returned to the table with mint tea.

Sabrina turned to me to ask about my family and how I was liking Damascus. Everyone I met seemed interested to know if I liked it here and if I was happy. I assured her I was when I felt Ali's hand find mine under the table. Electricity rushed up and down my body at his touch. I wished he would never let go and the night would never end. But, eventually, Sabrina checked her phone and jumped out of her chair.

"Sorry I have to go, it was so nice meeting you, Laila." She jumped up and kissed Ali's cheeks again and said, "I hope to see you again." She left and Omar followed her to walk her to her car.

"I hope it works out for them. It's a difficult situation."

"Yeah, he told me her family won't accept a Muslim guy for her. Does that happen a lot here?"

"Not like in the old days. It really depends on the family, if they are conservative or not. Anyway, that's the least of their problems."

"What do you mean?"

But before Ali could answer me, Omar was on his way back to the table.

"Wow, does she know she's gorgeous?"

"Omar knows he is playing way above his league."

"You see? I have problems up to here." He put his hand

up to his forehead but he was smiling. "And look who's talking!"

"True. We're both in deep shit." "Why? What will happen?"

"Everyone will give us a hard time for not showing up, I told them I had family stuff."

"Same. But they won't care what the reason is." "I hope it was worth it."

"More than worth it," Ali and Omar agreed.

I gave them a minute to finish their drinks before I said, "Sorry, guys but I should go too."

"Can I drop you home?" Ali asked. "If anyone even sees us, we can say Omar had to stay late." Ali stood and grabbed his phone and car keys.

When I stood to say goodbye to Omar I opened my mouth to say something that resembled a thank you for the incredible meal, and how much I enjoyed meeting Sabrina, but words wouldn't come and it wasn't just the wine. He blinked once to say 'You're welcome' and then he shooed us both out.

"*Yalla*, go."

In the car, I admitted to Ali that my mom said she didn't want me to make plans with him, but that she also didn't say anything about talking to him.

"I'm sorry, Laila, but with all due respect to your mom, I can't accept not seeing you."

"Me neither."

"Laila, at some point, it's your life. You have to make some decisions on your own. I understand you should respect your mother's wishes but what about your father's wishes? Or they don't count anymore?"

"No, of course, they do. It's just, that he never mentioned you. I never even heard your name in my house.

I don't know what he would think of us seeing each other. I mean, if I am really being honest I was never allowed to like 'date', you know?"

"Uh-huh."

"You do know. You seem to know everything about me."

He paused, before he said, "Not everything. Laila, why do you think I am finding every way I can to see you? I want to know you from you, by spending time with you."

"So do I. But I feel like you're already at an unfair advantage."

"Okay. What do you want to know?"

I had been meaning to ask about it since I saw it at the pool but didn't have the chance. "What's on your wrist?"

"A Rolex."

"The other wrist."

"It was a gift from my mother. She gave it to me when I was young."

"It's just a random green bracelet made with silk thread that doesn't mean anything? Ali, you have to meet me at least halfway."

"I wear it to remember who I am, where I came from, and where my loyalties lie."

"Oh." I did half expect him to say it was her favorite color or she was crafty or something equally mundane. Still, I wanted to encourage him to keep opening up to me "Was that so hard?"

"Excruciating."

"Next time, we'll talk about your exes." "Haha, no fucking way."

CHAPTER
14

BLONDE BAR

"You want me to braid your hair?" My mom poked her head in my doorway as I struggled to get my hair untangled in the morning. When I nodded she came in and stood behind me to face the mirror. She eyed the poster but said nothing about it. She had made her point that she didn't like it, but she also understood my humor and hers weren't the same. "Was it a busy night at Omar's?"

"There were a few people there."

"In case you need a break from him, I found a new spot for you to hang out. All people your age from everywhere, it's super fun." When my mom said things like 'super fun' I knew she was plotting or at least laying the groundwork to get me to do and like what she did and liked. "I thought we could grab some dinner there tonight, just you and I?" Seeing Ali last night made me feel a little guilty so I agreed. Also, I had not seen my mother excited about anything since we got here so I decided to indulge her. I also got the sense she was getting bored in the house and didn't have much to talk about with my aunt. She was never domestic before so the chances of her becoming a housewife now were slim to none.

"How are the squatters?"

"Gone, thank God. I don't know how Mazen managed it but he did."

"Oh, that's good." Even though I had been secretly hoping they would keep us here longer.

She brushed my hair all the way through first, carefully untangling the knots. When she started braiding it, she said, "I wanted it to be a surprise but tonight is actually a little bit of a celebration."

"Oh, really? What are we celebrating?"

"You know, the landscaping lady I told you about? Well, it turns out she knows everyone and she can get us people who can do the work at the villa and finish quickly. According to her, we can have everything done in a maximum of four weeks."

"Four weeks!"

"I know! I told you having connections here makes all the difference. I could never have found those people on my own."

I felt sick at the thought of leaving already. I knew deep down I couldn't stay forever, but four weeks felt impossible.

"I mean, hopefully nothing happens but if all hell breaks loose . . . we will be out of here." She looked at me in the mirror and I nodded, not trusting my voice to sound steady. I handed her an elastic as she finished my braid and left me to get dressed.

We entered the tiny restaurant in the Christian part of the old city, and it smelled of old wood, cigarettes, and spilled beer, though I immediately liked its cozy atmosphere. A waiter seated us at a tiny wooden table, the lighting was dim, with nothing but candlelight flickering from the few tables crammed into corners and a television screen playing karaoke songs perched in the far corner above the bar.

When my mom and I got settled in, we noticed the girls sitting at the bar.

"Air-dried hair, loose jeans, henna tattoos?" I asked. "Foreigners." We said at the same time, giggling.

"I don't know why European girls don't feel the need to wear bras," my mother said more quietly, a hint of envy in her voice. Though she was far from bohemian, I got the sense she longed for freedom from the constant upkeep required of a plastic surgeon's wife in Orange County. At least her idea of what a surgeon's wife should look like was totally different than what made my father happy.

I looked over at them while my mother went back and forth with the waiter about the cocktail menu. They looked to be slightly older than me but not more than college-aged. On each stool a young blonde perched, some half standing, leaning with their elbows on the bar, drinking beer out of glass bottles, their hair air-dried and pulled back in half ponytails and messy buns. They mostly wore tank tops and baggy jeans, revealing arms toned and tan, I guessed from carrying backpacks around the world. They were shouting at each other in several languages, but none sounded like English or Arabic, and they gestured to each other wildly, with cigarettes between their fingers. Mom was right about the bra thing. No one seemed bothered by them even though they were starting to get a little loud. My mom and I watched them from our corner, and I knew what she was thinking before she said it.

"Don't you think it would be fun to travel like that? Just being young and free, not staying in any one place too long?"

"Yeah, super fun."

"You have a passport that is easy to travel on, you're not in school, I'll be here for another month why don't you go? Paris? Rome? What do you think?"

Before I could answer, all at once, the blonde bar turned, noticing us at our tiny table. "Amy!" They yelled, waving their arms above their heads, which seemed unnecessary given how small the place was.

"Mom, they know you?"

She shrugged and smiled. "Oh yeah. They're so cute. They have the best stories. Come." "Laila!"

"I told them all about you," my mother grabbed my arm and pulled me toward the bar.

If I was honest I needed a little break from Omar and even Ali. Everything was going well but it seemed fast and I just wanted to catch my breath.

We drank margaritas, sang Madonna karaoke, and they told me their outrageous travel stories of sleeping on trains, making just enough money in every city to get to the next, and even bathing in city fountains when they had to. When the conversation inevitably turned to the men they mixed with, the blonde named Anna had the most to say and she was definitely into the bad boys.

"He is so sexy," she said, breathlessly describing one of the many men she ran into during her travels.

"He was wanted by Interpol!" the rest of the girls reminded her.

"Interpol! Who takes them seriously?" she winked at me and drained her beer bottle.

The blondes were actually fun, not defined by their last names or who their fathers were but by how many places they had been, the stories they told, and the people they met. Their lives were totally unstructured, unplanned, and free from judgment and rules. They definitely stayed in the shallow end of the Syria pool, living close to the surface, and enjoying the sunshine.

"So, have you been seeing the sights? Met any cute guys?" Anna asked, as soon as my mom left for the bathroom.

"Um, it's funny. I am supposed to go sightseeing with a guy. He is very cute."

"Oh, tell! How does he look?" she asked, the other girls tuning in suddenly.

"So, he's tall, dark hair—"

"Let me guess. Was he, by any chance, with big muscles but beautiful green eyes? Ali?"

"You know him?"

"We all know him." All the blondes started giggling. "He is the playboy of Damascus; it's difficult not to know him."

"He's like a passport stamp." "Unofficial customs agent." "No blonde shall pass."

They stopped laughing when they saw my face.

"Oh God, I am so sorry. Are you . . . in love with him?" "No! Of course not. I just met him; I mean I barely know him."

"Sorry. It's just Ali, he's actually a good guy, but not for a relationship."

"So you all ended it with him or what?" I asked, taking a sip from my drink and pretending not to care one way or the other, even though my heart was slowly sinking.

"We've all dated him off and on while we've been here. He has these VIP friends that we have no interest in, and he has obligations to them. But he never lied to any of us. He never promised anything. He was, you know, fun."

"Right. So, do you guys still see him?" "Not since . . ."

"Petra," they all said together.

Just then my mom came back from the ladies' room and said, "Petra is spectacular, I will take you there before we leave."

I nodded, grateful for the small gift that my mom didn't hear any of that conversation. Thankfully, they moved on to other subjects like all the other sites in Jordan that are worth checking out, and then Lebanon too. My attention started to drift back toward Ali and it triggered all my insecurities to think of him hanging out with these girls. Maybe my mom had been right all along. Ali was ten years older than me; he had an experience that I didn't, and we were only going to be here for a short time anyway. The last thing I needed was a broken heart so soon after losing my dad.

As if on cue, my phone started ringing and it was Ali. For the first time, I didn't pick up. I put my phone back in my bag and welcomed any distraction from thoughts of him. I drank more margaritas, asked for more stories, and by the time I left, I was seriously considering Paris.

CHAPTER 15

WHAT'S OBVIOUS

I woke up in the morning with a pounding headache. The sun was high so I knew I missed my chance at an early run again. At first, I didn't remember anything from the night before. Then the memory of a dark bar full of wild blondes, all Ali's old conquests, then calls and texts from Ali that I ignored. I wasn't sure so I checked my phone to confirm I had in fact texted him back at an obviously drunk hour that I was going to Paris and would let him know if I was ever coming back. Now I wasn't sure I could even get out of bed.

I pulled myself up and took a hot shower, letting the water run down my back, hoping I could get Ali out of my head or at least find some way of organizing my thoughts so everything didn't hurt so much.

When I came back to my room, after guzzling a whole bottle of water, I was slightly refreshed, so I talked it out with the Future President to get his take on it. As usual, he was a great listener, he was never as "judgy" as I thought he might be, but he always helped me work things out in my mind before I spoke to anyone real.

It was decided that I would call Ali and act as casually as possible in the hope that he didn't notice my passive-aggressive tone from last night. I was nervous to call him, and I didn't trust myself not to mention the blondes right away but I promised. When he answered he sounded busy and distracted anyway, so I told him I was going for a run and maybe he could meet me in the park after. He agreed though he didn't seem too thrilled with the idea. I couldn't tell if he didn't like the idea of me running or he didn't like the idea of seeing me.

Luckily, my mom was still in bed when I left the house, so she didn't have a chance to ask me about booking my plane ticket to Paris.

The run helped with the hangover and with feeling better about the situation with Ali. I realized it was not unsalvageable but we had some hurdles, the least of which were the foreigners, but still, it was going to bother me if I didn't bring it up. When he came into view, the hope of keeping our conversation upbeat was fading the closer he got to me. I wiped the sweat from my brow and smoothed my ponytail. He didn't kiss me on the cheek or make any small talk.

"Paris?" He was pissed. He stood in front of me, his arms crossed in front of his chest.

"Have you been?" I asked, still hopeful I could keep it light.

"Many times."

"Of course you have. Sorry about the late text, I—"

"I thought we had a nice time the other night. Now you don't even take my calls?"

"I loved the dinner." Just the memory of his hand touching mine and the electricity that coursed through me helped me put my guard down. "I just—"

"Laila, what's going on with you?" He seemed genuinely confused so I took a minute to get my breathing under control.

"We ran into some friends of yours last night. My mom and I."

He relaxed his arms and gestured to the park gate. "My car is parked here. Come."

When we got in his car, I didn't trust myself not to unleash or, worse, cry. Even I didn't understand why I felt like this, how was I going to explain without looking like a total psycho? I was relieved when he spoke first.

"So, who are these friends?" he asked.

"You know exactly who I'm talking about." My guard was up again as my thoughts went back to the braless blondes at the bar.

"Okay."

"They don't even wear . . . they all seemed so free, so cool, so . . . unattached to anything."

"You think being unattached is cool?" "You obviously do."

"Laila—"

"They know you, all of them. All!" Now I was pissed. "Before you judge me, can you at least give me a chance to explain?"

"That's the thing, Ali, this was before I came so I know I have no right to be pissed, but I still am. You don't have to explain."

"The problem is your mother, I get it."

"It just looks bad, Ali. It gives her more ammo than she already has and—" I figured I might as well admit it.

"And what?"

"I was crazy jealous. Like sick, out of my mind. I hated that feeling. I just wanted to get away from you."

"I don't want you to be out of your mind. I never want to hurt you like that."

"But you are enjoying my jealousy," I pouted.

"After you didn't pick up the phone last night and you didn't answer my texts and then all of a sudden you are leaving for Paris, *my* mind went to the worst place."

"Paris was a drunk idea. I'm not going."

"You put me through fucking hell last night, I have waited all this time for you—"

"Okay, I'm sorry. I am trying to grow up, it won't happen overnight."

"Laila, I'm not going to pretend I don't have a past, but it's a new thing between you and me. We will make our own memories. *Sah walla la?*"

I nodded my head, wiping tears with the back of my hand.

"And for the record, I've only been to Paris with my family. Believe me, they were hilarious trips and not even a little bit romantic."

"Now I feel stupid."

"So, if I am more open with you, then you will stop running from me?"

"When I saw you in the street that day, I felt like I knew you. And last night hearing the girls talk about you..."

"You do know me, Laila. And I know you and I know you are not like those girls. Not at all."

"You honestly think I'm better than them?" "You are better for me."

"Well, when you say it like that..."

"Unless you want to be free, cool, whatever..."

"I don't want to be cool. I don't want to go to Paris by myself."

"I got zero sleep last night and my assistant is ready to walk out on me. So, let me call the office and tell her to go. Can I drop you back home?"

By the time he dropped me off, I felt happy and exhausted and in need of more water and sleep.

As soon as I stepped into the courtyard my mom came down the stairs.

"Laila, there you are! I have been waiting all day! We need to book your ticket."

"Mom, I changed my mind about Paris."

"What? Why? You were so excited about it last night.

The girls were so excited for you."

"Yeah, I just don't want to spend what little time we have left here in Paris. Sorry."

"I don't understand what changed your mind."

"Paris will always be there, Mom. I will go one day, for sure."

"Damascus will always be here, too," she said and followed me up the stairs, "Didn't the girls talk to you?"

I turned around to face her in front of my bedroom door. "Yeah, they did. Did you know they knew Ali?"

"I mean, they may have mentioned him one evening while I was there," she said.

"I know what you're doing, Mom."

"And I know you've been seeing Ali behind my back. It's not like you."

"It's not behind your back, Mom. He is just, it's a small city. What am I supposed to do?"

"All those *wasta* people are spoiled brats! They've run this country for decades and they do whatever they want . . . they don't give a damn about anybody but themselves. You heard last night . . . Ali is a total player.

They don't take foreigners seriously. Why would I want my daughter involved with people like that?"

"Ali is not like that, Mom. He really isn't. I just wish you would give him a chance. And by the way, he doesn't see me as a foreigner."

"Are you sure about that? Sometimes I feel like I'm having the same conversation with you that I've had with your dad a million times."

"Why are you so convinced he would break my heart?

How do you know I won't break his?"

"Because he's ten years older, Laila. He's traveled, he's been educated. I'm sure he's been in and out of pretty serious relationships. I'm sure he's been to Paris with some girl."

"Actually, he hasn't. I asked him and he said he went on a family vacation to Paris. So?"

"Still, this is your first time even being interested in anyone."

"That should tell you something."

"Fine. You want to go sightseeing with Ali? Go. But in four weeks, we are both out of here. I want no arguments from you."

"Fine."

Before she left me, she turned in the doorway. "One more thing. I don't know how you will pull it off, but I would keep this from the family if I were you."

"If you are okay with it, what's the problem? Why would they care?"

"Isn't it obvious to you by now?" "Isn't what obvious?"

"Ali is an Alawite."

CHAPTER 16

ALAWHAT?

The only thing that was obvious to me was that it was 2011 and no one cared about religion. Maybe some people, like Sabrina's parents, but not Ali. I was too embarrassed to admit to my mom I had no idea what 'Alawite' even really meant other than the president's family was from the same sect. Anyway, Ali was a big-time Syr and his loyalties were clear, at least to me.

I was much more myself as I dressed that morning and updated the future president about everything that happened the day before, giving him a wink when I told him Ali was one of 'them.' I was more relaxed knowing I was free to see Ali as long as I didn't let the family know. Since I was leaving in a month there seemed no reason to cause a problem in the house even though I disagreed with Mom that Ali's religion would even be an issue. I didn't want to upset her since she could easily change her mind. We decided Omar was the best person to talk to about Mom's latest plan of attack on Ali.

I planned to take a run and then call Ali but he called me first instead. I told him about some parts of the conversation with Mom about the villa's renovations and how we would probably be gone in about four weeks.

"She might even have a buyer already but she has to get the work done first."

"Four weeks?" he asked, obviously surprised by her aggressive timeline.

"I know, it's the best I could do. I promised her before I came that I wouldn't push back on the return date. At the time, I just wanted to get here but I agreed to it."

"So when the renovations are complete and she has a buyer and she sells the house, then she can take you. But not one minute before?"

"So for now, I'm all yours. What part of the city do you want me to see?" I asked.

"Actually, I was thinking to get you out of the city."
"Okay. Where are we going?"

"You'll see. I'll pick you up tomorrow. Bring your bathing suit."

Before I could meet up with Ali, I stopped in Omar's bar to chat and pretend I was casually hanging out when really I needed his help to get one step ahead of my mother for a change. I didn't know what her angle was going to be, but I was tired of being the *ejnabeeyay* who always seemed to have missed an email.

When I walked into the bar, Omar's first reaction was, "Whoa. How did you get your hair like that?"

"I got a *sayshwar*. I'm obsessed. I'm never washing my own hair again."

"You're getting so Syr, Laila."

"Me? No one is more Syr than you, always scheming and eating *bizr*." When he handed me a margarita full- to-the-rim, I made sure to get to the point quickly before the bar inevitably filled up with people. "So listen, tell me whatever I need to know just so I don't look like a total idiot."

"On which topic?" "Ali's religion." "Fuck no."

"I can't ask Mazen! What, you think I should ask Ali?"

"I've known Ali a long time, even I would never ask him about his religion. Ever."

"Why not?"

"Because it's super rude and invasive."

"Okay, so they're not Sunni, they're more on the Shia side, right?"

"Kind of. Take the Sunni–Shia thing out of your mind, we don't care. This is more . . . tribal," he said, arms outstretched at his sides. "So, this conversation is exactly why we need all of these wild groups under one, strong, nationalistic identity, or else we have—"

"Democracy?" "*Jnan*. Chaos."

"Oh, right, sorry."

"Laila, all you need to know is that there are good Christians and there are bad Christians. Good Sunnis and bad Sunnis. Good Alawites—"

"Dude, I got it."

"You'd be surprised how many people don't get it." He paused before shaking his head and adding, "Your mom, the American, pulled the Alawite card. She's really . . . something."

"Omar, where am I going to hide him? He's like 6′2."

"And he's wide," he said, arms outstretched at his sides. "We call him 'the tank.' Mostly, because he's slow."

Ali picked me up the next day and drove us out of the old city and beyond the edges of Damascus. The space between buildings widened and more trees were lining either side of the highway. We passed through smaller villages with goats and vegetable markets and old men wearing *keffiyahs* and riding bicycles.

"Will you please tell me where we are going?" "My family's farm."

"Farm? You don't seem like the farming type."

When we finally arrived, black iron gates opened up to a gigantic, white home, made of chalky stone and glass doors. The gardens bloomed with pink roses and fruit trees. Like so many places in Damascus, this place felt vaguely familiar. When I stepped out of the car, I said, "Omg, Ali—"

"You remember?" "It's crazy."

He took me by the hand and led me into the house. He pushed open the double doors that led to the patio, crystal clear water in the swimming pool.

Later, we changed into running clothes and took a run around the perimeter of the 'farm', which was a massive orchard where you could see for miles without seeing another house or person.

I could hear him behind me, trying to avoid holes in the ground and clearly unprepared for this terrain. The soft uneven earth was similar to the beach, and I was grateful to be prepared for it.

"Seriously, you know what your problem is?" I asked when I noticed how much he was panting and holding his side.

"A girlfriend who wants to kill me?" He bent over, one hand above his hip.

"Your breathing. You are all up here." I put my fingertips lightly on his chest, making him stand. "You can't breathe deeply enough from here. Take a deep breath from here. This is where all your power is."

"Here? Is all my power?"

"Yes," I said, touching his abdomen and feeling for the first time like his equal and not like a little girl in front of him. He was genuinely listening to the advice, taking a deep breath through his nose. I pulled his bottom lip open and continued, "Let it out from your mouth." I could feel the tension leaving his upper body and he smiled his half-smile. "It takes some practice but you'll have more stamina."

"There is more to running than I thought."

"It took me a while to learn how to do it right." I turned to one of the fruit trees. "Did you know the Portuguese word for apricot is Damasco?" I reached up to grab one I had my eye on.

"I didn't know that. Now you speak Portuguese?"

"Just the one word, to be honest. Languages aren't my thing." I pulled one down and handed it to Ali.

"I noticed. We will work on that, too." He sunk his teeth into it and then grabbed my hand pulling me back toward the pool.

We collapsed on cushioned lounge chairs and drank from our water bottles. We didn't speak for a few minutes, watching the sun just as it was beginning to set.

"It's so pretty here." "Do you remember it?"

"I think so. I remember running and climbing the trees, I remember you chasing me."

"Seems like so long ago." His breathing was heavy but was steadier than before. "You want to swim?"

I checked my watch. "Sure, 15 minutes max?"

"*Yalla*, baby."

Before we left, we grabbed a coffee from the kitchen and headed back to the car when I realized I forgot my bathing suit in the shower upstairs.

"Leave it," he said.

"Yeah, no one will find it?"

"Nobody comes here but me. And the workers. It'll be dry for the next time you come."

We listened to music, the windows rolled down, and watched the countryside go by. I realized the last time I felt this bliss was at Amou's vineyard in Sonoma. I was running when I saw the apricot, the apricot that changed the course of my life or maybe put it on the exact right path.

I glanced over at Ali, droplets of water still glistening in his black hair. Before we left I pulled my hair up into a bun on top of my head so it didn't look wet. That way, I wouldn't have to explain too much about where I had been and why yesterday's *sayshwar* was ruined.

"You think they will find out about us?" I didn't even know who 'they' were but somehow it seemed like a reasonable question.

"Sooner or later, baby, sooner or later. And honestly, I don't care." He exhaled what sounded like a sigh of relief.

"Me neither."

His driving didn't scare me anymore either. No matter how fast he drove, how much he ignored other drivers and traffic lanes, with one hand on the wheel and the other holding my hand, I never felt safer.

CHAPTER
17

SAME LETTER AS ARSE

"I'm not even going to say the Lakers suck; it's that they have no class, you know? They play dirty when they're desperate," Omar said as soon as we walked in. He stood behind the bar, his phone in his hand.

"It's not their year. And you should talk." Ali and I sat down at the stools, three of Omar's regulars next to us.

"I am all class when I foul, first of all. And secondly, I wasn't desperate; I let you win." Omar seemed never to run out of energy or topics. "Anyway, this is Dallas's year," Omar said.

"I have two words for Dallas: LeBron James. Or is that three words? Anyway, you can't stop him," Ali said.

"Nobody can be bigger than the game. Nobody. And I'm telling you the gods will punish LeBron until he goes back to Cleveland," Omar said.

"Dallas will choke like they did in '06, you'll see."
"Then I have two words for you, Ali: Tony Robbins."
"Oh fuck, here we go."

"This asshole, he had the electricity to my office cut. We were days without electricity, and by the time I found out it was him, he had forgotten about it. You should see what I went through to get it back." Omar pointed at Ali as he explained to me.

"Seriously, man, I forgot about it! That was the week Laila came," Ali said, everybody at the bar laughing.

"Blame it on Laila, yeah," Omar said. "Why?" I asked.

"Why what?" Ali asked. "Why did you cut it?"

"He's so, what's the word? Like he gets nervous, he has to have control over everything?" Ali said.

"Anal?"

"*Laama* can I say this word, anal?" he asked, looking at Omar, who shook his head to say no. "Uh yeah, he's super anal. We enjoy watching him, his hair on fire, spending his whole day running around, trying to solve all these problems, and he never asks for help."

"In the end, I solved everything. I didn't even need you to get it back on," Omar said.

"He came back from a seminar in the States, some self-improvement thing." He snapped his fingers at the other guys at the bar. "Say his name again?"

"Tony!" they said, clutching their hearts.

"Omg, Omar, you went to a Tony Robbins seminar?"

Omar blinked once.

"I had to settle him down a bit, bring him back to earth, back to reality," Ali said.

"Back to Syria!" the others at the bar said in unison. "Tony is amazing," Omar said.

"Tony!" they cried in high-pitched voices, clutching their hearts again.

"Tony Robbins stuff doesn't work in Syria," Ali explained.

"What do you mean?" I asked. "This is for Americans," Ali said.

"Self-improvement is not just for Americans," I insisted.

Amer, the one Omar called 'the chubby one', chimed in, "Make your own destiny, you can have and do whatever you want. This doesn't work here. Our families tell us what our lives will be like. K*halas*, we get what we get."

"He's helped so many people all over the world achieve their big dreams. He's pretty amazing." I had my own memories of my father listening to his audiobooks and I grew to love the gravelly, booming sound of his voice.

"Oh, yeah? When he comes to Syria, I will believe in him. What would he say to this?" Amer asked.

"He would say 'believe in yourself first,'" I replied.

"I believe in myself completely. I also believe in reality. We do the best we can with our situation. And in my opinion, it's not so bad, huh?" Amer lifted his whiskey glass and tipped it toward me.

"Of course. I didn't mean . . ."

"They talk a big game, but they never dare come to this part of the world. If they believe in their message why don't they come here? They won't last one day. As soon as the electricity is cut, they'll run."

"Maybe no one's invited him?" I suggested.

"*Yalla*, Laila, send Tony an email. Tell him Omar sent you!" Another of his friends offered from the other end of the bar.

"You see, Laila? They eat my food, drink my liquor, they come on my boat and they harass me non-stop." Omar still stood behind the bar his arms crossed across his chest, but he was smiling so I could tell this was a recurring conversation. Ali turned toward the other guys and their conversation turned back to Arabic.

"I forgot you have a boat," I said to Omar.

"*Khalas* we'll go soon. Can you?" he asked, lowering his voice so Ali and the others wouldn't hear.

"I don't know."

"Sabrina wants you to call her. She wants to have lunch. Maybe she can help you out?" Omar said, throwing a towel over his shoulder.

I don't know why I didn't think of it before. Sabrina was fun to hang out with and happened to know how to keep a relationship under wraps. I hadn't said a word to Ali about Mazen and the family not wanting me to hang out with him, but I didn't want to give him the real reason. That conversation was unavoidable and I had no intention of turning into another Omar and Sabrina, but for the short term, I had no other options.

I turned my attention back to Ali and somehow they got on the subject of me and my lack of Arabic skills. Ali told them I didn't speak Arabic, so they politely went back and forth between languages, but when they got animated they couldn't help but speak in rapid-fire Arabic, and I didn't want Ali to keep having to translate every word. When he noticed how quiet I had gotten, he said, "I will teach you, don't worry. I know you have it all up here," as he put his finger to my temple.

Amer chimed in again and spoke to me, "Say his name. This is the hardest thing for Americans," he said, pointing his finger at Ali.

"Ali," I said, knowing they all pronounced it differently and I was too shy to try it the Arabic way.

"Ali," Amer mimicked, "so nice." Amer was smiling and batting his eyelashes at Ali and the other guys sitting at the bar howled with laughter.

"Don't listen to them. *Khalas*, Amer," Ali told him.

"She needs to learn! Laila, the letter *ain* comes from deep down, it is like a roar! You have to open your mouth like you are taking a bite. Ali," Amer commanded, his hand in a fist. "Say it."

Omar looked down the bar at us and raised his eyebrows. The volume on everything else in the bar was suddenly turned down as it seemed the whole place now was listening to our conversation. Though many people spoke English they appreciated foreigners who at least tried to speak Arabic. Now, all I could hear were people clearing their throats and the sound of the bubbles in the *sheeshah* pipes. I wiped my sweaty palms on my jeans, certain I would screw it up. Ali's expression was encouraging, and for whatever reason, he was confident I had it stored somewhere in my memory. I pushed the others out of my mind and focused only on Ali. I cleared my throat and took a deep breath, making sure I was taking all his direction without overdoing it.

"*Ali,*" I said, this time finding the sound in my throat familiar and correct. The bar erupted in laughter and applause and I nodded in appreciation.

"*Arse* is the same letter." Omar guided me quietly from behind the bar and when I repeated it, shouted, "Double points!"

"What is *arse?*" I asked.

"*Arse* is a bastard slash man-whore," Ali explained, then after considering added, "More on the man-whore side."

"Oh. Sorry."

"It's okay."

"You could just say 'whore', you know? You don't have to specify it's a male-whore."

"No, it's in the masculine tense." "Oh, right."

"But that was good. We'll work on your vocabulary next time."

By the time we left the bar that night, I was still laughing at the image of Omar running all over the city to get his electricity back on after Ali had it cut off. Even when he was speaking to his friends, and I couldn't understand more than a few words, having Ali next to me was enough—enough to make me feel like I was home.

CHAPTER 18

WAINUK, AKHI?

(WHERE ARE YOU, MY BROTHER?)

On the days I thought I could get away with it without anyone asking questions, Ali and I drove out to his farm to swim and run. He didn't complain too much about the running, and I could see improvement in his pace the more time we spent together, but he definitely preferred swimming with me.

"What happened to 'look, don't touch'?" I asked, giggling when he wrapped his arms around my waist pulling me into the deep end of the pool where I couldn't touch the bottom while he was on solid ground.

"That doesn't apply to you and me," he said, matter-of-factly.

"Why wouldn't it apply?" "Because you belong to me." "Says who?"

"ALI!" an unfamiliar male voice echoed loudly through the house and out to the pool. "*Wainuk, ya akho al sharmout?*" *Where are you, brother of a whore?*

"Fuck," he said, under his breath.

"Friends?" I asked, when he burst through the French double doors and out to the patio, dressed in white shorts and a t-shirt, his chest broad with the confidence of someone walking into his own home.

He stared down at us for a minute before he said, "This is where you've been hiding." He was standing so close to the water his white sneakers came out over the edge. "When I went to your house, they didn't mention you had a guest." He held a half-eaten apricot in his hand.

Ali and I stayed in the water, my arms still wrapped around his neck, while his friend stood at the edge of the pool staring down at us. I could not think of anything else to say and nobody moved. "Hi," I finally said, breaking the uneasy silence. "I'm Laila."

He finished eating the apricot and tossed the pit into the garden. "Laila." He let my name drop out of his mouth almost like he knew something in my name that I didn't.

When neither of them spoke, I released Ali and swam to the edge of the pool, where his friend stood. There was no other way to get out so I climbed the stairs hoping he would move by the time I got to the top. He didn't budge. He was not as tall as Ali, but somehow he held a huge amount of space, and he stood like a statue. He seemed angry with Ali, like he had 'caught' us, and I had to get uncomfortably close to get past him.

When I reached him at the top of the stairs I couldn't contain my curiosity and surprise at his aggressive entrance, "You look so familiar, have we met before?"

"No." His voice was cold, his tone firm, and he clearly had no intention of making himself seem more friendly.

"Oh, sorry."

The two guys that had come through the doors behind him were looking away and trying not to laugh, but Ali wasn't laughing. He stayed in the pool as I grabbed my towel and dried myself off. Omar and two other guys that played basketball at the school came through the open doors.

"Ali, you asshole, we've been calling you! You are like a girl—" He stopped when he saw me. "Oh."

"Girls don't answer your calls," Omar said, as he came outside behind him. They all stopped talking when they saw me.

"Hey guys, I was just leaving so—" "Laila, what's up?"

"What's up, O?"

"Damn girl, okay. Where've you been hiding?" "Not hiding, we were just, you know, swimming."

"I see that. You and Ali are Olympic swimmers by now." Omar seemed unfazed by any of the scenarios that were unfolding so that helped calm my nerves, but I knew something was wrong.

"Why is everyone acting weird?" I lowered my voice, wrapping a towel around my body and suddenly feeling really self-conscious.

"Don't worry, I've got you." He turned back around to the pool where Ali still stood in the water, his friend in white still at the water's edge.

It was one thing to be here with Ali; it was another to be the only girl with a whole group of guys. I retreated into the house, showered, and changed into dry clothes. When I came out of the upstairs bathroom, I looked out one of the windows I knew you could see the pool from because I had spied on Ali many times while he was swimming laps after I had got out. I saw that his friend in white was still standing over him and they looked like they were arguing back and forth.

Eventually, Ali's arms were stretched out to his sides in what looked like surrender. I had learned over the past few months that some Syrians took socializing very seriously and it really wasn't okay to disappear. If they were good friends it was odd Ali never mentioned me to him or vice versa. Maybe I could help smooth it over. Ali and I had enough challenges already; we didn't need a disgruntled friend he had been ignoring added to it.

I pulled my hair into a wet bun and headed downstairs, determined not to let anything or anyone ruin what was a perfect day.

Ali was in the main living room waiting for me when I came down.

"I'm sorry about them. I didn't know they were coming."

"It's fine, I should get back to the city, anyway. I told Sabrina I would call her."

Just as I grabbed my bag, his friend in white walked into the living room where we were standing.

"Ali tells me you're from California," he said, removing his sunglasses and placing them on the counter.

I caught Ali's eye behind him and he nodded so I said, "Yeah," without elaborating like I usually did. "Sorry, I didn't catch your name." I offered him my hand, noticing how blue his eyes were.

"Jamil. My name is Jamil," he said and I was grateful he was nothing like the religious people. When the guys behind him started snickering again he merely turned his head toward them and they stopped.

"Jamil. Beautiful," I said, determined to thaw the iciness from our meeting outside.

"Now that we know you exist, I would like you to join us for dinner tomorrow evening," Jamil said.

"Sure." I couldn't, at that moment, think of a reason why not.

"Ali will bring you," he said and then just stared back at me. He was more comfortable with silence than anyone I had ever met, which made me feel slightly tongue-tied. "My driver will take you back now."

"Oh. Thanks," I said, not realizing before that Ali would not be coming with me. Of course, now he had guests so he couldn't leave.

Ali had been quiet through our entire exchange, so I brushed off the feeling of disappointment that our time was cut short. "I had fun today. Thank you for the run and the swim," I grabbed his face in one hand and kissed his lips. "*Yalla bye.*"

On the ride back to the city I hoped that if it ever came down to me or Jamil he would make the right choice.

Something about Jamil was so familiar, although he was adamant we had never met before. Then it dawned on me as his driver raced me back to the city, the sun setting in the distance, lighting the earth on fire. It was true we had never actually met before, but he knew all of my secrets. He had seen me naked many times, laughed with me when any of my relatives overheard, and whispered in the hallway that I was *majnouneh*. He was the one my father mentioned in his office in California on my birthday a few years ago. His face had been hanging on my bedroom wall since Omar gave me the poster. It was Jamil, the other son.

CHAPTER 19

V IS FOR VISA

I took my run near Omar's office the next day and popped in to see him.

"Dude, you could have mentioned when you gave me the poster that you were best friends?"

"Uh, we're not in Kindergarten to have 'best friends', but if Jamil had one it would be Ali. So if he didn't mention anything or introduce you he must want it that way."

"I mean, it's weird that I see his face every morning."

"Excuse me?"

"The poster you gave me?"

"Laila, I was joking with you. You said you threw it away."

"I lied." I sat down in the chair across from his desk. "I hung it up in my bedroom, as a joke at first, but now . . . we talk."

"You talk?"

"He listens. In my defense, he wasn't real to me until yesterday."

"You didn't think he was real? How many times do we have to tell you? Everyone—"

"—knows everyone," I said, finishing his sentence for him. "How is that even possible?"

"Wow, that must have been awkward for you." Omar leaned back in his chair, bouncing his left knee under his desk. He ate *bizr*, flicking the seeds into a cup, and stared at me. I was hoping he would say something about Jamil's attitude towards me or 'catching' Ali and me at the farm, but he didn't give anything away.

"He seemed pretty pissed off at Ali?" I prodded.

"He is."

"Why? I mean, it's not really any of his business."

"Don't worry about it. You can smooth things over at dinner tonight. Just be sweet, be charming, be . . . foreign. You can get away with a lot."

"But we didn't do anything wrong!"

"Wrong. He knows Ali. He knows what he's trying to do, and it's not going to work."

"You mean hiding me?" I asked, but before he could answer his phone started ringing and Nadia came into his office carrying coffee and stacks of files. I took it as my cue to leave even though I would have liked to get more out of him. Although, even if I stayed, I didn't think he would.

When Ali and I stepped into the elevator of Jamil's building the first thing I saw when I turned to face the doors was a button at the top. It was a circle with a lion roaring and standing on its hind legs.

"Family crest?" I asked casually, as though we all had one. He nodded, but said nothing. He hadn't mentioned anything about Jamil since he 'caught' us in the swimming pool but I got the sense Ali was worried about it. I continued to make conversation, probably just to calm my nerves and take down the intimidation factor. "Lions are lazy. Did you know the females do all the hunting?"

"Lazy? Their job is to protect the females. That's why they can only have one dominant male in the pride. Did you know a lion can mate up to 100 times in 24 hours?" As soon as he said it, Jamil opened the door. "Ali, you're late. Laila, you're welcome. Please."

Jamil's home was nothing like I expected. There was no gold or mirrors or fancy chandeliers. In fact, it was clean and simple, the furniture looked new, but there was nothing flashy about it.

In his entryway, a simple table, a lamp next to it, held an open wooden box filled to the top with cell phones. Ali suggested before we got out of his car that I leave mine in the glove box. He automatically dropped his in, like someone who had done it a hundred times.

Jamil led us back to the living room area where the girls were already chatting. It was clear they had also been there many times before as they were all stretched out comfortably, lounging on his sofa, dressed in leather pants and diamonds, a couple of them smoking cigarettes. The guys stood by the balcony door dressed in white shirts and jeans, and I was relieved to see Omar had come along with a couple of his basketball friends. Maya perched on the ottoman in the center, her legs crossed and hands open at her sides, while the others listened passively. It seemed like they had heard her rant before, and I sensed this time was for my ears, even though we had only just arrived.

"The problem is the foreigners. These girls open their legs for everyone. Then they say Arab girls are shit on by men as if we are the ones with no self-respect? In our culture, men give us everything before we give them anything." Then looking directly at me, "Don't you think this is true?"

"I didn't know there was a 'problem.'" If I agreed I was totally allowing her to insult my American side and all my American girlfriends which felt wrong, but if I disagreed I would look defensive as though I were one of these loose girls she was describing. "Maybe a bigger problem is girls who only eat salad? They always have *tabbouleh* in their teeth."

Only the curvy redhead snorted and chuckled while the rest of the girls took their cues from Maya and glared back at me. Maya quickly closed her mouth, putting her hand up in front of her face and frantically running her tongue along her front teeth even though we hadn't even sat down at the table yet. Something told me that was the last chance I would have to be Maya's ally. I sensed there were always strings attached to that one, and I had no interest in being one of her followers. Though we had still not been introduced, it felt like we already had a long history.

"*Yalla*, let's eat!" Jamil clapped his hands together and everyone quickly moved toward the table.

"Everyone, this is Laila. I know Ali will introduce you properly."

Everyone came to the table, and we sat down.

"How do you and Ali know each other?" Jamil asked me, taking his seat last at the head of the table near Ali and me.

"We met at Omar's bar." "You met in a bar."

"Well, we knew each other before, our families knew each other, but I don't remember."

"You forgot him." "I was four."

"This story keeps getting better." Jamil passed the fish down the table, while Maya and the other girls pretended not to laugh.

"I mean, what do you really remember from when you were four?" I asked him, taking a plate from his hand to pass to Ali.

He leaned in close to me, smiled, and said, "Everything." Maya and the girls were clearly big Jamil fans, laughing at all of his jokes and loving our conversation.

"Where are you from, Laila?" a woman with a thick accent and even thicker lashes asked me. I loved how they rolled the letter *r* even when speaking English, but I dreaded this question my whole life. I answered with my usual spiel.

"My dad is Syrian; my mom is from California. I was born here, but we moved when I was very young."

"What is your family name?" She narrowed her eyes, her false lashes swallowing the whites of her eyes. She tilted her head to the side, pursing her red lips while she studied me.

"Abdullah."

"Ah, you are from Damascus. Yes, I know Doctor Abdullah, *kan iktir shater*, but he moved suddenly to the United States many years ago. I remember."

"He's my father."

"He returned? *Walla*, I didn't know," she said, looking around the table.

"He passed."

"Oh. *Allah yerhamo*, God rest his soul. Laila, I am very sorry." She sounded sincere and then gave Ali the look I wanted to give him about why he didn't tell them before I came.

Later when we got up from the table, I was able to pull Ali aside and ask him why he didn't tell them anything about me.

"I don't want us to be close with these people," he whispered in my ear and left it at that.

Ali stood still, allowing everything around him to move, but Jamil was agile, moving like cool water making sure you never knew exactly where he was. He moved with ease among his guests, not spending too much time on anyone, but giving his full attention to whoever he was speaking to.

Ali tended to speak to everyone at once giving you the sense he was with you but with an eye on everyone else at the same time, always assessing any threat level. Omar never stopped moving or talking. It was a good thing Omar kept his girlfriend hidden. Sabrina would have to be super confident and independent because his attention deficit would drive most girls batshit crazy. Omar could be mid-sentence and start a whole other conversation with someone else before he finished.

It was exhausting, trying to keep up with Ali and his friends; they were always socializing. It seemed they never spent time alone, away from each other. I still had an American side that needed space to be by myself and collect my thoughts. Though Jamil's decor was understated, his view was the most spectacular I had seen anywhere in the city. Maybe that's why there was really no need for opulence inside.

Jamil's place was also at one of the highest points you could get in Damascus, and I wanted to check out the view for myself. I snuck away while Ali was talking to Omar and a couple of other people and opened the door to the balcony.

There was a breeze in the air but it wasn't chilly. The lights of the city stretched for miles it seemed. I leaned against the balcony railing, breathing in the air of Damascus, wondering how I could have ever forgotten this place, how my father survived leaving this city. I hardly noticed Jamil opening the sliding glass door behind me and stepping outside. My moment of solitude was shattered, but if Jamil was a very close friend of Ali it wouldn't be a bad idea to get to know him a little bit better. I turned around to face him, keeping my hands resting on either side of me on the railing.

"Hi," I said.

"Hi." He stood directly in front of me, hands in his pockets, working something out in his mind about me.

"Your view is breathtaking." I couldn't help but gush. It was so freeing to be up there. "It must be the best in the city, huh?" I asked, hoping to break the awkward energy that had been between us since I met him and hoping flattery about his place would win him over.

"Yes, I believe so," he said, as though it was a decision made by others, and hadn't much to do with him. He stood, still staring at me. "It's strange, Ali usually prefers blondes."

I absently pulled my ponytail back around close to my face, finding I was losing my confidence and wanting to take back anything nice I had said about his place. "Things change," I said, my tone more curt this time.

"People don't." He shook his head slowly from side to side, never taking his gaze off me.

"Okay, whatever." I shrugged my shoulders, thinking it was my last attempt at being friendly with him. What was his problem? Why did he care what color my hair was?

"Ali said you are a foreigner, but I think you are a Syrian girl." He smiled for the first time, meeting my eyes. He moved in even closer to me.

"What's going on?" Ali came up behind Jamil.

I saw several pairs of eyes through the glass behind him pretending not to stare out at us. "I was asking your friend Laila whether she considers herself American or Syrian." He addressed Ali without taking his eyes off me. They both stood in front of me waiting for an answer.

"I'm both," I answered, although now instead of feeling resigned I had anger bubbling up inside of me.

"You cannot be both." Jamil smiled, looking to Ali, clearly unconcerned with my feelings.

I could feel Ali's eyes on me, but I couldn't read his expression. He pulled me by the hand and said goodbye to Jamil. We walked back through Jamil's living room, his guests no longer trying to hide that they were watching us. Omar was the only one who met my eyes, but I couldn't read his expression exactly; I could have sworn I saw a slight smile playing on his lips. If Omar is enjoying this or thinks this is funny I am going to kick his ass.

By the time we reached the elevator, I was fuming. "What the hell was that about? Why is he so concerned about my nationality? My visa is still good for another few months, I think." Why hadn't he just told Jamil I was Syrian *and* American? "What is his problem? I just don't know why he doesn't like me. How can you be friends with someone like that? Who cares if I am blonde or brunette? If you like me, he should—"

"Laila, are you a virgin?"

My mouth dropped open in shock and my cheeks flushed with embarrassment. What the hell did that have to do with anything? "What?"

"I'm sorry it came up like this, but I'm asking. Just tell me the truth."

I felt the walls of the elevator start to close in on me, the roaring lion seemed to be getting bigger, but there was nowhere to escape. "I don't think it's anyone's business. Least of all Jamil's."

"You're right, it is only between you and me." "It's between me and me, Ali, just so we're clear."

"Okay, what about me? You didn't think this would ever come up between us?"

"Not now, not like this!"

"Laila, I honestly don't care either way."

"You don't care so why do you need to know?" "Jamil says he can tell if a girl is a virgin just by looking at her. So?" "So what?"

"Laila, it's a simple question."

"Yes, Ali, I am a virgin! Okay?" I pulled my t-shirt down as the elevator door opened.

"Okay," he said, holding the door open for me.

"Is Jamil trying to get rid of me, is that why he wants to find something wrong with me?" I asked as soon as we got in the car.

"No, Lailla, don't say that. In our culture, this is a good thing. There is nothing wrong with you. You're perfect. You're more than perfect."

"Are you?" I asked, my blood now boiling. I didn't understand how he could be so calm.

"Perfect? No."

"It's a simple question, Ali."

"Laila, don't get pissed at *me*, this is exactly the reason I kept you from him."

When Ali dropped me back at my uncle's, and I was back in my bedroom, I went straight for the poster.

"Really?" I asked. The other two were silent as always, but I thought I saw a hint of a smile on Jamil's face.

CHAPTER 20

MEEN INTI?

(WHO ARE YOU?)

I paid another visit to Omar's office the next day. I hadn't slept well, and I wasn't sure exactly how to feel about dinner at Jamil's. I needed Omar's take before I spoke to Ali any more about it. I walked into his office and sunk into the chair in front of his desk.

"I hate to burst your propaganda bubble, but your guy is a dick."

"He's a dictator, what's he going to be?" he answered and kept typing.

"Jamil basically outed me as a V at his dinner party, who does that? Then Ali interrogated me in the elevator, and between the two of them, I almost died of embarrassment."

"Yeah." Omar didn't seem fazed by any of it. "Everyone just assumed, you know, you were 'Americanized.'"

"That's rude."

"That's reality." Omar picked up his phone. "Smile." He raised his phone and leaned across his desk, closer to me as I smiled and he snapped a picture of us.

"How does Jamil even know?" I asked. "Intuition. He's so good at it."

"He needs to mind his own business."

"Welcome to Syria, where no one minds his own business." He looked up from his phone temporarily. "This one time we went to Beirut . . . he's never been wrong." He shook his head and finished texting. Thankfully, Nadia came in to ask if I wanted Nescafe.

When she left, I asked, "How do you verify? Wait, no. Never mind. I don't want to know." I sunk further into his leather chair and crossed my arms. "So, Laila's a V, this is now public information?"

Omar stood and went to his open window. "Hey everyone! Laila Abdullah is a big V!" As soon as he spoke, I jumped up and went to the window beside him.

"God, Omar!"

A guy riding by on a bike spit on the sidewalk and two women walking on the other side of the street waved politely, confused but disinterested.

"See? No one cares."

"Omar, I can never show my face in the city again." I needed Omar to be on my side on this one.

"You can and you will. That's how you let people know you don't give a fuck, or however you want to phrase it."

"Thanks, O, for always lending a helpful spin."

"Listen, Laila, being outed as a V when everyone assumed you weren't is a good thing. Chastity, in our culture, reflects on your family and affects your marriage prospects. So even though you were embarrassed, believe me when I tell you it's much better than the other way around."

"I see why Ali didn't want to introduce me, that's obvious now, but I don't understand why Jamil's trying to come between us."

"For now, Jamil wants to see Ali sweat a little. Jamil knows Ali has only ever been with foreigners. He's going to see how long he can last with you."

"Then Jamil is going to be waiting for a long time because Ali and I are awesome."

"Are you?"

"Yeah," I said, without mentioning the abrupt way I left him in the car the night before. I told myself we would be awesome again as soon as I returned his texts. "I think so."

"So, despite the temporary humiliation, it seems lost on you that you are not 'Laila the *ejnabeeya*' anymore but certified by the president himself 'Laila, the Syrian girl.' This is better than your tourist visa. Isn't that what you wanted?"

"This was not what I had in mind." Although it occurred to me maybe Maya would have to shut her mouth now, and I was starting to see the situation from a different vantage point.

"Maybe this had an isolating effect on your life in California, but not here."

"It's Ali's reaction. Do you know what I mean? I can't read him sometimes. I couldn't tell if he was happy or disappointed or I don't know. I start to feel like I have known him all my life and then in one second he seems like a stranger to me."

"Ali, believe me, the only thing he is thinking about right now is how to keep Laila *and* Jamil happy. Neither of you is super easy."

When I got back home, everyone else was already out. My mother was probably cracking the whip at the villa and my aunt was out doing her daily errands so when there was a knock at the door I was worried it might be Mahmoud again. I was ready to tell him, once more, that Mazen was working. But it was even worse. Maya, with her high cheekbones and sunglasses, dressed in a starched, white button-down shirt, a few buttons undone at the top to show off her gold chain with the letter 'M' prominently wedged between her breasts standing in the doorway, blocking my uncle's street with her car.

"I don't think you can park there."

I was surprised that she knew exactly where I lived, but I was more curious as to why she was on my doorstep in the first place. Cars were not allowed in the narrow streets of the old city and for good reason, as most modern cars were too big to fit but that didn't stop Maya. She seemed unfazed that no one could get around her and the car doors couldn't even open all the way.

"Who are you?" was the first thing out of Maya's mouth.

"I am Laila Ab—"

"I know you're 'Laila Abdullah from America,'" she tried to mimic an American accent. "But, why are you here?"

"I'm from here."

"First of all, I never heard of you before. Secondly, you don't look at all like you're 'from here,'" she said, as she looked me up and down and then tried to peer around me into the courtyard.

"Maya, what do you want?" I asked because we were clearly never going to be friends.

"Jamil asked me to come and pick you up. He wants to see you at the riding stables."

"Stables? Horses are not really my jam."

"You're not riding; you're a guest of Jamil's. You'll watch the competition."

"I'm busy, sorry," I said and tried to shut the door in her face.

She was quick to hold the door open with her manicured hand. "You don't look busy. Jamil will not accept this as an excuse."

She was probably right. Even though he was going about it the wrong way, it crossed my mind that maybe Jamil felt badly about the way the dinner had gone and how Ali and I left. He might have been trying to make amends. After talking to Omar, I did feel a little bit better about the whole thing and considered that I may have overreacted. I was the one who was learning about the city and its ways, and I shouldn't expect it to change to suit me. Also, a small, shy voice inside reminded me that I was finally where I was supposed to be.

I told Maya I would be out in a second, and I ran upstairs to make myself somewhat more presentable. There was a good chance Ali would be there and despite how mortified I was he had been texting me non-stop since the night before.

When I came back out, Maya's driver was waiting with the door open as far as it could go, and I nodded hello to him. I couldn't even imagine what this guy must have seen working for her family. She motioned for him to wait outside the car as she and I got in the back seat.

"Listen, Laila," she said, removing her sunglasses. "Let me give you a small piece of advice. This can be the best city on Earth or it can be a living hell if you don't know your place. His is the only family that matters. If he tells you to jump, you say *tikram ainek*, how high?"

"Are you serious?"

"And, one more thing, I would stay far away from Ali if I were you. Or keep him as a 'family friend' only."

"Why?"

"He only dates foreigners. He is known for this. It's not good for your reputation."

"*My* reputation?"

She laughed and shook her head. "People will talk about *you*, not him." She motioned to the driver that he could get back in and we could go. "Do you enjoy living in the old city?" she asked, as we raced through the narrow streets.

"Yeah, it reminds me of my father." Even I was surprised by this sentiment and even more surprised that I shared it with her. I was sure she would tell Jamil everything I said. She put her sunglasses back on and was quiet until we arrived at the riding stables, leaving me to wonder who the 'people' were and why they cared if I was seeing Ali.

The 'stables' turned out to be more of a country club for horses, and when I saw Ali, he looked back toward the entrance immediately, almost like he sensed I was there. Ignoring Maya's advice, I walked toward the fence that enclosed the rotunda. It looked like the competition had already started, and I stood next to him as we watched. A small crowd seated on the benches behind us applauded for a young girl who looked a little wobbly on her horse, jumping through the rotunda.

Maya had been following closely behind me and stopped to kiss Ali on both cheeks. "Jamil is asking for you, he's at the bar."

"*Moo intay*," she told him as he started to move. I knew enough to know she said 'not you' to Ali, and she tilted her head at me. She stood in front of me until all I could do was go to him. I was not used to being summoned and ordered around. I didn't even have a chance to say a word to Ali.

I found him at the bar talking to Omar and a couple of others that I remembered from the dinner.

"Laila, Maya found you." "She did."

"You and Ali left so abruptly I didn't have a chance to invite you ahead of time."

"To be honest, Ali saved me." There was no point in being shy and, if he was, in fact, trying to smooth things over, here was his chance.

"Then please accept my apology, but I like to know who's around me," he said, not sounding at all apologetic.

"Well, do you need every detail?" I kept reminding myself he was the one who should feel embarrassed.

"Yes. But I would also like for you to feel welcome here." He handed me a glass of champagne. "Do you ride?"

"No," I said, taking it from him. "Maya will be out soon, shall we?" "Maya?"

"She is an equestrian. I thought you might enjoy seeing her compete."

"Sure," I said as we walked back out toward the fence where Ali still stood.

"Maya is one of our best. She is disciplined and ambitious. She is never more than fifty kilos, even when she comes back from vacation."

"You keep track of her weight?" I asked, suddenly feeling sick that I had made fun of her for eating salad, thinking it was all out of vanity.

"Her trainers do. Maya uses whatever she can to her advantage. Her size helped her become a champion. The trainers love Maya." When he saw my face, he added, "We don't have the same personal boundaries that you have in America."

"Clearly," I said, but by this time the champagne had relaxed me and I felt less hostile toward him. I had to admit I was now eager to see Maya compete, and even though we hadn't spoken I was happy to be by Ali's side again.

Jamil and I stood on either side of him and we all turned our attention to the rotunda. Maya came out on a white horse ready and waiting for her turn. Her hair was pulled off her face and tied in a ponytail that curled down her back. She wore minimal makeup, her white shirt now buttoned up and tucked neatly into her beige riding pants. She looked determined—one with her horse—her nostrils flaring and her face slightly flushed. She was in complete control of her horse, as soon she started out, easily clearing every jump and landing lightly but with precision. Jamil watched her intently, and I couldn't decide if it was attraction or ownership, or pride that held his attention. While he was distracted, Ali and I moved slightly away from him so he couldn't overhear.

"So, how are you?" he asked.

"Good, nothing's changed. Haha," I said, as he turned to me and smiled.

"That's a relief."

All of a sudden I wanted to move on from the dinner party and the heaviness I felt that night.

"But you didn't answer my texts," he reminded me.

"I was going to. I went to see Omar and then Maya showed up at my door . . . I didn't know what to think about the dinner and then the elevator . . ."

"Listen, Laila, I should have told you about him. I like what we have and didn't want to share you, for this exact reason. I'm sorry."

"It's okay. Omar actually helped me see it differently. I mean, I just hate to be stereotyped one way or the other, you know what I mean?"

"Laila, you think I don't know what it's like to be stereotyped?"

It was funny that I had never thought about what he must look like on paper in the US. He was perfect in my eyes and I couldn't imagine him any differently. It was also weird that I was standing there with Ali and the future president of Syria who, for whatever reason, probably because of Ali, wanted to know me. When I thought back to how I got to that place, how Omar let me in the American school and then introduced me or reintroduced me to Ali. It was my American blood that got me in the door, but it was my Syrian blood that kept me there.

CHAPTER 21

YELLI AAJBO ...

(WHOEVER LIKES IT)

"I can't breathe."

"Perfect," Sabrina said as she finished zipping my dress up in the back.

"Are you sure this is a good idea?" I asked, trying to take as much of an inhale as the dress would allow.

"Laila, Ali is a man. You can't keep dressing like a little girl next to him." Sabrina wrapped her hair up in a bun on top of her head, looking like she was ready to work when I came into her room. She lived with her parents but had a massive wing of their apartment to herself. She wore almost no makeup, just clear gloss on her lips, and always managed to look flawless.

I cringed just thinking about the jean skirt and flip-flops I wore to dinner for the first time at Jamil's house. Still, the dress Sabrina lent me was on the opposite end of the spectrum, and I wasn't sure how much I actually wanted to stand out at this dinner.

"It's just so . . . yellow. I look like one of my uncle's canaries." I turned in front of her mirror, seeing the bandage dress from the front and the back. It left little to the imagination from any angle. It wasn't short or even that revealing, but every inch of me somehow showed through. It showed more cleavage than I really had, but I didn't mind that part. As much as I wanted to focus on how I looked, new territory for me, I couldn't shake the conversation I had with Mazen about the schoolboys outside the city.

"You are not yourself today, Laila. What's going on with you?" she asked as I sat down at her vanity table. She gently pulled my ponytail holder down to release my hair and started to brush out the knots.

"Mazen told me something today, and it really bothered me. Something about kids being arrested for painting graffiti on a wall. Do you know anything about it?"

She nodded slowly before she answered. "Everyone is talking about it. Behind closed doors, obviously." Her lips turned down in a frown, and I was pretty convinced I wouldn't get much more out of her. "They were young. Some people say they were tortured, even. But, listen, we don't know for sure. We never really know what's happening." Maybe that was all she knew, and it was clear that was all she was willing to say.

"So, yellow is *the* fashion. Everyone in Beirut is wearing it this year. You want to be a regime queen, don't you? This is the uniform. *Yalla* march!" she ordered, but she was already returning to the more playful mood she was in when I arrived. I wasn't the only one who didn't want the story about the kids being tortured to be accurate, and it was easier to push it from our minds and focus on what we knew for sure.

"I can't even lift my leg."

"Hmm, I am going to have to teach you how to get out of the car. You will have to practice a few times. The problem is keeping your knees together. Never EVER open your legs; we die before we open our legs."

"We die?" I giggled, amused at Sabrina's only occasional flair for the dramatic.

"Yes, or we will find another way. Don't worry, we will practice a few times here." First, she dried my hair with her hairdryer and sectioned it out so she could use her flat iron. I rarely left my hair down, but I was starting to notice it made me look older to part it in the middle and smooth out the ends with shiny serum. "Now, do not even dream of wearing a sports shoe with this."

"I have flip-flops," I said innocently.

"Haha. I have nude sandals, they are a little big for me. All that running, and you never even wear heels to show your work?"

"I used to wear shorts to run, and that ended up being a huge problem for everyone."

"Because running in the streets in shorts is stupid. Wearing a beautiful dress to a nice restaurant away from *shabbab* who are thinking dirty thoughts is very different."

"When they're sitting in a nice place, they aren't thinking dirty thoughts?" I asked, genuinely curious about how much she knew on the subject of male thinking.

"At least they keep their thoughts to themselves."

"Well, Ali isn't like that," I insisted.

"They're all 'like that' *habibti.*" She furrowed her brow as she pulled a section of my hair with the flat iron.

"I mean, our relationship isn't. The first time Ali kissed me, I had to make it totally obvious that I wanted him to. And that was after three weeks of seeing each other."

"He's for sure very handsome. He's known for it. That group of girls, Maya and her gang hate that he only goes with foreigners. You should watch out for them."

"Yeah, I keep my distance from Maya. But it's Ali that scares me sometimes."

"Scares you? You just said he's too respectful. What did he do?" She paused, holding my hair in her hand and staring back at me in her mirror.

"Not like that. I'm afraid of how I feel about Ali. Honestly, Sabrina, I don't know how I can leave him now."

"I'm sure he feels the same."

"I don't know if he does. It's hard to explain. I can sense where he is in the room, you know, and just the sound of his voice makes me . . . " I stopped talking when I saw the face Sabrina always made when she heard something scandalous. It was a combination of blushing, a raised eyebrow, and parted lips. I wanted her to take me seriously and know it wasn't only lust that I felt for him. "Ali feels like home to me."

"Shit." She used her comb to untangle a piece of my hair before continuing with the flat iron.

"Did Omar say anything? I mean, they're pretty good friends."

"About you and Ali? Yes, to be honest with you, Omar loves you together. He said he hasn't seen Ali so happy, ever."

"That's good." I caught her eye in the mirror again. I sensed she kept most of her opinions to herself, which only made her more alluring, somehow fairer. "But you don't like Ali?"

"It's not that I don't like him; it's that I don't really like what's around him. Everything is about *wasta* and money and who's important and who is not . . . Omar and I argue all the time about his friends. It's too complicated."

"Welcome to Syria?"

"Exactly. That's why I stay completely out of it. Do you think your mom will let you stay?"

"My mother will throw a fit if she thinks I am staying, especially if my reason is Ali. No, I have to come up with some other plan."

"Just make sure you put your own plans first. That's all I'll say. What about going to school, university plans?"

"I'll figure it out." I shrugged my shoulders, relieved I could talk to a real person. It was exhausting trying to hide our relationship and my feelings. Omar said I was in his 'inner circle,' but I understood his loyalty was to Ali first.

She finished my hair and handed me the nude sandals. I had to admit the whole look was much more than I was used to, but it would have to do. Although Ali never mentioned it, I knew Sabrina was right. It was time for me to at least try to dress a little more sophisticated than ripped jeans and sandals. After all, we really were nowhere near the beach. It reminded me of Jamil's visit to the farm, and as we walked out to Sabrina's balcony to wait for Ali, I wanted her opinion if she would give it.

"Jamil came to Ali's farm once when we were there. It was like he 'caught us' or something. It was weird. He seemed annoyed that Ali didn't introduce us. I mean, why would he care?"

Her eyebrows were raised, her honeyed eyes wide. "Is this dinner tonight with Jamil?"

"Yeah," I answered, and before she had a chance to respond, we both looked down from the balcony to see Ali's car pulling up in front of her building.

"Remember *teezek* first on the entry, knees together on the exit," she said, clapping her hands together.

"Sabrina, thank you. I love you," I said, heading towards the balcony door to go back inside and finding I was slightly more steady on my feet. I knew with practice, I would get better.

"Listen," she said, and I turned back towards her. "Don't mention the schoolboys."

"To Jamil?"

"Of course not. But even to Ali. It's better not." she said, joining me at the door so she could flip my hair behind my shoulders one last time.

"Keep my legs closed and my mouth shut. Got it," I smiled, feeling so lucky to have a fairy godmother.

"See? You're learning!" she said, laughing and shooing me out. "Go."

I teetered out to Ali's car as gracefully as possible, hoping he wasn't watching. His driver waited patiently with the door open until I got to the car and lined my backside up with the backseat of his car. Sometimes when he let the driver take us, he would sit in front, but somehow he ended up in the back seat. He was on the phone when I pulled my legs in.

He switched his phone to his right hand to reach for mine with his left. I was always amazed at how good his touch felt and how firm his grip was around my hand or waist. He didn't seem to notice the dress or the heels, which was odd considering it was canary yellow, and you could probably see me from space.

I exchanged pleasantries with his driver, feeling more confident in exchanging greetings in Arabic. When I ran out of things to say, and Ali continued his phone call, I looked out the window, comforted by the city lights. Damascus came alive at night, the sidewalks bustling with shoppers and traffic snakelike in its crawl. Most drivers, including Ali's, ignored marked lanes so much that I could see pretty clearly into the cars next to ours. A little boy crammed into the backseat of a taxi, maybe ten years old, saw me staring and stared back, sticking his tongue out at me. I stuck my tongue out at him. Then he made a monkey face blowing up his cheeks and pulling his ears out. I pulled my hand from Ali's so I could put my thumbnail to my nose and wiggle my other fingers in front of me. We were both laughing when suddenly, he stopped and crouched down to his seat so I couldn't see him anymore.

"Laila, what are you doing?" Ali whispered, pulling his phone away from his ear and looking out my window.

Ali's driver glanced at me in the rearview mirror, and when I shrugged, he said, "*Khaf.*" He got afraid. He probably saw Ali coming into view next to me. I got a sick feeling in the pit of my stomach when I remembered the story from Mazen about the schoolboys and Sabrina's warnings not to mention them.

"I was playing with the kid. You scared him."

"Which kid?" He asked as he put his phone back to his ear.

"He disappeared."

What made me feel even worse was that I knew Ali, despite his size, would never hurt anyone. I wanted the boy in the taxi to know not to be afraid and that Ali was good and kind, a protector of kids like him. I reached for Ali's hand again; the material of my dress made it easy to slide over to his side of the car. When I sat in his lap, he didn't protest but put his arm around my waist, pulling me close to him. I didn't care what his driver thought or even that he was still on his phone. I put my head to his chest, wanting to feel his heartbeat and soak up his scent. I didn't realize how much I hated sharing him until that moment.

When we pulled up in front of the restaurant, his call was finally done; he lifted my chin with his fingertips to look at him. "I don't want to go," I said, worried that tears might start falling if I wasn't careful.

"To the dinner? Why?" He searched my face, genuinely concerned. "Laila, what's going on with you?"

"I don't know, it's nothing. I'm fine," I said, dabbing under my eyes with the back of my hand. He moved my hair behind my shoulders, sending a tingle down my spine.

"Is it . . . that time?" he asked, a half smile playing on his lips.

"Seriously, I'm going to punch you-"But I couldn't finish my threat because he pulled my face towards his and kissed my bottom lip, pulling my mouth open. He had kissed me many times before, lightly and politely, but this time I felt his desire match my own. I couldn't tell if it was the dress or the timing, but I knew something had changed in the way he saw me. Soon his tongue found mine, and I brought my whole body closer to his, and when he sucked my lower lip, I didn't want him ever to stop. The way he lightly traced my hip with his thumb, lighting my body on fire, it was as if the whole world had disappeared. "Definitely that time," he said as I pulled away, and he lowered his eyes to my cleavage. "God, Ali," And as soon as I said it, a heavy set of knuckles wrapped loudly across the car window, and Omar was standing outside with Ali's driver. He opened the door, sticking his face in the car, his sandy curls wilder than usual. I hid my face in Ali's neck, but we were both laughing by this time. "Out! This is not a hotel!"

"Isn't this the Four Seasons?" I asked, poking my head out pretty sure that's where we were. Ali nodded his head.

"Not for you! I don't want to see any of that shit! *Yalla la shoof!*" Omar shouted, pointing his finger at the hotel entrance. He then headed inside by himself, throwing open the double doors and talking to anyone lucky enough to be in the vicinity.

"This is our life." Ali shook his head slightly, smiling with his palms facing up, my face still buried in his shirt collar. "Omg," I said, still giggling at Omar's antics.

Although I wanted to try Sabrina's trick at some point, Ali lifted me quickly out of the car and placed me gently on my feet. As we walked through the entrance, Ali assured me, "We'll have a quick dinner, then you and I can do whatever you want. Good?" I agreed when he promised that there would be no more phone calls.

Jamil, seated at the head of the table, pointed to his watch, showing him we were late again. Everyone stood when we came in, and Ali gestured to them to keep their seats. After we said a quick hello around the table, we realized there were only two empty chairs left, and they weren't next to each other. I let Ali take the chair closer to Jamil, and I chose the other one at the far end of the table next to Tamara, the curvy redhead. As usual, Omar was close to the center, and he was already chattering away to everyone at the table.

Maya sat, of course, on the other side of Jamil, across from Ali. She wasn't wearing her usual pout but now smiling from ear to ear and passing around photos on her phone.

Tamara and I didn't have much in common, but she was always sweet, even to the waiters, so I was happy to sit next to her. She filled me in on what 'everyone' was talking about. Maya got a new horse, a snow-white Arabian, a gift from Jamil, and she was practically jumping out of her chair, squealing with delight and clapping her hands.

I couldn't have been less interested in Maya's news, but I was still on edge. Ali's kiss was a beautiful distraction, and I felt a bond with him we didn't have before, but my mind kept going back to the schoolboys and the kid in the taxi. I took Sabrina's advice seriously, but all I needed was reassurance that the whole story was made up and I had nothing to worry about. I found myself hoping someone at the table would bring it up, and when no one did, I kept checking my phone, wishing I had asked Ali for an exact time we could leave.

"Are we boring you, Laila?" Jamil asked, switching to English and raising his voice. I met Ali's eyes across the table while everyone seated turned and looked my way for the first time that evening. They all laughed uncomfortably, except for Ali and Omar, but then they all looked at me, waiting for me to answer.

"No, not at all. I was just . . ." I grasped for anything to say other than what was really going through my mind. The waiter I had just spoken to quickly removed himself and left me alone to face the whole table.

"You will come with us next time." Jamil offered from his end of the table. "Maya will let you ride her new horse."

"Her new horse?" I asked. He didn't seem to see or care that Maya and I didn't like each other.

Maya's giddiness from before vanished, and I couldn't decide which of her moods was more obnoxious. She was now open-mouthed, staring at Jamil like she might cry, but he ignored her, his attention still on me. "Laila can ride. After I break her."

When I looked at Ali, Jamil followed my gaze and added, "Sorry, Ali has no skills in this area." When the guys chuckled at Ali's expense, the women shifted in their chairs pretending not to hear, and Ali sat with a brooding look on his face but said nothing.

"Break her? Why don't you just let her be?" I asked, finally realizing no one was coming to my aid.

"It's an expression, Laila. It just means to train her, so she is rideable." Omar chimed in, his mouth full of food, apparently not reading between the lines.

"And so she doesn't embarrass herself and her country when we put her where everyone can see and judge her. We do it so she is safe." Jamil sat back in his chair and folded his hands together. "But Laila has something else on her mind. Something that has nothing to do with horses." He wasn't going to back down, and it was becoming more evident to me that although he said he wanted me to feel welcome, he had no motivation to make me comfortable.

"Fine, we could talk about what everyone is thinking."

"Please tell us, Laila, what is 'everyone' thinking about?"

Something in me shifted ever so slightly, and I sat up straighter in my chair. I felt a heat in my chest, and my breathing became more shallow—not only because of the dress. The group quieted down but continued to stare in my direction.

"Why don't you tell us what's really happening in Deraa?" An audible gasp and a cold air swept across the table. Ali looked at me in total shock, like I had somehow betrayed him. "I mean, you would be the one to know, right?"

Everyone froze in their chairs, probably waiting for Jamil to pounce on me and sink his teeth into my neck. They were all trying to decide whether they could get up from the table or pretend they didn't hear me. Jamil locked eyes with me, his steel-blue gaze giving nothing away.

Ali looked like he wished he had been sitting closer to get his hands on me. He finally broke the tension, "Laila doesn't know what she's—"

Jamil put a hand up to stop him. "Let her speak freely."

"They're kids, Jamil." "And what did they do?"

"They sprayed graffiti on a wall. Who cares? Let the school deal with them."

"What did it say?" He posed it as a question, but he already knew the answer.

"What difference does it make?" "What did it say, Laila?"

"It was something about . . . regime change," I said, swallowing the end of the sentence.

He nodded slowly before he said, "And you are in favor of such a change?"

"No, of course not. It's not the point-" I tried to keep my thoughts straight, realizing how Jamil had turned the whole situation to make it look like I was defending something that I wasn't.

"Those people you speak for would put you in the house with a veil on your head if you're lucky. You wouldn't be sitting in a restaurant with me drinking French wine in this . . . dress." An uncomfortable silence settled over the table while I cursed the dress that made me look ten times chestier than I really was. "Of course, they may be able to teach you proper manners." He shifted his glare to Ali.

"*Akeed*." Ali stood and threw his napkin on the table. "We have another engagement. Please excuse us." On his way out, he grabbed me by the hand and dragged me out the door before I could say another word.

"Ali, let go. You're hurting me!" I finally got out of his grip when we got to the parking lot.

"Laila, what in the actual fuck is wrong with you? If something was bothering you, you should have come to me first. If you had grown up here, you would know how to behave."

"That's the thing, Ali, you expect me to know everything, and you don't tell me anything!"

"Then let me fill you in. Like it, don't like it, I don't give a fuck. Either you want to be here, or you don't." His words stung me. I had seen him angry before but nothing like this. "This is who we are. And you are not going to change us."

"I changed for you."

"You are in our country now. If you don't like it, go back to the States."

"It's my country, too." "You left."

"How long are you going to punish me for my parents' mistakes? God help you if this country holds against you what your fathers did."

"What did you say to me?" "You heard me."

"You think your father was not a part of it? A part of all of this?"

"You just said he abandoned you. You can't have it both ways, Ali."

"Don't use your American therapy voice with me. I am crazy angry with you right now. You think you are better than we are, morally superior. You think everything is black and white."

"That is not my American or my Syrian side; it is my human side! I know when something is wrong."

"And the rest of us don't? We are all idiots, and you are sent from God, the speaker of truth? We do the best we can with what we have. We look out for the good of everyone, not just one group."

"Oh, yeah?"

"Don't even start with me. My religion has nothing to do with any of this."

"I was talking about Jamil."

Omar must have come out of the restaurant not far behind us. "Laila, I have to pass by the bar. Can I drop you off?" Ali nodded to him, and I followed Omar to his car, not even saying goodbye to Ali.

Omar was as quiet as I'd ever seen him, and he drove faster than usual through the busy streets of Damascus, running red lights and occasionally driving on the sidewalks. I was gripping the edge of my seat with one hand

and the window sill with the other in total shock at the things Ali had said to me and, of course, the things I had said to Jamil that started the whole thing. Before we reached my uncle's house, my phone rang, and it was Ali. Before I could speak, he said, his voice suddenly calm, "I'm going to Beirut this weekend. I'll call you when I get back."

"What is it?" Omar asked when I hung up without saying anything.

"He's going to Beirut. Unbelievable. With everything that's going on, they're taking a guy's trip!" I started to feel myself getting angry all over again, but Omar wasn't having any of it.

"Laila, you really messed up tonight." "But I—"

"Badly! Laila, Ali is going to have to fix everything you just did. This isn't a game. The less you know, the safer you are," Omar continued, "Maybe it will be good to take a break from each other." When I said nothing back, he said, "I'll walk you to the door."

"No, I got it," I said. Before Omar could say anything else, I took Sabrina's shoes off and ran to the alleyway toward my uncle's house.

I would need a minute between Ali and the family to get myself together. What little I had eaten at dinner was starting to come back up. I kept telling myself, 'Let him go to Beirut, let him go.' Maybe Omar was right; we could both use a break from each other. I stopped just before the door to catch my breath and wipe my tears away. My bare feet would definitely attract a word from the family. I took in as deep a breath as I could, hoping no one saw me in the alleyway, especially Mahmoud, but the street looked empty. I casually walked into the house, pretending nothing happened.

CHAPTER 22

AKBAR MINEK

I lay on the floor of the courtyard, looking up at a clear, blue sky, wondering what I would look like to someone looking down. I balanced a jar of Nutella on my belly button, hoping it would rain so I could open my mouth and drink, and maybe I would never have to move from this spot. Once I learned you could just eat it straight from the jar, I stopped looking for things to put it on.

Noura came into my view, her headscarf neatly tucked around the perimeter of her face, her lips red like American apples.

"You'll get sick," she said, standing over me.

"Yeah, definitely," I said, handing her my jar of Nutella.

"From lying on the floor," she said, taking it from me so I could sit.

"Oh, now I see what the problem is." I leaned with my back against the fountain. Noura sat on the fountain's edge, rinsing her fingertips in the water to wash off residual stickiness. Her daughter, Lulu, plopped down next to me and put her arms around my waist. I hadn't spent as much time with them as I originally intended to, and it was one more reminder that a break from Ali was probably good for everyone. It seemed so long ago that they were at the airport to meet me, Lulu sucking her fingers and waiting for American presents and Noura calling me a moon. It had just occurred to me that Lulu was the same age as me when we left Syria.

"Something happened?" Noura asked.

I hadn't heard from Ali in a couple of days, and I hadn't heard a peep from Omar either. I was thinking mostly about Jamil, but I wasn't sure why. I couldn't get his icy stare out of my mind. Not that I was afraid of him necessarily, what could he really do to me? Throw me in jail for ruining his dinner? Not likely. The worst he could do was make it difficult for Ali to see me, which was enough to make me resent him and want to make it up to him at the same time.

"I went to a dinner—" "Friends of Omar?"

"Yes, and I wore the wrong thing."

"You never care about these things," she said, tilting her head to the side with genuine concern.

"Yeah, I know. I guess I have to start caring now."

"Why?" she asked, giggling as though I had said something funny.

"Maybe it's time for me to grow up," I said, wrapping my arms tighter around Lulu and wishing with everything in me that she avoided the situations or maybe even the people I kept finding myself drawn to.

I had heard from Sabrina, and when she asked how the dinner went, I texted back that it was super awesome and the *baba ghanoush* was next level, which I realized later probably just made her suspicious. She must not have spoken to Omar. Either that or he didn't mention the disastrous dinner. I didn't say anything about the dress or the conversation with Jamil, but I had a strong feeling the dress looked very different on Sabrina. I figured she knew I was lying when she didn't answer back.

My aunt came out of the kitchen, a wooden spoon in her hand, and demanded Noura translate for her.

"I see these girls with lips, butt, boobs, and hair," she said, pointing with her spoon to the corresponding body parts.

"*Zayzat*, I know that one!" I interrupted, excited that I was learning new words. Lulu and Noura laughed, but my aunt was undeterred.

Noura tried to keep up with her as she waved her spoon wildly, translating, "Can these girls cook or clean the floors? How are these girls going to manage a household? For marriage, men don't care about that." She pointed down at me with her spoon. "I will show you everything you need to know."

"You're not going to wax my arms again, are you? That was painful, Auntie."

"All Syrian men want the same thing. Rich, poor, Sunni, Shia, it doesn't matter."

"Please don't say . . ."

"Food," she put her hand to mouth. "They surrender to you."

"But I don't want anyone to 'surrender' to me. I want them to leave me alone, so I can be by myself, without anyone else." Noura tried several times to translate this. I could see she wasn't getting through. My aunt continued to stare down at me, the backs of her hands resting on her hips.

"We don't like being alone," Noura explained. "Being alone means there's something kind of wrong with you."

I sighed, considering how much my aunt had put up with me, so the least I could do was humor her. And if I was going to be alone, I should know how to feed myself. Not that my aunt was really giving me any choice.

"I'm scared," I said as Noura helped me to my feet.

"You should be," she said, giggling as we followed her mother back to the kitchen.

I realized I had only rarely been in the kitchen since I arrived. I started to feel guilty for how little time I had spent with my family, treating their home like it was a hotel, choosing instead to hang out with Ali. I thought back to the conversation in Ali's car when he said his loyalties lie with his family. I should have told him my loyalties lie with mine. I was determined to push all thoughts of him out of my head.

"We start with salads, very important. You know fattoush. A basic salad of cucumbers, tomato, onion, lettuce, parsley, and mint, topped with squares of fried pita bread."

Noura showed me how to properly wash and chop vegetables, ensuring they were all the same size. We salted the salad first, then dressed it with lemon juice, minced garlic, olive oil, and sumac. They tossed their salads by hand, making sure every bite was dressed.

When I tried to put the fried pita bread on the salad, my aunt swatted my hand away to stop me. "Only before serving. They will get soggy," Noura explained, but I could tell my aunt was somewhat pleased with me because, after a while, she stopped yelling at me and just watched me out of the corner of her eye.

They showed me how to chop onions, fry them on the gas stove, and lay them gently over a bed of lentils.

My aunt said it was the easiest dish. Then we made fluffy, white rice topped with little fried macaroni. A staple on every dinner table. I scraped out the bottom of the rice pot, where there was a layer of golden brown rice. They also made spinach pies and stuffed zucchini as the kids ran in and out, grabbing bites. I couldn't even believe how much work went into making their meals. When I asked Noura if this was what they cooked for the whole family for the entire week, she said, "Only lunch and dinner."

Spending all day cooking took my mind off Ali. We weren't speaking made it easier to be with the family without feeling guilty for keeping a secret. It was not that I specifically denied hanging out with Ali, but I gave them the impression it was Omar. My mother left no room for me to wiggle out of any part of our agreement. I would have to go when she said and keep Ali hidden from my family until then. If they knew even half of the truth, they would just be worried. I thought if I just let everything die down, maybe we would have a chance to smooth things over. Maybe.

When Noura checked on the children, my aunt sat across from me at the tiny kitchen table where I had been chopping vegetables all day. I could tell there was more she wanted to say, and she didn't wish Noura to translate because she spoke in a hushed voice.

The words I could make out were *akbar*, 'greater,' like the call to prayer, or used to describe someone older in age, and *minek*, 'you.'

"Omar? He is old, yeah," I said, although as the words left my mouth, I knew instinctively that my game of hiding Ali had not worked. At least not with her. She knew.

She shook her head *al mishklay* the problem, *akbar minek*.

"It's my own fault." To my surprise, tears started to roll down my cheeks, tears that I had wanted to come, but I wouldn't allow. I felt like an idiot for challenging Jamil, and I was filled with shame for how much trouble I caused, not just for Ali but maybe for the family, too.

"*Moo al hah allaykee, al hah al abouki,*" she said, continuing to speak in a hushed but angry voice, pointing her finger at me. "*Allah yerhamo,*" she added.

"My father?" I asked, sure that I misunderstood.

What did my father have to do with anything?

Mazen must have overheard something as he came into the kitchen because he looked at both of us and asked what was going on. When neither of us spoke I got up to wash my hands in the sink, so my back was to him. I wiped my eyes with the back of my hand as my aunt went to set the table, leaving Mazen and me in the kitchen.

"Are you okay?" Mazen asked.

"Yes. You? Going to work?" I asked, already knowing the answer. All Mazen did was work now. He left Omar's office, came home for lunch, and then went to work with his father. His top pick of the marriage material girls happened to be Mahmoud's sister. Mazen was doing everything he could to please her family, working non-stop to be able to offer her a decent life.

Even though my aunt and I couldn't be more different and there was a huge language barrier, she understood somehow what was going on. She explained that the problem was bigger than me, and it came before me. And that I was actually not the problem, at least I wasn't the problem between Ali's family and mine. I should have been more sensitive to the conflict between Ali and Mazen that existed long before I got here. Ali had been born into tremendous privilege, more so than even he was aware. Mazen's military service didn't consist of sitting in an office ordering people around. Mazen went to Damascus University, Ali went to UCLA and got a master's degree. After he finished his undergraduate degree, he wasn't quite ready to come back to Syria and start doing the job that was handed to him along with a fuckload of money and a long line of people waiting to kiss his ass. Mazen had to save money so he could marry and build a life for himself, while Ali spent weekends partying in Beirut and wishing people would stop throwing their daughters at him. Mazen worried about the future, taking care of his family, and having the means to care for his parents when they got older. Of course, Ali didn't know any other life, and Mazen didn't see it as an injustice, just fate. His concern was for me, getting hurt, getting in over my head, knowing these people could ruin lives like ours without thinking twice.

My aunt had to stop cooking because it was time to pray. I watched her from the courtyard as she put on a floor-length white skirt and a white headscarf that covered everything but her face. She unrolled a small prayer rug, making sure it faced toward Mecca. She kneeled and rose, kneeled and rose, whispering praise. I envied the simplicity and richness of her life. She knew who she was, whom she prayed to, and the cosmos of her life ruled by the certainty and direction of her faith.

CHAPTER 23

DON'T BELIEVE ME, BELIEVE IN ME

I woke up to the sound of my mother screaming at the top of her lungs. I rushed out of my room onto the balcony. Mazen came out of his room running to the bathroom. He called back to her, 'Auntie, I'm coming, I'm coming!' but she couldn't hear him over her screaming.

She stood in front of the sink in her robe. She was in a total state of panic.

"My wedding ring fell down the drain! Please get it for me, Mazen! Nobody turn the water on!"

Noura and her kids were staying with us, and we crowded around the bathroom door, totally shaken from our dreams by the intensity of her screams.

"Auntie, I will open the pipe. It's no problem, no problem," Mazen kept saying, trying to get her to calm down. He took the stairs down two at a time, raced to the kitchen, and came back up just as quickly, carrying a wrench.

Still in a daze, the entire family stood sleepily in the hallway in their pajamas. Noura, a long braid down her back, held her daughter in her arms as she sucked her fingers and held on tightly to her mother's neck. My aunt, who without her scarf, had a head full of wild, gray curls, rubbed her eyes with the backs of her hands. I felt embarrassed, worried they would think she only cared about her diamond ring and didn't mind waking up the whole house. In all of my years as my mother's daughter, I had seen her cry, maybe twice. Tears streamed down her face, and soft sobs came from deep inside her as she clutched her fingers to her chest and rocked back and forth on her feet. We moved aside so Mazen could get through. He was not the plumber type, but we silently watched him dismantle the entire sink, listening to the sounds of clinking and clanking, and though she had quieted down, her screams still hung in the air. I was surprised all the noise didn't bring one of the neighbors to the door.

When Mazen handed her the ring, we all breathed a sigh of relief. She took it and shoved it back on her finger so hard I thought she would hurt herself.

"Thank you, Mazen," she whispered.

"It's okay, Auntie, everything is okay," Mazen assured her as he wiped his hands dry with a towel.

"The plumbing here, who knew where it could have ended up?" she said, smoothing her hair and realizing what a scene she had just made.

"Mom." We all knew Mazen would tear their whole house down to get it back, and there was no need to try to justify how upset she was. She was the only one who couldn't admit how much pain she was in over losing my dad. It was like if she showed one crack, everything might come bursting out.

"I overreacted. I'm so sorry. Excuse me." She threw her head back and pulled the rope of her robe more tightly around her waist. She slipped past my uncle, who was standing closest to the door.

As for Mazen and my uncle, they looked as steady as they always did. I hoped the responsibility of taking on my mom and me was not a source of stress for them. After Mazen politely refused my offer to help clean up, I followed my mom back to her room.

"They all think I'm insane," she said, lying back in her bed, the back of her hand across her eyes.

"They think you're human." I climbed into the bed with her and snuggled up next to her as close as I could get.

"It still doesn't seem real." "I know."

"I go over and over it in my mind. I keep thinking Dad's going to walk in the door. That it was all a misunderstanding."

"I feel the same way."

"My heart is broken, baby." "I'm so sorry, Mommy."

"I have to get out of here, Laila."

As if the night couldn't get weirder, I heard my phone ringing in my room. It was three in the morning, so I thought maybe it was Amou calling from Sonoma, but something told me it wasn't. I rushed back to my room to answer it, afraid I would rattle everyone again if I let it keep ringing. When I saw Ali's number, my breath caught in my throat. The last time we spoke, he said he was going to Beirut. I didn't think he would return in the middle of the night. I thought of the yellow dress, the screaming at each other in the parking lot, and the way Jamil looked at me when I mentioned the schoolboys, as I picked up my dad's phone.

Despite the heaviness I felt, the sound of his voice brought me relief. Even if we were angry with each other, I missed him, and his voice brought me comfort. He sounded as tired and drained as I did, which didn't seem possible considering he just spent the weekend doing God knows what.

"I'm sorry to wake you," he said.

"Where are you?" I asked, not wanting to explain why I was already awake.

"On my way home." "From Beirut?"

"Deraa." He paused, maybe waiting for me to ask for more. "Jamil sent me. I want to see you. And I want to give you something."

"Now?"

"Yes, now. Can I come?" When I hung up the phone with Ali, my mother came into my room.

When my mother came in asking who on earth I was talking to and I told her Ali, she seemed too exhausted to argue. When I told her he wanted to see me, she wordlessly turned back toward her room, softly shutting her door behind her.

I waited until the house was quiet again and tiptoed out the door. It was getting to the hour I would have been running in my early days in Damascus. It took me back to the days before I knew Ali or even Omar, and the city was full of possibility.

There was a crispness in the air, and it felt fresh on my face as I walked to the parking lot where he usually waited when he picked me up. When I saw Ali's car, I momentarily forgot about the way we spoke to each other just days before. When I got in the passenger side of the car, I noticed his beard, usually cut close to his skin, looked like he hadn't shaved in a couple of days.

"Were you not sleeping when I called?" he asked. I shook my head. "I will tell you about it later."

"I'm sorry for the way I handled you the other night. I worry that you will get yourself into trouble that even I can't get you out of." When I just nodded, he said, "Laila?"

"Okay, Ali. I get it. I don't know what else to say."

"You get it, but do you forgive me?"

I turned to face him and said, "I'll think about it."

"You want to make me suffer first."

If even half of what Mazen told me about those boys was ever confirmed, it was unimaginable, but I didn't want Ali to suffer. I didn't want anyone to suffer. "No."

"There's something else you need to know about Jamil and me. And I should have told you before you and I got into this."

"I think I already know."

"Our fates are tied. If he goes down, I go down with him, Laila. He is not my enemy. If you want to be with me, you need to understand that."

"I understand, but I don't like it. It feels like you are choosing him over me."

"I'm choosing my family. I'm choosing the path that ensures I can provide a very nice future for you. If you want it."

"Why don't you come back to California with me? You speak the language. You like the beach. We can come here and visit whenever you want."

"Laila," he pinched the bridge of his nose with this thumb and forefinger, "I can offer you exactly zero in California. I will have to build a life from nothing-"

"But we'll be together. That's not nothing. We can get a cute little apartment, maybe a puppy? We'll get jobs and buy furniture from IKEA like everyone else. No *wasta* bullshit, you know?"

"Laila, I love nothing more than the idea of spending the rest of my life with you. But it has to be here. I can't abandon my family and my country, especially right now. I can never live there, Laila. In that way, I'm not like your father."

"You think my father abandoned his family and his country, really?"

"I didn't say that. When he left, it was a different time. And he's a doctor, Laila. I'm not smart like him."

"You are an engineer Ali; you're not stupid." We were both silent for a few minutes, lost in our thoughts about the future. Then I remembered where he had been. "So, what happened in Deraa?"

"The boys were released. They are home with their families." I didn't expect a positive outcome. The most I hoped for was talking and plans to do more talking, but when he said the boys were released, I couldn't even speak at first. I had to hold my breath so I wouldn't cry again as his words sunk in.

"Before you say anything, please don't think in any way that it was because of you. I was already planning to go—"

"Then why didn't one of you just say that at the table?"

"Because he doesn't owe you an explanation. A lot of what I do, I can't discuss with anyone. There are lives at stake, and we had to handle that situation carefully."

"What did the families say? They must have been happy to see you?"

He took a sharp inhale and said, "Not exactly."

"Oh." I had envisioned Ali as the savior from Damascus, but it sounded like he was treated as part of the issue, maybe even the source of it. I remembered my aunt's words about the problem being bigger than me, which was the same for Ali. "I'm happy the boys are home. They are back with their moms."

"I want you to have this." He pulled a green threaded bracelet from his pocket and took my hand. He carefully tied the threads around my wrist, which matched his now. "You need a Rolex, too."

"I like this better. It makes me feel safe. Thank you." I kissed his lips before getting out of the car, where of course, Mahmoud stood at his usual lurking spot, then averted his eyes, pretending he didn't see me. This time I didn't care. I didn't know what the future held for Ali and me, but for now, I felt a closeness to him that I never had with anyone.

The sun was starting to come up as I walked back to my uncle's house. I felt calmer than I had in the last few days, Ali's effect on me when things were going well. Ali went to Deraa instead of Beirut, and my heart was lighter than it had been since Jamil's dinner. I couldn't help but smile at the sunrise. The boys are home, I thought as I pulled my wrist close to my heart, and the silk threads felt good against my skin. I was learning to trust what made no sense.

CHAPTER 24

MIN EEDI

(From My Hand)

"Omar wants to take me out on his boat," I said, coming into my mother's room as she got dressed for the day.

"He has a boat? Where?"

"The coast, Mom. La-something?"

"Takia? It's called Latakia. We used to take you there when you were little. You wore these adorable little bathing suit bottoms and ran around the beach, yelling at the waves..."

"So fun, but anyway—"

"You had more of a Syrian accent back then, so you said your p's as b's, so it came out more like stob!" She put her palm out in front of her, laughing at the memory. "You had such a cute little booty—"

"Mom. Focus." I loved it when she was playful, but I wanted to get her approval as quickly as possible while skimping on as many details as I could.

"I am focused, and I know Latakia is too far to just go for the day."

"We'll just spend one night and come back the next day."

"Okay, so Sabrina will be there? Are you staying in a hotel?"

"No. Maya is going; I will share a room with her. On the boat."

"With Maya?"

"Yes, she's fine, Mom. Can I go?" "Who else?" She eyed me in the mirror. "Jamil."

"Jamil, Jamil?"

"Yes, Mom. He's just a person."

"Just a person who also happens to be the president." "Future president. And no one has elected him to anything yet."

"What difference does that make?" she asked, smiling and showing all of her teeth. "I do hope his father hangs in there at least until Jamil turns thirty. He's in a tough spot."

"I don't know. Omar says it's not looking so great. So I can go?"

"You will have tons of security all over you and Ali." "I never said Ali was going."

"Is Ali not going?" she asked, raising one eyebrow.

"Is Jamil the only reason you are letting me go?" "With Jamil, I know you're safe. And Laila," she said, pretending to zip her lips. "It will scare the shit out of them, just don't." She reminded me to keep details about Ali and even Jamil away from the family, and it did seem to make them nervous, though no amount of Omar bothered them.

"I'll tell them it's Omar and his sister. They'll love that."

"What do people wear in La Takia?" I asked Poster Jamil when I got back to my room. If Maya was a regular there, I assumed lots of tiny bikinis. I packed my version of a two-piece, tanning oil, flip-flops, and my Khalil Gibran book, which was always a good luck charm even if I didn't open it.

When Ali picked me up at dawn to drive us to the coast, I asked him as casually as possible, "So, Maya?" I said as we started making our way out of the city.

"Yeah, what about her?" he asked, distracted by early morning traffic but trying to pay attention to me at the same time.

"Are her and Jamil like a thing?"

"A thing . . . uh, they have a special bond." Typical Ali answer. I didn't consider myself a gossip, but literally, everyone in the city talked about who Jamil would end up with, and Maya always seemed to be around him. I rarely saw him without her somewhere nearby, and the only other girls around him were either married or engaged to one of his friends.

"They would have beautiful babies together, don't you think?"

"Laila, since when do you care about any of this stuff? Marriage? Babies?" he asked, genuinely surprised by my interest.

"You're the one who said you want me to fit in with your friends, so now I just want to make sure I don't say the wrong thing, you know?"

"Okay, but why the sudden interest in Maya and Jamil, specifically?"

"Aren't they the only other couple going with us?" When he nodded, I continued. "I thought if Jamil got engaged, especially if it's to someone like Maya, then maybe..."

"Maybe what?"

"Maybe he'll be too distracted to bother with you, and you don't have to pretend just to be my 'family friend' anymore?"

"You think he's going to stop after he gets married?"

Maya and I were laying out on the deck of Omar's boat, which seemed more like a yacht, on a sparkling Mediterranean sea. I flipped over onto my stomach and asked Ali to put suntan oil on my back. He always did it for me when we were at his farm, but now he just squirted some out and sloshed it around sloppily on my back.

"Ali, you are making a mess of it! Maya, will you do it?

Ali stood up as Jamil and Omar came out on the deck, "Jet ski?" he asked.

I jumped up, making Maya spill the oil all over me. "We want to go too, right, Maya?" She had her usual bored look and wiped her hands off with my towel. "Can I ride with you?" I asked Ali.

Jamil threw me a life jacket and said, "No, you come with me. Maya, you ride with Ali."

As I put the life jacket on, I noticed I was the only one wearing one, and I was annoyed to see Maya in just her bikini climb on behind Ali. I sighed, swallowing my urge to complain about how the rules only seemed to apply to me. Or maybe it was because I was American, and they were always making fun of us for being into 'safety.' Although the fact that Jamil was shirtless made it easier to wrap my arms around him. Omar got his own and took off in front of us.

We all followed Omar's lead, away from the boat, crisscrossing in each other's wakes. Ali kept turning his head to talk to Maya. Whatever he was saying was making her laugh. My annoyance disappeared quickly as the turquoise water sprayed me and sunlight bounced like diamonds off the surface of the choppy waves.

Jamil pulled in front of Ali and Omar, probably knowing they would follow, and picked up his speed. As soon as I thought we couldn't go any faster, Omar and Ali behind us, Jamil cut the engine, let them pass us, and then turned us in the opposite direction and took off, putting the jet ski at full speed again.

It wasn't even a few minutes before I couldn't even see them behind us anymore. I had to hold on to Jamil tighter to avoid falling off; the water would have felt like hitting cement at this speed.

We pulled up to a dock next to a small fisherman's boat when he finally slowed. Two young boys ran out, eager to greet us and happy to see Jamil. One of the boys looked like a young Ali with a sweet smile, green eyes, and thick lashes. He stretched his hand out to help me onto the dock. I took off my wet life jacket, embarrassed that all I had on was a bathing suit underneath. Jamil took a blue button-down shirt out of the back of the jet ski and handed it to me.

"What is this place?" I asked, buttoning the shirt. "This is where I'm from. We came to this restaurant a lot while I was growing up."

"That's nice," I watched him take candy out of his pockets and hand it out to the boys on the dock.

"And you said you like fish."

"Yeah, uh, what about those guys?" I neglected to say 'Ali' specifically.

"They will find us if they need us." He didn't seem concerned at all that we left Omar, Ali, and Maya in the middle of the sea and took off.

"You do whatever you want to do. You never think about other people?" I wrapped my wet hair up in a bun on top of my head.

"They like me like this." He took the cement steps up to the restaurant, which looked all outdoors, with cracked flooring and chairs made with colored wires in yellow, green, and red. This was nothing like the white tablecloth dinners I was becoming used to having with him, either at his home or a restaurant in the city with at least fifteen other friends. This time it looked like it would be just he and I.

I didn't have my phone, so I had no way of telling Ali where we were. I felt justified as I thought of him and Maya laughing on his jet ski and how much he had been ignoring me since we arrived at Omar's boat. I wondered if they just went back or would come to find us.

Jamil was unusually chatty with me, telling me how he and his brother used to run around the restaurant wreaking havoc. At the same time, his father entertained local politicians and military people.

"Does your family still come here?" I asked, realizing he had never discussed his family with me before, especially his father.

"Not since my brother died. And my father doesn't travel at all anymore." Because I didn't have siblings, Mazen was the closest I ever felt to having one; I would die if anything ever happened to him. People always surrounded Jamil, but he seemed alone.

"Why did you bring me here?" I asked.

"You don't like it?" he asked, his focus only on the restaurant as though this moment was all that ever was between us.

"The night on your balcony . . ." "I was right," he said.

"You had a 50/50 chance," I refused to let my embarrassment over that night give him any power over me.

"I was sure. Ali wasn't."

"He could have asked me himself." "But he didn't."

"What difference does it make? Ali may not show it to you, but he loves me, okay? And I am in love with him." Jamil's pale blue eyes met mine, his brow raised and lips slightly parted, but he said nothing, so I continued, "The rest of the stuff doesn't matter to either of us."

"Are you sure?"

Only God knows why I revealed myself to him like that, telling him something I was not even willing to admit to myself until that point. Jamil was much more challenging to read than Ali, but I was pretty sure it was not jealousy that drove him, so that was a relief, but his interest in me seemed odd however I looked at it. The only conclusion I could come to was he had an interest in whoever Ali spent his time with. Maybe this is how he vetted all his friends' girlfriends.

We sat in silence for what seemed like forever, just looking out at the water, the waves quietly lapping at the rocky beach below us. I was hoping Ali would appear at some point when Jamil nodded slightly, and all of a sudden, the staff started bringing out dishes of every imaginable seafood. They brought chilled white wine and a whole fish platter with halved lemons on the side. I wondered if they knew we were coming and looking at the spread, they couldn't have possibly just whipped this up with no notice.

One of the young boys, who looked like Ali, brought a white plate piled high with tiny fish that looked deep-fried. Finally, Jamil broke the silence when he picked one up and said, "You just eat the whole thing like this," putting the whole fish in his mouth.

"The whole thing with bones and eyes and everything?"

He nodded. "You never had these before?" He picked one up and held it up above my mouth for me to eat.

I tried to take it from him with my fingers, but he pulled it away. "No. It's an insult to an Arab if you refuse to eat from their hand. It implies you don't trust them."

"Seriously?" As awkward as I felt, I couldn't help but laugh. Now that I revealed I was in love with Ali, it seemed harmless to become slightly less hostile toward Jamil. I ate the whole thing right out of his fingertips, and it was delicious, salty, and deep-fried; the little fish were addictive. To my surprise, he laughed as he watched me.

"I never heard you laugh before," I said, my mouth still full, my fingers now greasy.

"I am not used to girls like you." "What kind of girls are you used to?"

"The ones trying to impress me. It's not as cool as it sounds."

"What about Maya? She seems to care for you." I didn't buy Ali's theory that Jamil's father's position was all she cared about. "I mean, everyone thinks—"

"Maya and I have a special bond. We always will."
"That's what I've heard."
"What else have you heard about me?" "Oh, nothing but good things. Obviously."
"Then you should probably find some friends besides Omar."
"Working on it." As soon as I said it, Jamil nodded for the bill. As we headed back, I hoped it was apparent that Jamil decided he was hungry and wanted fish, and I just happened to be the one on the back of his jet ski.

When we got back to the boat, only Maya was on the deck, sunbathing. Her bikini, this time, was a bronzy beige color that made it look like she wasn't wearing anything. Her skin shimmered with suntan oil, her fingertips the same color as the icy Jamaica she sipped. I wondered if hers was virgin. As Jamil went to speak to her, I took the chance to find Ali.

I pulled the sliding door open and found it was quiet inside. The air conditioning hit my skin, giving me goosebumps. I kept moving past the bar and downstairs to the bedrooms. I tiptoed into his room, hearing the shower running. I walked past the pristinely made bed and into the bathroom. I rationalized it was the only way to speak to him in private.

"Ali?"

He opened the shower door and looked at me. "Did anyone see you come in?" he asked and then noticed me wearing the blue button-down. "You're wearing his shirt?"

"No." I took it off and stood in my bathing suit, pretending to busy myself by looking in the mirror and pulling my hands through my wet, knotted hair to try and untangle it before I washed it. Mine and Maya's room had the most comfortable bed, but we didn't have a private bathroom and shared one with Jamil. "I have to shower, too."

"So get in."

When I got in with him, I realized it was big enough for the two of us, but just barely.

"God, it's so cold! Turn the hot water on a little bit." I turned the tap toward the hot water. I wet my hair under the water stream, trying to get the salt and sand out.

"You could have got in with Jamil."

"Are you serious? The guy kidnapped me, and I have to defend myself?"

"How were you on the back of his jet ski to begin with?"

"You were there! You saw what happened. You could have said something."

"You're turning this on me?"

"You looked more than happy to be with Maya." "Oh for fuck's sake, Laila—"

"Why are you pissed at me? Get pissed at him!"

"I am!" His words sounded much harsher, especially since we were in such a small space. I watched the water running down the front of his face, fists clenched at his sides. It was the first time I had seen his anger toward Jamil. He had never spoken one word against him. At least it was a start.

"Ali, this is what he wants. How can you not see that?" He relaxed his muscles, letting his arms fall to his sides. "He wants us to be jealous of each other. And I feel like you've been avoiding me since we got here."

"I have been avoiding you." "Why?"

"I don't want him to know about you and me. I want him to think it's more casual than it is. We are old family friends, that's it."

"You have to tell me why." "It's complicated."

"I love you. You love me; what's complicated?" "He is."

"But I already told him . . ."

"What? What did you tell him, Laila?"

"What's wrong with telling the truth?" I bit my lip to keep from spilling that I had revealed to Jamil that I was in love with Ali. Now, the only thing I could do was stop talking. I thought being honest would make him realize that Ali was serious about me, and then he would mind his own business. "I'm sorry. I just thought—"

He sighed and lifted his head back to let the water run over his hair and face. He looked back down at me, his anger dissipating. "You'll learn. You'll learn to keep secrets. Because you have to." He put his hands on the sides of my arms, his voice softer now. His eyes were the same color as the sea, traveling the length of my body. "Turn," he said. When I hesitated, he made a circular motion with his index finger. I turned around slowly, so my back was to him. "Move your hair."

I pulled my hair off my back and to the side of my face. I liked feeling vulnerable with Ali, and I wasn't as shy as maybe I should have been.

He gently washed my back with a washcloth, careful where he touched me. "I'm sorry I spilled oil on you earlier. Maya doesn't know how to do anything properly."

It was slowly dawning on me that the more I told the truth, the harder it was to spend time with Ali. The best things happened when no one knew what we were up to and when we kept our relationship private. Why it took me so long to realize didn't matter so much as that I did learn. I turned back around to face him, got on my tiptoes to kiss his lips, and then got out of the shower. I assumed Jamil would probably be coming back down soon.

When I left Ali's room in a towel, my hair still soaking wet, the air conditioning hit my skin, still warm from the shower. Jamil came down the spiral staircase just as I pulled Ali's door shut behind me. He was still shirtless but now wearing white linen pants hung low on his hips. He stopped when he saw me, and I couldn't tell if it was evident that I had come from Ali's room. I smiled and moved toward the door to our room, being careful to hold my towel close to my chest.

"Your shirt, I . . . Sorry," I said, knowing I left it in Ali's bathroom when he put his hand up to stop me. "Thank you for lunch today. It was fun."

"You're welcome."

"Friends?" I asked, extending my index finger.

"*Akeed*," he said, linking mine with his.

He pushed the door to Ali's room open, not bothering to knock. It was true he was beautiful in a different way than Ali. His porcelain skin was flawless, his blond hair always slicked back, and his blue eyes framed by almost colorless lashes. It was a shame that even if he wanted to be good, he probably couldn't.

When I opened the door to our room, I was surprised to find it empty. Maya must still be on the deck with her Jamaicas. She must not have washed her hair or even changed out of her bathing suit.

When I finished getting dressed and came back out on the deck, Maya was dancing, a cocktail in her hand, dangerously close to spilling it. I had seen Maya drink quite a few glasses of red wine, but I had never seen her drunk. Guess that settled the question of whether her drinks were virgin.

"Laila! Come dance with me!" she shouted and waved at me. She had thrown on a short, white lace dress over her skin-colored bikini. Probably, it was the first time since the day she was born that she wore nothing on her feet; her toes painted the color of apricots. She wore little makeup and looked relaxed and without agenda. Long, blonde waves hung halfway down her back, her bronzed skin made her curves more sculpted, the blue-green of her eyes sparkled like the sea, and I could still catch the scent of her suntan oil when she moved.

"Maya," I felt the need to explain even though everyone knew that Jamil had kidnapped me. What was I supposed to do? Scream, yell, jump off the jet ski going at top speed like it was an actual kidnapping? They had to know I had no choice.

"I know," she said, quickly dismissing me and throwing her glass off the side of the boat. I panicked for a minute, hoping no poor fisherman was in the vicinity at the wrong time. Luckily, it was just us with the sea to ourselves, all the locals back safely in their homes by now. I turned my attention back to Maya.

"You know what?" I half expected her to say she thought I had feelings for Jamil and that it was some sort of secret between her and me. She stood on the stairs leading to the hot tub, and threw her arms around my neck, and put her lips close to mine. "Laila," she said, and for a moment, I thought she would kiss me full on the lips, but she just stood as close to my face as she could, looking like she might cry or laugh. There was a small smudge of black mascara under her lash line, and her breath smelled of alcohol. I could feel eyes watching us from inside the boat.

She leaned as close as anyone had ever been to me, and I thought she might say she loved me or some other drunken classic that I had heard from many of my wasted friends on the rare occasion I went to parties. Instead, she let her eyes close, leaning her head back. "I wish we could trade places." She popped her head back up and laughed in my face. "I would be perfect for California, don't you think so, Laila?" Now she took her dress off and threw it on a deck chair.

"It's not that different from here, actually . . ."

"It's wasted on you because you don't even care about how you look! Dance with me, *hebla!* Move your ass!" Then she shouted to whoever was on the top deck to turn her music up and started waving her arms and moving her hips in figure eight. "Don't you think I could be famous? If I lived in California, I would be famous." She jumped down from the stairs and grabbed a pair of sunglasses on the table.

"It's not that great to be famous." It seemed like it should go without saying.

"How would you know? 'I'm Laila. I like to exercise and sit at home,'" she pulled her lips down and out into an exaggerated pout, still wearing the sunglasses. I had learned not to take offense to anything she said, and I couldn't help but laugh at seeing her imitation of me. Now that the sun had set, there was no way she could see anything with those sunglasses.

"See? We can't escape ourselves," I said, now having to shout over the music, but I had already lost her.

She continued to dance around the deck in her bikini,

occasionally singing the lyrics when she knew them. She wouldn't make it far as a singer, that was for sure. I wondered if the fish could hear and if they were annoyed.

"Laila, you will stay for the wedding?" "The wedding?"

"You have to stay. After that, you can go back, but not before."

"Wait, you're engaged? When is this wedding happening?" I had to shout even louder over the now blaring music as she had moved away from me.

"Shh! They will hear you!" She jumped off the chair and came back toward me. "It's going to be on Valentine's Day."

"Valentine's Day? I mean, I wouldn't miss it."

"At first, I was scared, you know, to get engaged. Honestly, he's more the one who wants it, *bas yalla*. It's better to get married young. I want so many babies, our families are best friends, and we look perfect together," she said, very matter-of-factly.

"It's true. And your babies would be so cute." "I know."

"I think you guys are perfect, too. And about the lunch, you know there is nothing between us, right? Like, at all."

"Of course not!" She laughed out loud. "Everyone knows the truth."

"Good, I'm relieved."

"But we didn't tell anyone yet. So it's between us, okay?" Even though she put her finger close to her mouth, completely missing her lips, I got her point.

"Of course, I will keep it to myself." And I meant it. Whatever I had to do to convince my mother to stay, I would do it because, my feelings aside, a Jamil and

Maya wedding would be epic. I was relieved to know she understood Jamil's interest in me was not romantic at all, and they were the ones destined for each other. As I thought more about it, there was nothing I was looking forward to more than their wedding.

She released me from her grip and moved her hips to the music, sashaying toward the moonlight, her hair floating in the breeze, lost in her world. Suddenly, I felt Jamil standing next to me, his hands in his pockets. We both watched her shimmy and shake and move her body in a way I could never make myself move. I was happy the deck, except candlelight on the outdoor bar and lights from the hot tub, was mostly in shadow, and the sea was completely black, except for moonlight. For the first time since I had met her, at least, I could tell she wasn't performing.

"She thinks she wants to be famous," I said, finally breaking the silence.

"Not for singing, I hope."

"I wouldn't underestimate her."

"No, never. Do you have ambitions, Laila? Beyond running and convincing your mother to stay in Syria, even though we know she hates it here."

"You can't take her personally." "No, but I would love to meet her."

"Yeah, any time." I still felt embarrassed, and I resented that she couldn't just enjoy the experience instead of putting all her efforts into getting out. Although if anyone could convince her to stay . . .

"Laila, will you do me a small favor?" "Okay."

"Will you please put her dress back on, braid her hair, and bring her to the dinner table? The chef has something special prepared, and I would like to eat by ten."

Maya's hair was a matted mess from the saltwater, wind, and her performance on the deck. I thought it looked better wild. I didn't know if it had anything to do with his position or personality, but we all did what he asked. And now I had a favor to ask of him, too.

Jamil and I became friends, and he and Maya were planning their wedding. And according to Maya, I was the only one who even knew. When Ali said I would have to learn to keep secrets, I didn't think it would be so soon.

CHAPTER 25

M

Maya pushed my hand away as I tried to put her dress over her head, swearing at me in Arabic. She almost kicked me in the face when I tried to slip her wedges back on her feet. She finally held still, letting me braid her hair, and when I finished, she pulled it all out and messed it up with her fingers.

I frowned at her but decided to change my approach. "Maya, don't you want to look pretty for your fiancé?" I asked, waving her tube of lip gloss in front of her. When all else failed, her vanity was highly motivating.

"I always look pretty," she said, as she sat on the bed, pouting and kicking her shoes off again, "and he doesn't care. He ignores me."

"Maya, he wants to marry you!" "A lot of people do."

"They're all like that. Ali does the same to me in front of people. I know he's crazy about you. He doesn't know how to show it. He told me you guys have a 'special bond.'"

"Laila," she said, as she allowed me to slide her wedges back on her feet and even let me put a gloss on her lips, "you should never have come here."

When Maya and I finally got to the table, dinner had already started. Luckily, the guys were already deep in conversation when we sat down.

"What do we want with these old Russian planes and tanks? It's a joke. I don't need this kind of army." Jamil looked at Maya out of the corner of his eye and met my eyes. I shrugged and said, "She didn't let me."

"What kind of army should we have?" Ali asked, wiping his mouth and putting his napkin back in his lap.

"This." Jamil held up his phone. "An army of hackers, the best in the world, trained for a fraction of the cost of old-school artillery and useless foot soldiers."

"We're behind," Ali said.

"We can catch up." Jamil said, not showing even a trace of doubt.

"How?" Ali asked, though it was rare for him to push back on anything Jamil requested of him.

"We have youth; the numbers are there. And if we don't, they will turn against us."

"What if they already have?" Ali asked, glancing down the table at Maya and me.

"There's still time. If we grab them now." "What about Israel?"

"Who gives a fuck about Israel?" Jamil looked around the table, his palms open in front of him.

"Our people." I could tell Ali was trying to keep his temper in check, but Jamil was pushing all his buttons.

"You think people believe our story of the amazing *Jaysh A Soori*? C'mon, man. Our enemies and Israel's enemies are the same."

"If we end the draft, it will be seen as weak," Ali said.

"It will be seen as reform," Jamil said as he cut into his steak.

"He's right, ya man," Omar chimed in. "This is falling out of fashion everywhere. Laila, how many of the guys you knew went into the military?" he asked, pointing across the table with his steak knife.

"I didn't have any guy friends," I said, hoping they would go back to ignoring Maya and me.

"Oh. Did you know anyone? Did you go to an all-girls school?"

"No, I went to public school."

"Okay, how many times did a guy in your class say he was interested in joining?"

"None of them."

"She grew up in a wealthy area," Jamil said, taking a sip of his wine.

"It's all volunteer anyway. Nobody has to go," I said, but when Ali shot me a look, I stopped talking. I thought they were interested in my opinion, but Omar was only trying to make Jamil's point.

"You seriously think an army of nerds is going to protect our borders?" Ali asked.

"Our enemies are inside. You and I both know this to be true," Jamil said.

"You're talking major changes; we're not ready. What we need are highly trained special forces on the ground. And we have options for funding," Ali answered.

"I don't like these options. I want to bring the country into this century. And you will help me." Jamil held his ground.

"We will lose critical support from our own people," Ali said.

"Who?"

"You know who." Ali wasn't budging either. "What does he want?"

"We all know what he wants, and it's impossible." Whatever was impossible, I had never seen Ali stand up to Jamil like this.

Jamil leaned back in his chair and said nothing for several minutes. He looked down the length of the table between Maya and me. I had to strategically place my arm in front of Maya's chest to keep her from face-planting in her salad. If he was bothered by the fact that his soon-to-be fiancé was so drunk she couldn't see straight, he didn't show it at all.

It was quiet for a minute before Jamil turned to Ali. "End the draft. Get them off my payroll. And do what you have to do. *Khulusni*." Omar pumped both fists in the air, but Ali looked less than thrilled.

"I'm going to bed. Good night." He stood and placed his napkin on the table, not even looking my way. I wasn't interested in being ignored by Ali for the rest of the evening anyway, regardless of his reasons, but being abandoned, caught me by surprise. When I thought about excusing myself early, too, Jamil asked me to take Maya to bed. When I stood and tried to take her arm, she swatted me away.

"She has no fashion! She couldn't even find a hairdresser until now!"

"Maya, I went to the hairdresser."

"One time? My family would not speak to me if I go around the city like this!"

"My family likes me the way that I am." "Well, then I feel sorry for your family."

"I will take her." Jamil stood, and then he did something I never thought I would see him do. He kneeled in front of her, put her hips against his left shoulder, and stood, her body now draped down his back. She, of course, loved it and wrapped her arms around his waist, giggling and letting her hair tumble all the way down the back of his body. "Good night."

As soon as he slid the door closed behind them, I looked to Omar. "I thought we were becoming friends."

"Do you want to get in the hot tub?"

Even though I was tired, I didn't want to be anywhere near Maya, and now Jamil was with her; I wanted more to stay on the deck with Omar. "My bathing suit is . . ." and then I remembered my bathing suit was still hanging in Ali's shower.

"We can just sit." Omar didn't need any explanation. As much as we bickered like siblings almost, I loved having him as my friend. Some days, I felt like he was the only one I could trust besides Ali.

We settled in the lounge chairs with towels wrapped around us. The wind had picked up, and it was much chillier now that the sun had set. Jamil's sunglasses, which Maya had worn earlier, were still lying on the side table.

"One minute, she's telling me her biggest secret, and the next, she tries to slap me. I don't get her."

"She's a scorpion. Always has been. If it makes you feel better, she hates me too. Wait, what secret?"

"I can't tell. Ali thinks I can't keep a secret, can you imagine?"

"You can't keep a secret."

"Wait, why does Maya hate you? And I never told anyone about you and Sabrina." My mom surely didn't count as 'telling,' and the only reason I told her about Sabrina was that she was convinced Omar had a crush on me. I guess I could have let her think that, but it seemed disrespectful to Sabrina, and my mom wouldn't and couldn't do anything to put them in jeopardy.

"Now, you owe me one." "I can't."

"Why not?"

"I promised. And I want to prove to Ali that I can keep a secret as well as he can."

"This is my boat, number one, and number two; no one keeps a secret from me. In conclusion, no one keeps a secret from me on my boat."

"You just like saying 'number two.' Did they teach you 'in conclusion' at DCS? You say it a lot."

"Laila—"

"What? I don't know anything, remember?" "That was before."

"Before what?"

He paused before he said, "Before you started having lunches with Jamil."

"One lunch. And who says my secret has anything to do with Jamil?"

"What did you talk about?"

"Nothing. Jamil told me it was where he grew up, and his dad used to entertain people there while he and his brother ran around."

"Laila, I'm super drunk. Please just tell me."

"Maya's engaged. Shit. I seriously can't do it, like it's unbelievable."

Omar sat up suddenly, more alert. He took the towel off and turned to me. "What are you talking about, engaged? Jamil told you?"

"No, Jamil didn't even mention it. Maya told me when she was drinking and dancing. She was wasted."

"She told you she's engaged?"

"Yeah. I just think it's weird Maya isn't way happier. I thought she would be over the moon. Even I'm excited. Why is there not more celebrating going on?"

"Because it's Maya. She can never be happy. Because he's not the one she wanted."

"What do you mean?"

"Maya was crazy about Jamil's brother, Munir. As much as they tried to hide it from everyone, it was undeniable chemistry."

"Omg, Munir was the one who died? The one who was supposed to be . . ."

"Yes."

"How do you know he felt the same about her?" "Because Munir was my best friend. I was in the car with him . . ."

"Oh." An image popped into my mind of the letter 'm' in gold calligraphy, encrusted with yellow diamonds. The necklace always hung around Maya's neck no matter what she was wearing. I just thought she wore it to show off her breasts, but it actually was not for her own initial but the love of her life. "I had no idea. Ali never said anything about him. I'm sorry."

"You weren't here. You would have no way of knowing."

Omar told me about Munir's popularity, the excitement around his future presidency, and the differences between Munir and Jamil's personalities. It also clarified why Maya treated Omar, despite accepting all his invitations, like a used tissue.

"When she looks at me, she thinks of him and wishes it was me that died that day. Some days I wish the same."

"Omar—"

"No, seriously, I'm not trying to be dramatic. Everyone wanted Munir to be the president, everyone."

"Well, if that's how you feel like it shouldn't be you that's here, think about how Jamil must feel."

"I do think about it. But he doesn't care what anyone else wants."

"I don't know. I used to think that about him." "You're changing your mind about Jamil?" "You think Munir was better?

"He was better because we knew him. He didn't hide anything. He was open about all his wild ways, his crazy spending, his drinking, and even his obsession with Maya. We always knew what we would get with him."

"Obsession?"

"Seriously, Munir could literally have any girl he wanted. He was crazy about her. He told me everything. I know more about Maya than anyone."

"But she wishes you were dead, and you still invite her on your boat and put up with all her shit?"

He shrugged. "After Munir died, Maya was one more responsibility that got passed to Jamil."

"Maybe it's all part of the plan. How did I know something you didn't?" I asked, but Omar was snoring and I was barely able to keep my eyes open. Sleeping on the deck with Omar seemed like a bad idea, so I forced myself to get up and go downstairs. When I opened the bedroom door, Maya was alone and sounded asleep. Her hair was still a mess, and she didn't take her makeup off. Even though Maya was an asshole to me, I couldn't stop thinking about Munir. She was in love with him and lost him forever. I couldn't imagine having Ali ripped from me. In fact, I was becoming more and more determined to find a way to stay near him.

I slipped into the bed next to her and shivered when my legs hit the cool sheets. Forgetting all the tension and Jamil's interference, my mind went back to earlier in the day when my body was still warm and tingly from my shower with Ali. I could still taste his lips on mine and feel his hands all over my body. If paradise was anything like today, it was worth the wait.

CHAPTER
26

BOUKRA BIL MUSHMUS
(TOMORROW IN THE APRICOT)

"Hey."

"Hey." I stretched, smiling at hearing Ali's voice first thing in the morning, and wiped the sleep from my eyes.

"Why do you sleep so much? You are like a cat."

"I'm assimilating." I put my phone on speaker, so I didn't have to hold it. Once I got over the first few weeks of jet lag when I was getting up with the sun to run, I slowly but surely adjusted to local time. Late nights at Omar's were keeping me out until all hours.

"Maybe you don't have enough to do?"

"Did you call to tell me I am *kaslanay?*" I opened one eye.

"Yes," he said, but I could hear the smile in his voice. I giggled and turned on my side, catching sight of the poster. I completely separated the Jamil on my wall from real life. Mine was much easier to talk to; 'Poster Jamil' was more accessible and could be whatever I needed him to be, whoever I imagined. "I was a straight-A student all through high school, by the way."

"Yeah, because you couldn't go anywhere!"

"True." My life in California seemed a lifetime ago like it happened to someone else. None of my friends would have believed I had more freedom in Syria than I ever had in Orange County. It brought memories of my dad and the rare occasions I would ask him if I could go to a party or gathering where we both knew there would be boys. I spent time with my girlfriends until they got boyfriends, and before long, I was on the honor roll. I could still hear his voice in my head "*ya Laila, habibti*, we don't have boyfriends," he used to say in his thick accent. "A queen, after she finishes medical school, will get married to a king, and I don't see any kings in Orange County."

"Daddy, I don't think they like kings in America."

"You're right. Americans only love beautiful people."

"I also called to tell you the groundskeeper from the farm called me. He needs me to come and take care of a few things. Will you come with me?" Lately, I have been thinking more about what my father would think of Ali and what he would think of me spending time with him.

"Right now?" I sat up in my bed, rolling my neck from side to side. I wanted to see him, but it would be a while before I could get myself ready, and I would need at least an hour to run.

"Yes. Right now." Ali never really meant right now; sometimes it was '*heleh, baadain*,' which literally translated to 'now, later.' I was still figuring out so many things about him.

"Laila?"

"Okay, but I have to go for a run," I said, throwing my covers off to check the state of my legs. The excruciating leg wax my aunt and cousin did on me worked and lasted for weeks. It was true we had thick, lustrous hair on our heads, but that meant thick, not so lovely hair, by modern standards, everywhere else on our bodies. On the upside, Arabs figured out a lot about hair removal centuries ago. I ran my hand down the length of my legs and found they were still smooth as silk. It was worth the pain for sure.

"We can run there," he said absently. "You're going to run with me?"

"If you swim with me."

"Fine, but I am wearing shorrrrt." I rolled my r and my eyes as much as possible. When he started grumbling, I insisted I wasn't compromising this time. "Ali, it is so hot out there. Are you serious? I am wearing whatever I want today." And every day after that.

I never thought I would be in a couple, the concept was so alien to me, but compromise was becoming more a part of my routine with Ali. Maybe people with siblings learned earlier, but better late than never. I hopped out of bed, quickly brushed my teeth, and washed my face, and by the time I threw my stuff in a backpack, he was calling me to say he was in the parking lot down the street from my uncle's house. It was the first time he was on time, ever in his life, probably. What was the rush today? I wondered as I told the Poster Jamil goodbye and yelled to my aunt that I would be back later.

We finally got out of the city, leaving the traffic and chaos of Damascus behind us. There were two ways to get to his farm that I knew of, and one was a little bit quicker, though I was in no hurry. Ali didn't hesitate to take the mountain road, avoiding the circle, the sword, and the autostrade. We had to stop once in Muhajireen.

Then we were on our way out of the city, with some rolling hills spotted with green and the occasional sheepherder.

"Is everything okay, Ali? You are a million miles away." "Sorry?"

"I said you seem a little distant," I said, my voice raised. How could he not hear me?

"Yeah. No, I'm not." "You can tell me. Jamil?"

"It's nothing." But when I raised my eyebrows at him, he continued, "What? I don't have a rainbow up my ass all the time, Laila. That's all." He was always teasing me about how, despite their internal battles, Americans overdosed on external cheeriness. Still, I could tell that was not all. "Sorry, thank you for coming with me. I just don't want to talk. I only want to be with you today.

Please, okay?" I nodded, actually not minding because I was still sleepy from the night before and perfectly content to be with him too. I finally figured out how to change the music in his car. When I found Arabic pop music, I filled his Range Rover with *'habibi, habibi.'* He looked over at me, shaking his head. I used to complain that all the music sounded the same, but now I liked the upbeat tempo and that all the songs were about love. It used to annoy me to no end that Ali always wanted to be with me, but he spent so much time not talking to me. He didn't like to be away from me, but that didn't mean he always wanted to talk either. It made me happy that we could sit in silence together and not feel the need to fill space between us because it was already full. He only turned down my music once to ask me if I brought my bathing suit. I told him I had, feeling pretty sure I tossed a white bikini in my bag along with my running shorts before I left the house.

"You have the upper hand in the water. I get it."

He smiled for the first time that morning but said nothing, so I turned my music up. He drove like he always did, maybe even faster, ignoring lanes, all traffic laws, and other drivers. It occurred to me on the way how many things used to bother me that no longer did. I liked how he drove with one hand so he could hold mine with the other.

As soon as I got out of the car, something felt different. When I walked into the house, I stood in front of the glass doors Jamil had burst through when he 'caught' Ali and me together in the pool. I smiled just thinking of times we spent together running and swimming and laughing, away from all the complications in Damascus.

"It's so quiet here today. Where is everyone?" "They went back to their village. Are you hungry?" "I'm always hungry."

"I will find you something."

I followed him into the kitchen and sat on the countertop while he rummaged around in the fridge.

"Their season is over, but best for last." He pulled three apricots out of the fridge, one between his teeth, the other two in his hand. He came towards me, putting the other half of the apricot he was eating in my mouth. He stood in front of me, resting his palms on either side of my thighs.

"I hate when things are over," I said with my mouth full of apricot.

"But you said you like new beginnings. After the rain washes everything away, new things can grow, right?"

"That was after two of Omar's apricot margaritas." He pulled me closer to him and said, "You drink too much." I didn't want to continue that conversation, so I kept on the same train of thought I was on before, "I guess I don't like the space in between."

"Everything has its time and place."

"I thought you didn't want to talk today." I didn't want to talk anymore either, so I jumped off the countertop, wanting to get outside and run before it got too hot. I opened the sliding glass door and stepped out. "*Yalla*, baby."

I started off in the direction of the apricot trees, turning once to find him following me. I wanted to see if he could keep up this time, and I increased my speed to what I usually run. Come on, Ali, I thought as I forced myself to run as I usually would and allow him to meet my pace instead of slowing down to meet his. I was pleasantly surprised when he was right next to me within a few seconds. Our steps matched in speed and tempo; our breathing found alignment the same way the muezzins found each other's voices during the call to prayer. Not that I ever doubted we were physically compatible. He was everything I didn't even know I wanted, what I had been waiting for. I could not imagine being more in love, and wasn't that the whole point? – aside from a piece of paper and a party I wasn't that interested in ever having. Still, I was nowhere near ready to get married, and it didn't seem he was either.

We ran for at least two kilometers and worked up a respectable sweat. When we got back to the house, I went inside to change into my bathing suit. When I heard my running shoes squeaking on the marble floor, I realized it was much quieter than usual. I poked my head into the kitchen, but I found it empty. Except for the whir of the fridge, it was silent. It was strange because before, maids and drivers and people who worked in the orchard always seemed to be coming and going. Music spilled from the cars, their doors open as the drivers cleaned them with soapy buckets of water and sponges. Aromas usually drifted from the kitchen as the housekeepers prepared lunch. Phones would be ringing, knives against cutting boards, pots clanging in the kitchen, and the sound of the neighbor boys playing basketball. It felt still today, as though it was only Ali and me. It made me realize how little time Ali and I spent alone together and how little time Ali spent alone, period. I took the stairs two at a time up to one of the bedrooms, and as I peeled off my sweaty running clothes, it occurred to me that Ali may not know we were the only ones here. I pulled my bikini bottoms on and quickly tied my top.

When I came back outside, he was already swimming laps in the pool. I admired him for a few minutes, the water gliding over his bronzed muscles as he moved seamlessly through the water. I walked over to the deep end of the pool and let my legs dangle into the water up to my knees, enjoying the cool relief and waiting for him to come back toward me. He swam all the way underwater until he reached me, coming up for air in between my legs. He effortlessly lifted himself out of the water, so his face was close to mine, droplets spilling down his face. I pushed him back in and dove over the top of him.

When he caught me in the shallow end, he pulled me toward him, moving all the space between us. He definitely had more speed in the water, and I felt the upper hand slipping more in his favor. Somehow I just didn't care, and I let him lift me off my feet, wrapping my legs around his waist.

"*Kameshtek*," he said, spinning me around in circles as I clasped my arms around his neck. Whatever was bothering him before was fading into the background, and he was just here with me and not thinking about anything else.

"Hey, I thought you said this wasn't 'your style'?" He smiled, nodding at the strings holding my top up and reminding me of our conversation at the hotel pool about Maya's skimpy bikini. My breasts definitely didn't round out the sides the way hers had, and my butt cheeks were almost totally covered where hers were not even containable. Still, I had to admit it was weird that there was a time when I was defending Maya. It all seemed so long ago, and now it was like everything was falling into place, and my true destiny was finally unfolding.

"People change," I decided.

"As long as it's only for me, I like it." "We'll talk about it."

"Nothing to talk about."

I giggled, allowing him to think for a minute that he had some control over me. Although, for the first time since I ran into him outside the hotel, I finally allowed myself to get totally lost in him. My legs stayed wrapped around his waist as he pushed my back gently against the pool's wall. I didn't care anymore about who had the upper hand. All of the warnings from my family and people trying to pull us apart faded away. His mouth tasted like ripe apricots and lust and maybe everything I loved and secretly desired.

He led me by the hand, out of the pool and back inside without saying anything. We had reached a level of comfort with each other, taken showers, and even changed together, so I wasn't surprised when he took me upstairs to the bedroom. We fell on the bed together, our wet bathing suits soaking the crisp, white sheets. He opened my palms, lacing his fingers with mine at either side of my head. His lips found my neck, and I welcomed the pressure of his hips between my legs.

I finally let go of all my worries and doubts about his love or his intentions. But I was puzzled by his somber mood; his eyes were clouded over in a way I hadn't seen before. Part of me felt he wanted more of me, part of me felt like he was retreating. Was he depressed by the thought of waiting for me until I was ready to get married? Was it impossibly far away for him? Was kissing just not enough for a man almost thirty? I pushed the thought away and instead savored the feel of his hands all over my body, my fingers entwined in his wet hair.

He slid his hands up my thighs and hooked his thumbs under the ties of my bikini bottoms, exposing my deep tan lines from so many days of playing in the sunshine with him. It wasn't until he started to pull them down that I gasped like I was waking up from a dream.

I pulled my mouth away from his, putting my hands over his to stop him. At that moment, he seemed like a grown man instead of like me. I started to feel the years between us, his maturity suddenly intimidating when I was usually so drawn to it. The feel of his thumbs pulling at my bikini bottoms brought me to reality as my breath caught in my throat.

"Ali, I—" I was surprised because he had never pressured me before. Looking back, he had not had that many opportunities. I guessed he could have brought me here before, though; there must have been many times when no one was here.

"No?" His eyes searched mine for an answer.

"Why are you in such a hurry? I'm saving myself for marriage; Ali, you know that." I never thought I would have to explain myself to him.

"I want to marry you, Laila."

"But we're not married now, Ali. I'm just not ready for all that."

"You're not a little girl anymore." The way he said it made it seem like he had said it many times before, though he had never said it to me.

"I know that."

"I'm sorry. I just want to be close to you. I'm sorry," Ali said.

Just then, both our phones pinged. It was a text from Jamil inviting us all to dinner that night. He told us where to be and when and added, "God help you if you are late."

"What is his obsession with being on time?" I asked, grateful for the interruption to such an awkward conversation.

"Tell him you can't make it." When I looked up at him in surprise, he repeated it more forcefully this time, "Tell him you can't come." He took the phone out of my hands and texted Jamil himself when I hesitated. He tossed it back to me. "I don't like having you around,

Jamil. Don't come to this, trust me. I will come to see you after."

"Are you going to the dinner?" When he didn't answer, I swung my legs over the side of the bed and stood in front of him, forcing him to look at me, "Ali, are you going?"

"I have no choice!" His voice echoed through the empty house, the marble floors suddenly cold beneath my bare feet. When he saw the look of shock on my face, he lowered his voice but repeated himself, "I have no choice."

"You should get back then." I managed to keep my voice calm, trying to process everything that just happened.

I went into the bathroom to put my jeans and t-shirt back on and threw my wet bathing suit and running clothes in my bag. I did my best to braid my hair, but my hands were shaking. I felt like I was moving in slow motion and, at the same time, felt the urgent need to get out of there. When just a few hours ago, I was blissfully happy. My mind raced with thoughts of why I never dated. It was partly my dad's rules and partly my own shyness. But I always thought Ali understood and respected me. Did I not make it clear? Did I lead him on? Maybe I shouldn't have worn the bikini. Then I got angry with myself for thinking it was my fault. Did he think that I was 'loose' because I was raised in California? Omar and his friends' prevailing attitude and conversation, who had all lived abroad, was that foreign girls would sleep with anyone. I set them straight a few times, reminding them we weren't all the same, and they were super judgmental either way. Who cares what people do in their own relationships? I had to keep reminding them to mind their own business.

By the time we got in the car, my blood was boiling. He was waiting by the car when I came outside, and I threw him my bag. Without even looking at him, I got in the passenger side and sat in enraged silence as he put my bag in the trunk. I was hoping he would say something, apologize or at least acknowledge that he was a total asshole. Still, we drove back to the city in silence.

I knew if I even opened my mouth, I would scream at him and say things that I couldn't take back. I was ashamed that I was also afraid to lose him as angry as I was. More than anything, I was just bewildered. I could understand Ali's frustration with Jamil, but why was he mad at me? I had only ever seen him angry once before when he dragged me out of the restaurant after I had challenged Jamil. That seemed minor compared to this knot in my stomach. Why on earth he reacted the way that he did, I couldn't understand. He knew I was a virgin; why the hell would he even put me in that position? Kissing was one thing, maybe even a little more was okay, but sex was never an option. I felt myself getting angrier on the drive home as he didn't say one word or even look at me.

Meanwhile, Jamil was texting me the entire way home, ensuring I knew about the dinner. Annoyed, I sent him a text back, reiterating what Ali had already said, adding I had made plans with my family. I was tempted to tell him Ali didn't want me there. Still, I didn't want to give him the impression we were more than 'casual friends.' It seemed like a bad idea to let him know Jamil had any influence on our relationship. Also, I didn't want Jamil to think I was some pushover. I didn't understand why I even cared what Jamil thought of me. I needed to be alone to think about what had happened. I wanted Ali to cool off, and I was not in the mood to deal with Jamil's bullshit too.

I was already afraid of putting Ali in a position where he had to choose between us, but maybe I was just scared of who he would choose.

Please reschedule with your family
I can't
Ali?
No, it's not him. He totally knew it was him. No one was buying Ali's story that we were just friends.
Then I insist you be with us this evening, it's a very special occasion.

Ali and I rode back to the city in silence. I knew he cared for me, loved me even. Before I got out of the car, he said, "Laila, I'm sorry."

It was reassuring that he did feel bad. "We will talk later. This is what couples do, right? They work out their differences, they fight, they make up. *Sah walla la?*"

"Yes. I will call you later."

Was Ali the only one who didn't see that tonight was probably the night Jamil and Maya would announce their engagement? I was proud of myself for keeping Maya's secret, but I didn't know how Ali didn't find out on his own.

Maybe now that Jamil was getting engaged, he would leave Ali alone. Jamil sent me a car, but I was running late because we had come home late from the farm, and I had to wash my hair. I hurried out to the car, running only a few minutes late. I grabbed my book 'The Prophet' to read on the way. He didn't say anything about sex specifically because he was too classy. Still, I wanted to see what Gibran had to say about marriage.

CHAPTER
27

KISS ME AGAIN

As soon as I entered the restaurant, I was met with the sound of *'lalalalalaleesh!.'* I saw Maya first. She stood smiling at one end of the table with Jamil, wearing a short, off-shoulder red dress, already setting the stage for a Valentine's wedding. As I got closer, I noticed she removed her gold 'm' necklace and replaced it with a pear-shaped diamond that hung right between her breasts. Jamil looked as happy as I had ever seen him. At a quick glance, it looked like the usual entourage, drinking champagne, all talking at once except this time an elderly man was seated at the other end of the table. He looked old enough to be Jamil's father, but knowing the condition he was in, it most likely wasn't.

I didn't immediately see Ali, so I scanned the rest of the room and spotted him standing at the bar alone, his back to the rest of the group.

I was a little disappointed to have missed the main event, and had it not been for us getting back late from the farm and me having to wash my hair, we would have heard the announcement. Maya and Jamil would be a match made in . . . wherever. At least I arrived in time for the rest of the celebration, and Ali would know now that I could absolutely keep a secret, even from him.

Tonight the restaurant was unusually crowded, loud music blared from the speakers, and everyone seemed to be in a celebratory mood. It was clear that I wasn't the only one excited to see Maya and Jamil get married. A hush fell over the table when everyone noticed me, but Maya smiled and reached her arms out to me. "Laila!"

"Congrats, Maya. You'll make a beautiful bride," I said, kissing both her cheeks. I meant it sincerely, but I was eager to leave them to go talk to Ali.

"Hey," I said as I came up beside him at the bar.

"Laila," he turned toward me, clearly surprised to see me, "why are you—what are you doing here?"

"Jamil insisted. He sent Hassan to my door, for God's sake." He pulled his thick black hair back with his hand. He looked oddly nervous; I had never seen him as anything less than calm and confident. Now he was fidgeting and kept picking up his glass and then setting it back down.

"So, it's official, the secret is out?" I took a sip of his scotch, feeling it burn in my chest. "What? Ali, why are you looking at me like that?"

"You knew?"

"I did! Maya told me on the boat. So, now you know I can keep a secret as well as you can." I smiled, genuinely proud of myself.

"I wanted to talk to you alone."

"We can talk about us later, Ali. I don't think this is the time or the place. It'll be fine, okay?" Eventually, I knew we would have to deal with the sex thing, but I didn't understand why he was still weird about it. Or maybe it was Jamil's demands that were getting to be too much for him. "Who is that?" I asked, trying to veer the conversation toward Jamil and Maya and the man who sat at their table.

"Maya's father," Ali said. "Listen, I don't think you understand-"

"Oh, right. He must be so happy," I said, imagining what it would feel like to unload Maya on another man.

"Laila, you're finally here." Jamil started coming toward us with Maya close behind him.

As they approached, Ali pinched the bridge of his nose with his forefingers and said, "Fuck."

"Ali, what is going on?" I asked.

"Laila, please listen to me." He tried to take my arm when Jamil pulled me by the waist toward him.

"*Mabruk habibi*, she is my gift to you," Jamil said to Ali, a drink in his hand. Maya came up on the other side of Ali, slipping under his arm. "Aren't you going to congratulate Ali and Maya on their engagement?" Jamil asked, putting his arm around my waist and holding me tightly against his body.

"Haha. Congrats to *you* on *your* engagement," I said, trying to remove myself from Jamil's grip. I was getting used to his dry humor, but a sick feeling came over me when no one laughed. Maya laced her fingers with Ali's, revealing a rock on her finger that might as well have punched me in the face.

"You'll be here for the wedding, Laila? Valentine's Day, you promised," Maya giggled, reminding me of the conversation we had when I was sure it was Jamil she was marrying.

"Yes, Laila, considering what a close family friend you are of Ali's, I know he will insist you and your mother attend the wedding," Jamil said.

When I finally found my voice, I spoke directly to him, blocking Maya and Jamil out, and for a moment, all the music and noise faded into the background. "Ali, this is your engagement . . . this is your engagement party?" I could barely get my lips around the word. It was as if everything was happening underwater or in slow motion. Ali and I stood silently, staring at each other for what seemed like an eternity. Maya stood with his arm still around her shoulder, a smug smile on her face, her eyes fixated on me.

"Laila, please, this is a delicate situation . . ." Out of the corner of his eye, Ali watched Maya's father, a smallish man with rounded shoulders, watery, gray eyes, and slow movements, approach the four of us at the bar. Despite his toad-like stature, everyone seemed to move quickly out of his way.

"You are engaged to Maya?" I asked, my voice sounding foreign even to me.

Ali cleared his throat, nodding at Maya's father, and then looked directly at me. "Yes. Yes, it's true." A smile I had never seen before crossed his face.

Jamil put his lips to my ear. "Laila, you are being rude. Please offer your congratulations to Maya's father."

Maya's father looked me up and down, a look of disgust on his face, then turned his attention to Ali and Maya as though I wasn't even standing there anymore. Like I was nobody.

All I could hear was the blood rushing in my ears, my heart pounding, and a weak feeling in my knees. I don't know if it was my pride that kept me standing or Jamil's steel grip around my waist. I removed his hand with some force and managed to get myself out of the restaurant. I didn't realize until I got outside that I had not been breathing.

Ali and Maya are engaged. Ali, my Ali, is marrying Maya.

I leaned up against the wall outside, and Ali's driver looked at me, probably wondering why I was leaving so soon as he had just seen me going in. He started walking toward the car to open the door for me. I did the only thing I knew how to do, the only thing I could do. I took my stilettos off and started running in the opposite direction. The only hope I had was that creating some distance from Ali and Maya and her father would bring some relief, which would make it not true.

I felt stones under my feet in the street, little pieces of glass with every step. I didn't think I could stop, but I knew I couldn't keep running. When I found myself in a totally unfamiliar neighborhood, I stopped to pull a rock from my foot when a black Mercedes pulled up beside me. The tinted window came down on the passenger side.

"Get in."

CHAPTER 28

SOS

When I flipped him off with both middle fingers upside down, Syrian style, he said, "Laila, get in the fucking car." Jamil got out of the car when I didn't move from my place on the sidewalk. "*Majnouneh inti?* Who goes running in the street with no shoes on? You also embarrassed me in front of Maya's father."

"*I* embarrassed *you?*" I hurled myself toward him, managing only to hit his arm with my shoe as Hassan effortlessly blocked me and pushed me back, putting his massive body between Jamil and me. I tried to get around him; Jamil and I were circling around Hassan and shouting at each other. "You need a bodyguard? You're afraid of me?"

"Ali had his chance to tell you about Maya. Don't blame me for his mistakes."

"Jamil, you knew I was in love with him! I told you in Latakia. Don't pretend you didn't know."

"Ali lied to you."

"He didn't. He lied to you."

"*Habibti*, Ali knows that he can never marry you. Never," he said, his voice softening, and he stopped circling. Hassan looked like he was getting dizzy, so Jamil carefully moved around him toward me.

"He told me today that he wanted to marry me! He can't stand her. I know him—"

"You don't know men, Laila." He didn't take his eyes off my face, and I was getting sick to my stomach thinking about how insistent Ali was on me not coming to the dinner. Was it only a few hours ago before everything fell to pieces? "He was waiting for you to leave."

"I don't believe you," I said.

"He's doing what is right for his family and what is good for his country."

"For his country or for you?"

"I am this country." His voice was firm but not aggressive. It was as if he was only pointing out a truth that everyone but me understood. "Laila, you're bleeding."

"What?" I looked down at my bare feet, a pool of blood forming on the sidewalk under me. I sat down quickly to examine the bottom of my right foot, where most of the blood was coming from. I still didn't feel pain, but I knew it was coming.

"Let me see." Jamil crouched down next to me.

"Laila, are you alright?" Mahmoud, of all people, appeared on the street corner nearest to us and a couple of other young guys I had seen in the neighborhood.

"Yes, it's fine. I just stepped on something," I said, blood now gushing from my foot.

"My brother is a doctor. His office is down the street.

Shall I get him for you?"

"Let's take her to him," Jamil picked me up and carried me down the street after Mahmoud. "You know these people?"

"Sort of," I said. "They are friends of Mazen."

I was sure they recognized Jamil; his picture was now all over the city. He was always on television and had been since his father got sick. But I couldn't even begin to imagine what Mahmoud was thinking. Or what he would tell his family. Or what they would tell my family. I was suddenly self-conscious about what I was wearing and tried to pull my dress down a bit without Jamil noticing what I was doing.

When we got to his brother's office building, a small crowd of people behind us, his brother opened the door, dressed in his white coat, a surprised look on his face when he saw us. We had never met in person, but we knew of each other. When he saw me in Jamil's arms, a bodyguard, a growing crowd of *shabbab*, and me with an open wound, he probably didn't know what to make of the whole situation. Still, he brought us back to his office, closing the door behind him. Jamil put me down on the white table, blood on his shirt and pants, while the doctor washed his hands. He examined my wound, the pain increasing, and picked a long shard of green glass out of the bottom of my foot with tweezers.

"Broken beer bottle." He examined the green glass against the light, then dropped it in a metal bowl. He had the same British accent as Mahmoud. "It's quite deep. You need stitches."

"Can you do it?" Jamil asked.

"Yes. I will numb it for you first. Have you had a tetanus shot recently?" The doctor asked me. "I would highly recommend it if you've been running barefoot in the streets."

"Wait, don't you need my medical history or if I have any allergies?"

"Do you?"

"No," I said, catching a glimpse of myself in the mirror hanging above the sink, Jamil leaning against the counter next to it. My mascara had streaked down my cheeks, my eyes rimmed with black eyeliner, and my hair had become a wild mess.

"This wasn't really how I envisioned this evening going either," Jamil said.

"What did you think was going to happen?"

"I expected you to behave like a fucking grown-up." "We've met, right? You can go, no one asked you to come. And by the way, you were the one who insisted I be there tonight, remember?"

"My mistake."

The doctor silently stitched my foot, but he glanced up when I raised my voice at Jamil, who stood seemingly unfazed.

When the doctor finished, he wrapped my foot and wrote me a prescription that I had no intention of filling. "Also, you will need help walking, I can send you a pair of crutches tomorrow, but until then, you will need help."

"I don't need anything, thank you." I tried my best not to unleash my hostility on the doctor as he was only trying to help. Having Jamil in the vicinity triggered me, and I couldn't seem to lose him.

From what I could understand from the scuffle at the door, the doctor didn't want to accept payment from us, but Jamil insisted and left Hassan behind to take care of it. I tried to hobble down the street by myself, but I could not make myself. Because we were not too far from my house by this point, I finally let Jamil carry me through the narrow alleyways to get to my uncle's house. Whenever I started to feel my heart soften toward him, I reminded myself that if it weren't for him, I never would have been injured to begin with. We were both silent; I could only hear his steady heartbeat, surprised he had one. But I was too exhausted to keep arguing, and nothing seemed real.

I tried to jump out of Jamil's arms ahead of reaching the front door. "Please just leave me here. I can get to the door myself."

Before he turned to walk back down the narrow alleyway, he said, "Laila, I promise I will keep you close to me."

"I don't want my family to see you."

By the time Mazen opened the door, Jamil had disappeared from view. Mazen was the only person I wanted to see, and I hoped that I could get past my mother and the others by some miracle. When he saw me with my bandaged foot and dress covered in blood, he opened his mouth to speak, but before he could, I buried my face in his shirt and cried all the tears I had been holding back. I couldn't explain what happened right away. He placed me carefully in a plastic chair by the fountain as my sobbing subsided, but I still couldn't speak.

He held my hands in both of his and said. "Ali?" Although we had tried to keep our relationship secret, the family knew.

I nodded, still unable to make the word 'engaged' come out of my mouth. The rest of the family started to come out of the living room, and when my mother saw the state I was in, she ran toward me.

"Laila, oh my God, what happened!" she screamed, which only made me cry more.

Mazen said, "Ali."

"What did he do to you?" My mom kneeled in front of me, like when I was a child, and I fell and hurt myself.

"I stepped on a piece of glass. I wasn't wearing any shoes," I said, finding it hard to get my words out, and my voice sounded weird even to me.

"Wait, what, why were you barefoot?"

"Because I was running away! I was running from Ali because he—, he—"

"Laila, what is it?" she asked, her frustration with me growing.

"... he's marrying Maya! He's engaged to Maya," I said, unable to keep my voice from breaking. When Mazen said the word *'makhtube,'* quiet anger in his voice, they all gasped in horror, with Noura putting her hand over her mouth and my aunt clutching her chest and clucking her tongue.

My mother's mouth dropped open as she stood, gathering her black maxi dress in her hands, "Engaged? To fucking Maya? Well, we'll see about that."

Everyone started yelling at once, and I tried to keep telling them why they couldn't do anything, but no one was listening to me. My uncle and Mazen were yelling back and forth at each other, my uncle trying to calm Mazen down.

"He needs to know he can't do this to you. His disrespect for you is disrespect for all of us!" Mazen insisted.

"You can't do anything!" I yelled as much as I could get a breath in me. They all stared at me, and when Mazen asked why, I answered, "Because it was Jamil. Jamil did this."

The courtyard was suddenly quiet, the realization hitting everyone at the same time that I was right. There would be no apology or confronting Ali. There would be no consequences for him, only shame on our family. Now that Mahmoud and all his friends knew, it was just a matter of time before the story got out in our neighborhood of what happened. I stood up slowly as Mazen came to my side. He helped me up the stairs one by one, and I managed to wash all the makeup from my face and brush my teeth like it was any other night.

I knew my mother was furious, and she would want to untangle the whole incident with me and start plotting against him, but I needed to be by myself. I went back to my bedroom, hoping I could find peace there, or at least be alone. I took off my bloodstained dress and slipped into my nightgown. When I crawled to my pillow, on top of my bedsheets, too tired to pull the covers back, I realized I didn't have my phone. I must have dropped it somewhere between the restaurant and the doctor's office. That's when I glanced at the wall next to my mirror. I had become so used to his presence that I hadn't realized I wasn't alone in here either. I should have ripped Jamil's poster off the wall, but the effort of getting back up seemed beyond what I could do. There was no fight left in me. I pulled my knees close to my chest and fell into a deep, dreamless sleep. All I remember thinking was, 'Let him watch me sleep' and praying that I would never wake up.

CHAPTER
29

RAMADAN

But I did wake up. A man clanged a pot outside the courtyard walls and yelled for us to eat before the sun rose.

Ramadan.

Today started the holy month of fasting and purification, which was the last thing I was in the mood for and I had totally forgotten about. "You are the worst Muslim ever," I told myself, reaching for another pillow to put over my head. My mouth was dry, and my head was pounding. Then I remembered all I drank was a single sip of scotch from Ali's glass that burned all the way down. Everything came rushing back—how Jamil sent his car to bring me to the dinner, Ali at the bar, Maya's red dress and massive rock on her finger... she knew that night on the boat, and she didn't even have the balls to tell me the truth. None of them did.

Running had saved me from heartbreak before, helping me move the grief from losing my dad, but now I couldn't even do that. I kept the pillow over my head, ignoring the calls to wake up, but I could hear other people shuffling around in their *shahatta*. It wasn't until I knew for sure the sun was high that I sat up in bed and listened to a soft knock at the door. When Mazen poked his head in my room, I motioned for him to come in. He asked if I needed him to call the doctor and if I knew it was Ramadan. I told him I would be fasting like everyone else in the house. I didn't mention that fasting seemed like the perfect way to hide in my bedroom, and the thought of food made me nauseous.

"Are you having pain? You shouldn't fast if you are injured."

I shook my head no, not trusting my voice, but he gave me a look that suggested he knew I was not okay and there was no use pretending.

"I don't know what to do. I should probably go back to California, but with my foot like this, I don't know if I can," I finally told him as he eyed the long row of running shoes I had on the other side of the room. Mazen, who was usually upbeat, seemed kind of down, and I wondered if it was my own mood I was projecting onto him. Maybe going back to the office with Omar worried him, or the first day of Ramadan in the middle of summer could bring anyone down one notch. I remembered a conversation, and there were many, with Mazen when he warned me not to hang out with Ali. When I asked for specific reasons why, he said, *"The people will talk."*

"Who are the people?" I had asked, not taking him seriously.

"You don't know them."

"Then why do I care what they say about me?" "It's not only about you, Laila."

Mahmoud was definitely part of 'the people', and though I was grateful he took me to his brother, I had a feeling it wasn't entirely out of concern for me so much as his own smugness. I wondered if he even remembered pulling me off the swing when we were young. Then again, maybe he was trying to make amends.

"You should stay while you are healing," Mazen offered now, cutting through my thoughts, though he seemed distracted. "Spend time with my mom and Noura. They will help you."

"Until when?"

"Until your mind is safe for you."

When he left to go to work, I finally moved my legs out in front of me to examine my bandaged foot. It was tender and sore, but at least nothing was broken. I was delaying getting out of bed because I knew I would have to accept what happened as soon as I put my feet on the ground.

Ali's engaged.

I sat on the edge of the bed, my feet dangling just above the floor. I replayed the night over and over again in my mind, from the time I walked into the restaurant, the loud music, the *lalalaleeshing*, and how they all stopped when they saw me and the look on Omar's face. How long did they think they could keep it from me? Would Omar have said anything to me?

I couldn't get Ali's expression when Maya's father came to the bar where we were all standing, out of my head. Ali acted like he didn't even know me. Like I was some random girl he was trying to end a conversation with so he could focus on Maya.

I would have to start all over again, again. No matter Ali's reasons or excuses or even how involved Jamil was, Ali could have told me. He did the opposite of trying to break up with me, which proved he didn't ever plan to say anything. Jamil was right. Ali was waiting for me to go back to California.

The worst part was knowing now I was that girl, the one I knew in high school that I was secretly judging from the safe perch of my virtuousness. My attitude was that I could never be hurt or humiliated and definitely not by a guy I met only a few months before. I imagined what the chatter around me was now, "*How could she not know? Why didn't she listen to anyone? Poor thing, everyone else saw it coming.*"

I put both feet down, finding relief in the coolness of the marble, at least on the foot that wasn't bandaged. I decided not to wear my *shahatta*, although my aunt's warning about going barefoot unless I wanted an illness that would most certainly lead to death still had a firm hold on me. They had all warned me in one way or another.

I checked my nightstand like every other day, but it was empty today, not even a glass of water. Not drinking was going to take getting used to. I wondered if Ali had called, and I wished I would have at least had the satisfaction of not answering. My phone charger next to my nightstand looked sad, still plugged in, not connected to anything.

I stood carefully, using the furniture to help me. I could put only a tiny bit of weight on my bandaged foot, enough to take a small step forward. I held on to the end of the bed and then the dresser, passing Jamil as I reached for the door.

I looked over the balcony railing down into the courtyard, but even the thought of trying to get myself down the stairs was too tiring, so after I used the bathroom, I hobbled back to my room and crawled into bed. I stayed there for, I don't know how long, from one call to prayer to the next. If I moved even slightly, everything hurt, so I stayed still and listened to the sounds of the house and the courtyard.

My mother came to check on me several times a day, always asking if I wanted to get on a flight back to California. She knew a guy who could make arrangements quickly. Although the villa was still far from finished, she wanted me to go by myself. I seriously considered leaving. I could forget about everything and go back to the vineyard. I could learn everything there was to know about wine and soil. Sonoma really was paradise. But I hadn't listened to Amou either, wanting instead to come to Syria and find out what it was and who my father really was.

But I wasn't ready to go back, so I used my stitches as an excuse not to travel, telling my mother I would wait until it healed, which seemed enough for her in the short term. She was surprisingly gentle with me, even allowing me some space to be alone and just feel sorry for myself.

When the house got especially quiet, and I couldn't stand being in my room anymore, I made my way to the balcony railing. Most of the family kept busy, probably to take their minds off hunger or avoid me; I wasn't sure which. When I looked down into the courtyard, only my uncle was there, and he looked up from the birdcage in his hand. His white hair stood out against his bronzed skin, and his brown eyes were warm and forgiving as he waved for me to come down.

When I finally got to the bottom step, he wanted to show me his canaries. I always heard their song but never paid much attention to them, like many other things I neglected to see. I felt a twinge of sadness that because I had spent so much time coming and going, I maybe missed the smaller, sweeter life in Damascus.

He showed me with hand signals that their wings were clipped and told me they were happy. When I asked why they needed a cage, he told me there were cats and made a claw motion with his hand. I smiled for the first time in days, nodding my head in agreement that cats sucked and should be avoided.

For the next several days, I spent most of the time in the house with my uncle. Every day I took my time coming down the stairs, and he approached me with the same gentle dedication he took to his birds or the way he might care for a young child. He showed me how to care for them, clean their cages, and give them clean water, things I could do sitting or standing without putting too much weight on my foot.

Even after Iftar, the fast-breaking at sunset, my uncle and I sat in the courtyard while the rest of the family watched a television series they were obsessed with. I didn't want to watch anything that would remind me of Ali, and my uncle never watched television at all. We drank our tea mostly in silence and listened to the fountain. Sometimes, he shelled pistachios for me and showed me how to peel an apple in one thin, bouncy curl. I was always amazed at how impossibly close he got to the fruit's flesh. He fed me and looked after me as though he were literally trying to keep me alive, and in a way, he was.

When nobody else could reach me, he was like a single beam of light. I drew strength from him, sensing the power of simple acceptance of life just as it is, just as it comes to us, one moment at a time. He brought strong memories of my father, but their hearts were oriented differently despite their resemblance. Where my father had fire, my uncle had peace. One evening after I made my way up the stairs, my mother knocked on my door.

"Lails, can I come in?" she asked. In fairness, she had given me enough time to mope and not talk to anyone. But I was going to have to face it at some point.

"As long as you don't say 'I told you so,'" I said, making room for her on the bed.

"I just wanted to give you a hug and tell you I love you."

"Thanks. So what else is going on?"

"So, Mazen's fiancé broke it off with him." "What? Why?"

She shrugged, nibbling on an apple slice. I would have to push to get more out of her, although I was a little afraid to ask.

"Is it because of me?"

"I guess we're toxic now," she said, matter-of-factly. "Shit."

"No, Laila, of course not. They probably weren't right for each other."

"Mazen was crazy about her; he was so excited to get married. What's he going to do?"

"Back to the stack of photographs, I guess. Mazen will find someone better for him. Anyway, who wants to deal with those people?"

"Mahmoud is the only difficult one. His brother was the one who stitched my foot, and I don't think he's religious at all."

"He's adorable," my mother said, using her apple to point to Jamil's face in my poster.

"Jamil? Mom, he is . . . the worst. He is, literally, the worst person in the world."

"Please, Laila, there is no such thing as the worst person in the world. Jamil is doing his job."

"Which is what exactly?"

"Keeping this country from blowing up. And from what I've seen, Jamil took care of you is checking up on you. I don't see Ali doing any of that."

"What do you mean he's been checking up on me? And by the way, Jamil is the one who arranged Ali's engagement to Maya. And that was after several failed attempts at breaking us up before that—"

"Maybe he knows Ali better than we do. Did it ever occur to you that maybe this whole time Jamil has been trying to protect you?"

"He threw kids who graffitied a wall in jail." "He didn't."

"I think he shoots people—"

"He shoots people? Laila, the guy went to Oxford." "Why does everyone wear blinders when it comes to him?"

"You're the one who's been blinded by love or lust or whatever it was with Ali. Now you're just seeing what the rest of us already knew to be true. Ali is a total player, and by the way, marriage won't change him. He'll probably cheat on this poor girl, too."

"Maya is a 'poor girl'? And who said he was cheating?"

"He got engaged to someone else. Do you think that just happened overnight? They must have had some kind of a relationship."

"The whole thing is so weird, Mom. I am not stupid; I would have known if he had a relationship with Maya. I was with him all day right before . . ." Hearing the words out loud, I felt sick to my stomach. The memory of the white sheets wet from our bathing suits and the way he slid his thumb under the string of my bikini bottom grazing my hips. The way he touched me in ways he never had before.

"Where? Laila, where did you spend the day with him?"

"At his farm. Sometimes we went running and swimming in his pool."

"Just you and Ali?"

"The house was usually full of people, maids and drivers and whatever."

"Usually, the house was full of people? Except for the last day you were with him? Laila?"

"He wouldn't do that to me, Mom; he would never, he just . . . nothing happened. Even if you hate Ali, you know me."

"Don't ever let him convince you he's anything other than what he is, which is not good enough for my baby girl. Never has been," she said and kissed my forehead.

The engagement dinner weighed so heavily on my mind that I had not given much thought to that afternoon with him. It turned out that I was a game to Ali, but at least in a small way, Ali didn't win either.

"Jamil did you a huge favor. He saved you from so much heartache down the road. So what if he has to crack a few skulls to keep the rest of us safe?"

"Laila, I was hoping to take a look at you. Make sure your foot is healing properly, and the bandages are clean," the doctor, whose voice I recognized, said from the other side of my closed door. "Also, I have something that belongs to you."

When I told him to come in, he carried my Gibran book, and I immediately remembered that I was reading it in Jamil's car.

"My book," I said, taking it from him and riffling through the pages, not knowing what I was looking for.

"And your phone." When he reached into his pocket, I was surprised that I had no memory of having it in his office. I assumed I had left it at the bar with Ali. "Looks like it needs to be charged."

"Thanks, Doctor . . . I'm sorry, I don't even know your last name," I said.

"We weren't properly introduced the other night. Please just call me Hani."

"I left these in your office?"

"No. Your friend, he brought them to me."

"Jamil?" I asked, seeing my mom raise her eyebrows out of the corner of my eye. I had left out the part about him carrying me through the streets of Damascus, first to the doctor and then home. "We're not friends."

"I see," he said, and as he started to unravel my bandages, my mother excused herself, but I knew I would have to answer more questions about Jamil later. I was already annoyed, and I could tell the doctor found my situation amusing.

"What's so funny?" I asked, throwing my phone across the bed, and then immediately felt bad for being rude when he was only being helpful.

"You have his picture on your wall. I have never seen anybody do this before."

"Oh. Yeah. It was an inside joke. Kind of. I don't know anymore."

"I try to base my opinions of people on what I see in front of me. Not what others have said or what I expect them to be like."

I sighed, reminding myself for the millionth time that every man was not my enemy, and the doctor had nothing to do with any of it. "You might know who he is, but you don't know him," I said, as diplomatically as I could.

"He seemed very concerned for you. When he brought me your things, he asked if I would make a house call. He also offered me an unnecessary amount of money. Which I refused, but I appreciated the gesture."

"He's good at getting people to do things for him."

"All my patients get the same treatment. I would have come to see you anyway, but I wanted to see if you would call me first. Of course, I didn't know until recently that you didn't have a phone."

"When can I run?"

"I would stay off of it for a while, to be honest. We don't really know how deep it is. If you come and see me in my office next week, I can check it again."

Dr. Hani was like *kinafeh*; he was sweet and warmed your soul. It was impossible to stay angry or even slightly annoyed with him.

"Do you think I will ever heal from this completely? I can run like I did before?"

"*Akeed*, no. You'll be stronger and faster than you have ever been." He flexed his arm muscles, making me laugh for the first time in a while. When he left, I put my dead phone in my nightstand drawer, deciding I was better off without it.

While everyone else in the family handled me carefully, my aunt took a different approach. First, she handed me a broom and I did whatever I could with my injury to help in the house. Every morning we stripped the beds, cleaned the floors, and did the laundry. The few rugs left out in the heat of the summer sun we pulled up and beat on the balcony with brooms. Some we rolled up and put away, others we returned to the salon. My aunt had particular ideas about how everything should be cleaned. Lemon and oil for the wood furniture, dish soap for the white, plastic table tops, disinfectant, and hot water for the floors and bathroom. We used white vinegar and newspaper for the windows, which was a daily routine for them, whether or not they were fasting.

When I cleaned the floors for the first time, I almost passed out from the cleaning detergent, an overpowering pine-like aroma that seemed out of place. I splashed water from a bucket across the floor and got down on my hands and knees to scrub it with a stiff brush. After that, I pushed the water toward the drain with a squeegee.

The first part of Ramadan was days of hunger, thirst, headache, and unbearable heat. The relentless sun that brought me to life when I first came now seemed like it wanted to kill me, but the courtyard shielded us. Even my mother helped. We hung the laundry to dry on a clothesline, and by the time we got to the end of the line, the beginning was dry. As my world got smaller, my past and future seemed distant, I found satisfaction in tiny details.

I prayed every day, five times a day. Noura taught me to wash my hands, feet, and face before prayer. She taught me the words and motions, all of which I didn't understand but which unexpectedly brought me comfort. I worried the rigidity of the ritual and not using my own words would make Him seem stern, but I found freedom in submission. I wasn't alone in my suffering; each of us had our own stories mercifully silenced.

Everyone was happy that I listened to Dr. Hani's advice and stopped running for the entire month. I knew I could make my injury worse if I did and I was sick at the thought of running into anyone. Like Noura and my aunt, I stayed in the house. I adapted to courtyard life.

When we weren't praying or cleaning, my aunt and Noura spent most of the day cooking. Mostly I got in the way, and patience ran short when people were thirsty and without morning coffee. I didn't understand how they managed to be around food all day without caving into the temptation.

In the privacy of my own mind, I only let myself think of Ali on occasion. I wondered if he was fasting and if he was also suffering. The smallest part of me hoped he was.

I was relieved to see my period as it is one of the rare exemptions from fasting. When it came, I was reminded time was moving forward, whether or not I was going with it. Seeing my own blood also reminded me I was a girl, and it seemed girls were never really exempt from suffering. I was proud of myself for not giving Ali my virginity, the only saving grace in all of it. A tiny part of me was resentful that Ali's power allowed him to pursue all of his desires, and my only power was in denying my own.

He came to the door once, at least once that I knew of. I was on my hands and knees, scrubbing the balcony floor. I watched him in between the wooden slats of the railing, and I could see him through the fruit trees. I pushed strands of hair away from my face with the back of my hand and wiped them on my sweatpants stained with cleaning products. When he called my name, I stayed kneeling, watching him, trying to decide if I hated him or if he was a stranger I never actually knew.

Mazen was the one who opened the door, but when my aunt saw Ali, she screamed at him, calling him every name in the book and cursing his relatives, his God, and his religion. Mazen carefully stepped out of her way, even though she was nearly two feet shorter than Ali. I watched with detached curiosity as she beat his legs with a broom until he finally left. I went back to my scrubbing as if nothing had happened. Later, I realized I was smiling in the shower as if I'd had a tiny triumph. My aunt was a ball breaker, and she didn't care that Ali was a big *wasta*.

As the days and weeks went by, my foot started to heal to where I could go up and down the stairs quickly and do the same chores as everyone else without any help. As promised, Dr. Hani came to remove the stitches and bandages and replaced them with smaller band-aids. Though I couldn't put much pressure on it, I knew the day would come when I could run again. After so many days of stillness and solitude, I could barely contain my excitement. The doctor did warn me not to push too hard in the beginning and reopen the wound, making the timeline longer for healing. I promised to wait until at least after Eid and then incrementally work up to longer distances.

As soon as the doc left, Mazen came to my door. "Did you hear? I can run soon!"

"Great." Mazen stood fidgeting in the doorway. "Listen, Omar is here to see you."

I paused at first, not hearing any of their names for so long. I felt myself deflate; the bubble of excitement over my healing burst. I finally decided, "Tell Omar to fuck off."

Mazen hesitated before he replied, "I cannot say this to my boss."

Why is everything complicated here? "Fine. I'll do it." I went downstairs to find Omar standing at the front door. He was sweating in his polo shirt and khaki shorts, his sandy curls out of control. I was wrestling with myself because my Syrian side told me I was beyond rude not to invite him in for coffee, and my American side wanted to punch him in the face for not telling me about Ali's engagement as soon as he knew.

"Omar, what can I do for you?" I asked, trying to keep my tone polite, at the very least.

"Your voicemail is full, so I came to check on you."

"I'm awesome, thank you."

"I see that," he said, looking me up and down, my ponytail probably a mess. "Sit bait, huh?"

"We're cleaning the floors. We might do all the windows, too. So, super busy . . ."

"How many windows can you possibly have here?" he asked, trying to see around me into the courtyard. Though he had a point, the way old Damascene houses were designed, there were not a lot of windows. Still, I was getting annoyed with him and his questions and pretending nothing happened.

"Did you come here to talk about cleaning?" I asked. "Can you come to the bar this weekend?"

"I stopped drinking."

"You can start again, celebration time," he said, pretending to shake maracas.

"I don't feel like celebrating."

"Fine. Gabby makes a very nice juice. Please, Laila, I just want to talk to you."

"Did you know the engagement was to Ali? On the boat?"

"I swear on my life Laila when you told me that Maya's engaged to Jamil, I had no idea what was about to happen."

"But you knew about Ali before I did. You were at the dinner, Omar. I saw you."

"It's complicated. There's a lot you don't know about." "I thought we were friends."

"We are. That's why I'm here." When I didn't answer, he continued, "Are you even curious what I have to say?" He started walking back down the alley, shaking his head.

"Omar?"

He turned his arms open at his sides. "Will Ali be there?"

"No. I swear, he won't. He's not even here." When I raised my eyebrows, he shrugged and said, "They're at the coast."

"I'll come."

"Thank you." He put his palms together in Christian prayer and bowed. I couldn't help but laugh in the same way I did when we hung out before. I couldn't deny I was missing my old life in Damascus, even the parts that didn't include Ali, a little bit.

As soon as I closed the door, Noura was standing there. She must have overheard my conversation with Omar about going out. "You should . . ." she said, gesturing to my messy hair and bleached sweatpants.

"Yeah," I answered, knowing she meant it was time for me to clean myself up. Even knowing Ali wouldn't be there, I wanted Omar to be able to tell him I was okay, even better than when I was with him. What I did know was that I couldn't unravel the whole thing by myself. As much as I hated swallowing my pride, I was eager to see Omar and hear his side of the story.

Mazen was coming down the stairs, and I realized it had been ages since I spoke to him. "Sorry about that. I shouldn't have asked you to . . . " I said, referring to Omar's visit.

Mazen smiled and shook his head. "It's no problem. I understand."

"Any improvement in your situation? Dr. Hani seems cool," I asked, hoping Mahmoud and Dr. Hani's sister changed her mind about breaking off their engagement.

"It wasn't because of you, Laila. Just so you know."

"Then, why did she break up with you?"

"Her family." He shrugged his shoulders and sat down on the stairs. "It happens."

"They suddenly changed their minds from one day to the next?" I asked, sitting next to him.

"It's not your fault."

"I was feeling so good, and then Omar shows up, and I am right back where I started a month ago. Maybe I didn't fast or pray enough?"

"This is not what Ramadan is for."

"It's about cleansing, purification, I get it."

"No." He said, rubbing his palms together. "It is about forgiveness. Part of it."

"Well, totally missed that part."

"When you forgive him, you will be free of him."
"You are a better person than me, Mazen. You're better than any of us."

"It's not true. I accept the life God has given me. That is all."

"That's the problem, Mazen. I don't want to accept life without him. I don't want to be free of him."

"You still want him?" he asked, unable to mask his disbelief.

"I want him, but not as he is, you know what I mean?" "This is not possible."

"I know."

The truth hidden beneath my pride and anger was that I missed Ali, the Ali I had seen on the street that morning in Muhajireen. I missed simple Ali, the soldier with the sweet smile and no *wasta* to speak of.

CHAPTER
30

STAY SMALL

"Shoo, shamay khara intee?"
I narrowed my eyes and sucked my cheeks in the mirror the way I had seen the regime queens do so many times. "This is called a smokey eye, Mazen," I answered without looking his way.

"Smokey eye? *Ma biyl belik*, it doesn't suit you," He said, but I could tell he was in a good mood today.

"Maybe it's the new me." The me who solved, instead of created, problems.

"I prefer old you."

"You complained all the time." "You're seeing him?"

"No. And anyway, I can't avoid them forever." "None of us can."

When I finally got to the bar, an hour after I said I would arrive, Omar was already behind the bar, pouring drinks for his regulars. Amer, 'the chubby one,' yelled my name and beat his belly like a drum. "How are you? Long time!"

I smiled and waved at Amer and it was like I pressed a back button before meeting Ali. As if on cue, one of the waiters came through the swinging doors from the kitchen, and I remembered the feeling I had when I first saw Ali come through those doors. The butterflies I got seeing him in his white collared shirt and jeans after his military uniform. He looked like a preppy kid from the East Coast, but he was nothing like that. And now I wished I had just ignored him. My life may feel very different, and my attitude toward Syria would definitely feel different. If only I had used the few Arabic words I knew and loved to say, "*khalas, yalla, bye.*"

"Apricot margarita?" Omar pulled me from my memories.

"I'll have whatever you're having."

"I've told you so many times, I don't drink when I'm working."

"You said you wanted to talk to me." "Yes, but it's my first day back—"

"Then grab a bottle, get Gabby out here, or I'm leaving."

"Damn, Laila, okay. Courtyard life made you a badass." Omar picked up a bottle of scotch from behind the bar. He handed me a bucket of ice and came around the other side of the bar.

"Don't be fooled by the exterior." As the words left my mouth, I remembered where I first heard them. Ali's words to me at the pool that day we ran into him and Maya in her string bikini when he explained how Syria was strictly 'look, don't touch.' I guess that only applied to Syrian girls, at least more Syrian than me.

I followed Omar upstairs to a small balcony where we could see the courtyard. We sat on chairs and faced the railing. After thirty days of good behavior, I felt a pang of guilt going straight to drinking scotch.

"Are we the worst?" I asked, taking a glass of ice from him.

"There are much worse than us, believe me."

"Like Jamil? The bigger the *wasta*, the bigger the asshole?"

"You haven't met his cousins yet." "Worse? How is that possible?"

"Lails, what's with the leather jacket, the tank top? Do you have tattoos under there?"

"What? It's the new me. What happened to your hair?" I asked, pointing to the wild sandy curls that seemed to grow up and out and never seemed to come down.

"Sabrina usually makes me cut my hair, but I haven't seen her for over a month," he said, reaching in his hair, his hand almost disappearing.

"Why? Did something happen?" I asked, afraid his answer might include them breaking up, too.

"Not really, we just have to lay low for a while, and I had so many family obligations. You're not the only one with problems, Laila."

"Well, that's good. I mean, it's good you didn't break up."

"You didn't answer me about the tattoo."

"Yeah, Omar, I went out during Ramadan and found a tattoo parlor to do all my lady parts."

"Never say the words 'lady parts' to me, ever again!" he said, pointing his finger at me.

"I missed you."

"Same. So are you okay?"

"Yeah. Definitely. Why wouldn't I be?"

"Now, you want to pretend nothing happened?" "Jamil tells Ali what to do, and Ali does it. What is complicated?"

"There's more to it than that."

"Did they end the draft? Did you go to the army, by the way?"

"I have sisters. If Jamil gets what he wants, it will be all-volunteer anyway."

"If? You mean Ali hasn't done it yet?" "Maybe you don't know the whole story."

"Maybe you don't know the whole story, either." "I know Ali loved you; he loves you still."

"He loves Jamil more."

"He loves his family, his country, yes, but not more than you."

"Right, he loves me so much he's getting married to Maya."

"Here's the thing. With Maya. Remember how I told you Maya was very in love with Jamil's brother, Munir?"

"So?"

"After he died, Maya's father wanted Jamil to marry Maya. He felt her reputation was tainted, and no one else would touch her. If Jamil took her on as one more responsibility that was passed from Munir, then Maya's father would return the favor with unquestionable loyalty to Jamil's presidency, at a time when Jamil needs this support."

"But Jamil still said no? I mean, he's always with her—"

"Optics. The next president would be wise to marry a Sunni to show they are willing to share bloodlines with us. Also, she's not . . . his type."

"How did Ali get stuck with her?"

"Who's the next most powerful man in the country? Ali's father, who, by the way, hates Maya's father. There has been bad blood between them going back to their soldier days."

"And now they'll be family."

"Yes, which you would think would make them too powerful, but the opposite is true. Because of Ali and Maya's fathers' hatred for each other, they will always have to compete for Jamil's favor."

"Omar, everyone on the boat knew but me."

"Ali couldn't tell you. Your mother already had it in for him, and he knew there was doubt in your family's minds. This would have killed any chance he had with you."

"And now?"

"Ali was hoping that if I spoke to you and you were willing to listen, then maybe you would . . ."

"What, like be his side chick? You've both lost your minds."

"Whoa, Laila, don't go there. It's not like that at all."

"Oh really? Did you know that the same day he got engaged, we were alone at his farm, and he . . . ugh, he was getting fucking engaged the same day!"

"I see. Listen, please understand I am not defending Ali—"

"You are!"

"Maybe he's in love with you, Laila, and he wants you, and he wants to be close to you! What is wrong with that? Why do girls always turn sex into a game of who has the upper hand?"

"Welcome to Syria. Are you kidding me?" "We're not all assholes, you know."

"Are we still talking about Ali and me? What do you want me to do? Stay home and wait for him to break off his engagement? Like a girl with low self-esteem and no brain?"

"Yes, that's what I want you to do right now. You're letting your pride get in the way of your destiny."

"What is my destiny, Omar? Do you know? Because I thought I knew; I thought Ali was my destiny ... But I was totally wrong. And now I don't trust myself, I don't trust you, and I sure as hell don't trust Ali."

"He feels bad about how it all went down that night—"

"He could have told me; he could have fought for us.

He could have told Jamil no."

"You still don't know where you are."

"Then maybe I don't belong here, and I never really did."

"Then why did you come?"

"I came for my father because it's what he would have wanted. But if he knew what happened with Ali, he would send me back to California in a heartbeat."

"Wait, you're going back? Are you serious?"

"I would have already left if it wasn't for my foot. You and I both know there's nothing here for me."

"Wait, what happened to your foot?"

"I injured myself running ... it doesn't matter. If it wasn't for Jamil—"

"Jamil?"

"Yeah, he is the one who sent me the car to come to the dinner in the first place. Actually, if it wasn't for him, I wouldn't have known about his engagement until God knows when—"

"I see," Omar said, not meeting my eyes.

"I mean, were you going to tell me? Like, ever?" "We were hoping we wouldn't have to."

"Well, now everyone knows, and I'm going home. Good luck with everything, Omar. Thanks for the drink. Drinks."

"Laila, what do I tell him?" "Ali? Tell him '*khalas, yalla bye*.'"

"He waited for you." He hesitated before continuing, "Outside, every day to see if you would go running. In the parking lot. Like a dog."

My pride definitely wouldn't let me forget how angry I still was with Ali, and the only condition I had to forgive myself was that I promised never to repeat the same mistake. Even to my own ears, my voice sounded like steel, but I meant it when I said, "Good. He should know his place."

As I left the bar that night, I thought maybe Omar was right. Even though it didn't change anything with Ali, two things that contradicted each other could both be true.

I understood the words strung together but having spent some time here, I finally understood what they meant when they said 'welcome to Syria,' the words that both warmed me and sent a shiver up my spine.

When I got back to the courtyard, Lulu, Noura's four-year-old daughter, was sitting on the steps. Now I felt silly in my black eyeliner and leather jacket, trying to appear bulletproof, when inside my heart still ached and the smallest thing could send me into a rage or, worse, make me cry. Now I was drunk on scotch and my liner was probably smudged.

"I tried being good," I told her and she giggled as we both knew it didn't really suit me, either. All thirty days of fasting and praying and cleaning weren't enough. I was in a small enough space to forget but as soon as I came out of the cocoon I was in, the world reminded me how fragile I was.

    I sat on the stairs next to her and felt like I was talking to my younger self. The same girl that was in Syria and knew Ali, whose mother tried to keep her away. The memory she thought was a dream of running through the apricot orchards, yelling his name at the top of her lungs as she got him to chase her and the thrill of him finally catching her, throwing her up in the air so high she thought she would never come down. She felt her mother was just ruining her fun. If only she'd known the heartbreak her mother was trying to protect her from.

    The thought of possibly keeping Lulu from future pain, in the same way my parents had tried to save me, gave me a little bit of hope.

    "So, you heard what happened?" I asked as she sucked her fingers like she always did, holding the doll my mom brought her. "It's my fault, you know. Everyone tried to warn me. Even Maya. Now you know to stay away from players, right? No players, no douchebags, no liars . . . don't make the same mistake your cousin Laila made."

    "No Alawie," she said, taking her fingers out of her mouth.

    "No, no, no. Lulu, listen to me," I said, coming down on my knees in front of her. "Ali is very bad. But it's not because he is Alawie. I am sure there are lots of good Alawite boys out there who are honest and loyal and . . . perfect gentlemen." She kept smiling and sucking her fingers, her wild hair held together by an elastic ponytail holder. "I don't know any of them, but I'm sure they are out there."

As much as Ali hurt me, I would not let him change me. The more I thought about it, the more I realized I did know another Alawite boy. He was brutally honest and very loyal to his friends, at least. He did have good manners. He was a perfect gentleman who also happened to be a gigantic *wasta*, a cannon who could make any problem look like a mosquito.

"You and I should probably stay away from the Alawie boys, too, just to be on the safe side." She smiled and nodded in agreement.

If only young Laila knew, fifteen years later, that same Alawite boy she trusted with her life would let her fall, shattering her in a thousand pieces.

CHAPTER
31

KIND OF SAFE

"*OUMI YA LAILA! HAJTEK NOUM!*" My aunt was yelling from the courtyard for me to get up.

"*Yalla jaiyeh!*" I yelled back that I was coming. I scurried out of my room in my *shahatta* to the bathroom. I splashed my face with cold water and looked at myself in the mirror. It was a new day in Damascus, and I was cleansed of my sins along with everyone else. The family seemed in better spirits, Ramadan was over, Mazen's engagement was back on, and my mom was anxious to get the workers back to the villa. As soon as Dr. Hani signed off on me running again (a very short distance), my mom booked my ticket back to California.

"How was I fasting for 30 days, and I gained five kilos?" I asked Noura as soon as I came down the stairs.

"This happens to everyone. We all say we are going to lose weight, but it never works."

"Bravo, Laila!" My aunt broke in, the only person I had ever known to applaud and welcome weight gain.

Noura added, "She said now you have an ass and some boobs."

"Awesome."

"Some! She wants you to gain five more now." Noura, the covered girl, taught me all Arabic curse words, and she swore the most.

"If only I could make sure those next five kilos go to my ass and boobs, too," I said as we walked into the kitchen.

"This is in God's hands, *habibti*," she said, handing me a tray of vegetables to chop.

"So, who's coming tonight?"

"Nobody is coming tonight. Just the family."

'Just us' was usually about twenty-five people. I was glad I was part of 'just us.'

"After, we will go to the park." "Like the playground?"

"Yes, you will like it."

"*Yalla*, I'm ready." Besides the one night at Omar's bar, which barely counted, I hadn't really been anywhere.

After dinner with the family, Noura gathered the kids and Mazen dropped us off at the park. It was more like a carnival with rides and cotton candy and bright neon lights. Noura hooked her arm through mine and released the kids to ride the rides.

"Is it safe?" I asked, eyeing the rickety roller coasters and Ferris wheel.

"Kind of," Noura answered, giggling. "You fell here one time, you remember?"

"My mom told me, but I don't remember that. Mahmoud pulled my hair, and I fell off the swing onto the concrete or something. My mom told me Mazen hit him in the face."

"He deserved it. He was always jealous of you."

"Weird."

She hesitated before she said, "But it was not Mazen, no. Ali hit him in the face, boom. He was on the ground." When she saw my openmouthed expression, she continued. "Yes, Ali, he punched him."

"Wait, why would my mom lie about—never mind, Ali was there?"

Noura shrugged. "He was crazy, like fire in his eyes. I remember until now, I was afraid he would kill him."

"It's so weird that I don't remember him from back then. Not really."

"Not even one small thing?"

"So I have this memory of him chasing me at his farm. I guess I made him chase me, I don't know, but that's all I remember."

Noura sighed. "Some things I love about here, some things it's very complicated. We can't always be with the one we love."

I had given Noura a lot of details about Ali, but I left out a few parts. I felt ashamed for letting it get that far. I didn't know what the family would do if they knew the whole truth.

"I don't care what anyone will say. Ali is a stupid idiot who is only doing what his family wants for him because they're scared. I know he always has, since he was a young kid, loved you too much."

"I don't know what to believe anymore, Noura. I feel like even if he does love me, he still chose Maya."

"But Maya will never be you. Anyway, was he really that handsome? You will find someone better, a gentleman."

"I don't want anyone else; I mean, I don't want anyone. I will never go through that, whatever you want to call it, I will never go through that again."

"Okay."

"Noura, I'm serious."

"*Inti amar*, you deserve the best in this world. A king.

I pray God brings you someone very special one day." "Yeah," I said, worried I would start crying again.

"*Yalla khalas*, no more tears, *habibti*, let's go have fun!"

Before we left for the park, I promised my mother I would start packing, which was more challenging this time. It didn't really matter what I took with me when I left California as long as I had clothes to run in. I decided to leave half my running shoes behind for Noura, who loved all the bright colors and almost all of my running clothes. That left me with my Gibran book, a few souvenirs I picked up in the old city, and several gifts from Ali. It wasn't that I wanted any of them, but over the months we were together, my dresser filled up with perfumes, jewelry, even stuffed animals that, at the time, I thought were cute but now looked childish as though they belonged to someone else. He had spoiled me in some ways, but all I really wanted, and the one area where he could be stingy, was his time. That and proclaiming publicly that he loved me and not caring what anyone thought about it. Nothing made me happier than spending hours in the sunshine at his farm swimming, running, kissing . . . of course, now it made sense. So much of it, I had forgiven, thinking he was trying to protect my reputation.

The thin green bracelet was still tied around my wrist, and I assumed it was one of those things that you never really take off . . . it just eventually wears away. But the emeralds Ali bought me that were like a tennis bracelet now felt too heavy to keep. Throw them in the trash can? Give them away? Most girls I knew would think it was tacky and bad luck to have gifts from a failed relationship. Selling them felt even worse. If Ali thought I profited somehow from our relationship, it would drive me insane, and I had no intention of giving him the satisfaction.

Mom suggested I give the jewelry back to him. I was starting to think my mom was right a lot more than I ever believed before. The thought of seeing Ali put my stomach in knots. The idea of Maya wearing the gifts he gave to me was even worse.

"I can return them for you," my mother offered.

"Can you do that without ripping Ali's head off and making a scene?"

"No."

"Then I guess I have to do it."

"Just get it over with. You'll be happy you did."

"Fine, I will."

"Your flight is in three days, Laila . . ." "Mom, I know. I'll do it."

After an hour of rides and sugar, Noura and I returned to the parking lot to enter the street that led home, and I heard Noura stop dead in her tracks and say, "Oh no."

When I saw where she was looking, I saw Ali in the parking lot, standing in front of a shiny new black Mercedes in sharp contrast to the other dusty cabs and trucks parked there.

The first thought was he had come to pick up the jewelry. For Maya. Had my mom gone ahead and told him to come to pick everything up? *He came for the jewelry.* Heat spread through my chest, and my hands started to shake, my anger already reeling out of control.

"If you came for the jewelry, you should have sent your driver." I walked right past him to the closest shopkeeper. I grabbed the metal pole that all merchants needed to pull the steel gate down at the end of the night when they closed. He looked a little apprehensive but let me take it.

"Jewelry?" Ali asked as I came back and started towards the car. "No. Omar said you're leaving—"

"Is this a new car? An engagement gift?" I whacked the mirror on the passenger side as hard as I could. Maya's mirror.

"Jesus Laila, what are you doing!" he said, not having considered the car's effect on me or anyone else.

"It's so pretty." I gingerly glided my fingers along the shiny black exterior, smooth as silk without a scratch or mark anywhere. I walked all the way around the car, as it only seemed fair to take off Ali's side mirror too. Ali had to jump out of the way as I raised the metal pole above my head and smashed the mirror on the driver's side.

"Laila, what the hell! I just came to talk to you." "So talk."

"I never wanted you to find out like you did. That's why I didn't want you to come to the dinner. I wanted the chance to tell you myself."

"So you feel bad about the way I found out? Not about the actual engagement?"

"All I wanted—"

"I know what you wanted. It's not for you; it was never for you."

"That's not fair, Laila. And can we not do this in front of everyone?"

"In front of everyone?" I scoffed. "Like you did to me when you got engaged, and I was the last to know?"

"Okay, you've made your point, Laila. It's enough!" Ali's shock was subsiding, and he was getting angry.

"Are these your special license plates, so you never get pulled over? The *wasta* plates?" I asked, smacking his license plate until it fell to the ground. "There is one on the back too?"

"Oh my God." Ali held his head in his hands, resigned to watching me destroy his car.

"Does this car 'belong' to you, Ali? This is what you let happen to your belongings?"

"Fuck, Laila!" He tried to grab it from me as I brought the metal pole down on his windshield with every ounce of strength I had left. "This is my father's car!"

"Tell him I'll send your fucking jewelry back." I didn't have the strength to hold tears back anymore, and it was the last thing I cared about. I left Ali, his car now smashed to pieces, open-mouthed, and glass under his feet. I told myself he deserved it.

CHAPTER 32

GOD'S CITY

Now I couldn't go home. Noura must have gone ahead of me, probably to get Mazen. By now, my mother would know what I did and be furious with me. I couldn't turn around and face Ali either. At least I had my running shoes on, so I picked up my pace and ran past my uncle's door and in the direction of the old city, my old running route from when I first arrived. Then I remembered my last run was with Ali before his engagement. Though it was crowded and stuffy, I moved through the ancient city and started running in the only direction I knew. Maybe I would go to the American school or further, I wasn't sure. All I knew was that I couldn't be home or anywhere near Ali. I couldn't even begin to understand what I had just done.

I loved running after dark when the mornings didn't work anymore, especially in Damascus. The city came alive at night. The wind was soft and inviting, the traffic and people sitting in outdoor restaurants releasing electric energy through the city streets. I could feel my breathing even out, and my pulse found its natural rhythm. People were out walking and exchanging pleasantries, stories, kisses, and gossip, children running around their parent's feet.

The farther I ran, the more I left the memory of Ali behind me. I couldn't keep hanging on to him, even in my anger. The more distance I got from Ali, the more pieces of him I left behind me, shedding his scent, the taste of his lips, the way he said my name, all of it. Everything I wanted to tear down Ali would have died defending; it seemed so obvious to me now that we could never work. The whole time I had been blaming Jamil for everything that happened. The truth was it was me who stepped on the glass in the street; it was me who had trusted Ali with my heart, and it was me who chose not to listen when everyone warned me I was going to get hurt. If I was humble enough to admit it, Jamil had tried to warn me more than anyone. When he told me on his balcony that Ali preferred blondes, that people don't change, he was the only one who cared that I knew about Ali's engagement and saw the truth for myself. He was also the one who came after me that night, not Ali. And it was Jamil who was there to hold me up so I wouldn't fall apart when Ali confirmed the engagement news in the restaurant, and it was him who carried me through the streets of old Damascus to deliver me home.

My foot was starting to ache, and I tried my best to ignore it. I had no plan for where I was going other than to keep running to the highest place I could get. Eventually, I found myself in front of Jamil's building.

There were guards and barricades, but when I spotted a familiar face, I knew he had to be home.

"Hassan, can I go up?" I asked as casually as I could. When he eyed me suspiciously, I said, *"Hooway talubni."* (He asked for me.)

I never saw Hassan have any expression whatsoever, but he raised his eyebrows ever so slightly at my claim. He got out of the car, got on his phone, and then waved me in. Not before patting me down and taking my phone from me, but still, I was in the elevator, this time alone with the lion on my way up. I stuck my tongue out at that lion just to remind myself not to be afraid or take him too seriously. By the time I reached the top floor, I still had no idea what to say to him, so I thought I would improvise. I smoothed out my ponytail and straightened my t-shirt, taking a deep breath to steady myself. I stopped when I reached his door as I could hear my own voice on the other side and the sound of glass shattering. *Shit.*

It was too late for me to back out, but I hadn't counted on him already knowing what I had done. Someone must have taken a video and sent it to him. When he opened the door, I couldn't speak, and I had almost forgotten why I had come in the first place. The last time I saw him was over a month ago. Before he left, he said he would keep me close to him. I always felt transparent in front of him, like he could see through me; it didn't matter what I was wearing.

"You smashed his car?"

"His father's," I answered, realizing after I said it that it was actually worse, and my voice sounded childish even to my ears.

"Did you run?" I nodded. "You still have bandages."

"Hurts," I said, clenching my teeth so I wouldn't cry in front of him.

"Come."

The moment I walked through his door, I felt different. Like everything had shifted since the first time I was there with Ali before I knew anything or anyone. He led me down the now-familiar hallway into the kitchen. "Sit." He knelt in front of me, a bowl of water in his hands. He gently removed my shoe and sock and plunged my foot into the water. He rinsed until my foot was clean and the water was bloody.

"I thought all Arabs hated feet." He looked up at me briefly but said nothing. "Sorry. You're pissed about the car?"

"Give me your hand." But when I gave him my hand, he said, "Your other hand." He brought out a steel knife and cut easily through the silk threads to release it from my wrist. I could feel the coolness of the steel against my hot skin, and it felt free to have it off.

"I don't care about the car. What I want to know is why he was there."

"Ali?"

"Yes, Ali! Who the fuck are we talking about?"

It had not even occurred to me until he said that Ali could be in trouble, too. I was torn between wanting to defend him and still being furious about what he did.

"He is engaged to Maya. He has no reason to be near you now."

"The jewelry. Ali wanted the jewelry back."

"Jewelry? Whatever he gave you is nothing to him, nothing to his family."

"My mom called him. She told him to come." Though I winced at Jamil calling gifts from Ali that I cherished so much 'nothing.' "She hates him. She doesn't want me to have anything from him."

He glared back at me, his jaw clenched and tension in his shoulders. If I backed down, he would find out I wasn't sure if my mom called Ali or not. I didn't stop at my uncle's house and came straight to him. I held his gaze until I couldn't anymore. "I should never have come here. It's funny, Maya was the one who told me that," I said, pulling my sock and running shoe back on.

I was halfway down the hall when he said, "Laila." I turned but stayed where I was in the hallway, unable to decide which way to move. I caught a glimpse of myself in his entryway mirror, and for some reason, I was reminded of what I felt in my white dress at my father's funeral. What seemed like a lifetime ago, looking at myself in my bathroom mirror and how I knew everything had changed. The destiny I had sensed but never really believed was unfolding, and fate had not forgotten or betrayed me.

"Why did you come?" He asked me a question that, for the first time, it seemed he didn't know the answer to.

"I was running—"

"I know why you came to me, I was asking—" "Why I came to Damascus. I'm telling you, Jamil.

I was running in Sonoma, outside the vineyard where I was working. I didn't know yet about my father's accident. I saw an apricot on a tree, just one, which was strange because it wasn't their season yet. The taste was unbelievable. And I thought of Damascus. Where I was born, where I entered the world, a few buildings from here, but a place I didn't know anything about. Something was calling me inside, but it was bigger than me. Then we got the news about my dad."

"You found God in an apricot?" I smiled and nodded, not wanting to explain more. Either Jamil understood me, or he didn't.

"I see."

"And just so you know, I came to you, not for your help but because you have the best view in the city. And I think it's unfair that you're the only one who sees it."

"You're welcome to enjoy it as much as you want." He said, smiling back at me. "At the moment, I have something I must do. If you're still here, I'll join you after."

When Jamil left me, I walked over to open the sliding glass doors that led out to the balcony. I wondered if Jamil felt the same way when he stood out here. I felt like I was flying high above the city, the wind pulling my hair from my face, where no one could touch me and no one could bring me down.

I opened my fingers, the green silk threads that had been severed from my wrist still in my hand, the last thing to connect me to Ali. I let the winds of Damascus lift it from my palm, and I watched it disappear into the city lights. *If you want me, come and get me, you bastard.*

I thought of myself when I first arrived in Syria. I came for my father and myself, but Damascus had greater plans for me. I fell into true love and unimaginable heartbreak. I learned what it means to be guided by loyalty and destroyed by betrayal. I discovered what hunger feels like, what paradise tastes like. I found Him, I found my father, I found where heaven and hell meet. In the oldest city in the world, I unknowingly found the frontline, and there was no going back.

When I heard the sliding glass door opening quietly behind me, I was taken back to the day at the farm when Jamil was shouting Ali's name, his voice deep and powerful, like divine authority. I didn't know who he was, but we had known each other. All the days and nights in my bedroom, I revealed myself to him, bits and pieces I couldn't share with anyone, not even Ali. As Jamil came out onto the balcony, I stayed facing the city, green lights randomly scattered throughout the city's skyline. He stood behind me, wrapping his arms around my waist. He put his lips to my neck, breathing me in, pulling my body closer to his chest.

Damascus got into your veins, seduced, enchanted, and then never let you go.

GLOSSARY

Akbar: greater than, older than

Akeed: for sure, yes, absolutely, without a doubt

Akhi: my brother

Albi: my heart, used as a term of endearment

Amar: moon, term of endearment

Amou: Uncle, a father's brother, also used as a respectful way to address friends of parents and relatives

Arse: bastard

Aweeyay: strong, aggressive (for a female); can be positive or negative depending on the context

Bahkheel: stingy man

Bint Nass: daughter of good people

Barday: cold, slow for a female

Daiyaa: lost, for a female

Ghaleeza: silly, for a female

Habibi: my love, term of endearment for a male

Habibti: my love, term of endearment for a female

Haram: a sin against God, forbidden in an Islamic context

Hayati: my life, term of endearment

Ibn Massoul: son of an important man

Inti: you, for a female

Iktir: a lot

Kaslanay: lazy, undisciplined, for a female

Khalas: enough, stop, something is over, finished, done

Majnounay: crazy, for a female

Melounay: tricky, sly, for a female

Mitlik: like you, for a female

Msayfay hay: "she summered," flighty, in her own world, unbothered, dreamy

Muy: Water

Sayshwaar: a blow dry

Shyfay hala: "she sees herself," meaning she is overly confident, arrogant, superior

Shway: a little bit, "shway shway" means to slow down

Sit Bait: grandmother of the house, the matriarch, highly complimentary

Taweelay: tall, for a female

Tayyib: okay, sounds good, alright, in agreement

Tuz: fart, used to mean "who cares?"

Useerah: short, for a female

Wasta: currency of connections, used as a noun to mean "a person of influence"

Yalla: let's go, hurry, in some context it can mean "ok, whatever"

Yainee: kind of, sort of, a little bit, also can be used as a term to mean "means"

ACKNOWLEDGEMENTS

To those who have been in the 'kitchen' with me. Thank you for reading drafts, helping with research, editing, and pushing me forward when I needed it. Shane, for all of it. I will never find words in any language to express my gratitude. James and Alex for letting me miss some football games to write. You are the greatest gifts of my life. Mom and Bobs, you have taught me unconditional love and adventure. Thank you for living fearlessly and truly, an unchartered life. This book simply could not be without you. Tarek for being my number one fan no matter what. Mickey, you have been such a gift to this family. Bes, the only one who will ever understand the magic of our shared story. Edna and Bernie, may you rest in infinite peace, for giving me the son who gave me sons. I am forever in your debt. Kate, for your unwavering belief in possibility. Dad, how I wish you could see this come to fruition. I know you are with me.

Nadine for believing in me from day one and blazing a trail for the rest of us. Samia, your insight, vision, and delicious sense of humor are invaluable, as is your sisterhood. My soul sisters, Kathy, Dana, Sara, Melva, & Alexia, for holding my hand. Zena, for your generosity and perspective about the spirit of the time. Abu Fares, for your own flawless and passionate work.

Dhanya at Notion Publishing, for your clarity and guidance. Avia, for your instrumental feedback on Laila's character. Colin, for the timely synergy and jumping on board when I needed help.

Thank you to my Syrian family, who raised me as one of their own, for teaching me how to love.

Finally, the city of Damascus, my forever love, for making me strong and showing me how to honor all that is greater than me.